The Frontiers of Love

by Diana Chang

THE
FRONTIERS
OF
LOVE

With a new introduction by Shirley Geok-lin Lim

University of Washington Press

Seattle & London

Library of Congress Cataloging-in-Publication Data
Chang, Diana.
    The frontiers of love / Diana Chang; introduction by Shirley
Geok-lin Lim
        p.   cm.
    ISBN 0–295–97326–9
    1. Asian Americans—Fiction.   I. Title.
PS3553.H2719F76   1993   93–35512
813'.54—dc20   CIP

INTRODUCTION

Individual and society are certainly beings with different natures. But far from there being some inexpressible kind of antagonism between the two, far from it being the case that the individual can identify himself with society only at the risk of renouncing his own nature either wholly or in part, the fact is that he is not truly himself, he does not fully realize his own nature, except on the condition that he is involved in society.

—Emile Durkheim, *Moral Education*

The Frontiers of Love was first published in 1956 to much acclaim. But nowhere was it hailed then as an Asian American work. The republication of Diana Chang's formidable first novel by the University of Washington Press is a belated recognition that the novel is one of the earliest transgressors of canonical frontiers. It queried categories of identity—national, racial, class, and gender—at a time when American readers in the main were not merely unmindful of issues of diversity but when powerful state forces were inimical to any suggestions of deviance from the jingoistic and hysterical brand of patriotism that Joseph McCarthy had hijacked as his terrain.

In fact, for the reader reading the novel for the first time, its themes, characters, actions, and stylistic textures appear strikingly contemporary. Appiah and Gates, identifying the thrust of disciplinary concerns in the 1990s, speak of "the politics of identity": contemporary scholars expand "on the evolving anti-essentialist critiques of ethnic, sexual, national, and racial identities" (1992,

625). *The Frontiers of Love* anticipates this "post-essentialist recon-
ception of identity" by more than three decades.

Like Sartre's characters in *No Exit*, the major characters in *The
Frontiers of Love* are bound together in a claustrophobic geographi-
cal space; however, their tormented relationships hold existential
dilemmas that function both as allegories for varieties of human
conditions and as material manifestations of sociopolitical forces.
Located in Shanghai's International Settlement, at the historical moment just months before and up to the Japanese Imperial
Army's surrender after the nuclear holocaust in Hiroshima and
Nagasaki in 1945, the novel constructs metaphysical problems that
cannot be understood apart from their historical and geopolitical
specifics. Large philosophical questions that are usually presented
as universal and abstract in nature—Who am I? How do I know
who I am? How should I act? What is good? What is evil?—are
dramatized, particularized, and finally have their premises sub-
verted as they are subtly and repeatedly reinscribed against, over,
and through the finely observed world of the Shanghai metropoles
in the period between Japanese imperialist dissolution and the
Communist takeover of China.

Set in 1945, *The Frontiers of Love* was already in some ways a
historical novel when it appeared in 1956. The experiences it represented, of the Second World War's exiled and interned characters in Japanese-occupied Shanghai, are even further removed for
the generation of readers in the last decade of the twentieth century. Thus, in crucial ways, the novel must be read in its historical
context. The dilatory yet tense, superficially pleasure-loving yet
paranoid intensity of the novel's social world suggests the tenor
of relations in a specific cosmopolitan milieu in response to eight
years of militaristic rule. The novel constructs the sensibility of
a particular society undergoing a crisis of an interregnum: the
characters are isolated individuals thrown together by the political violence of war into an inescapable community of transients,
exiles, aliens, and sojourners, each seeking solace and satisfaction
in the constrained space of a hostile occupied territory.

Shanghai and China frame the narrative as sites for the contestations of territory and naming, the place for economic and political power struggles recognized today as colonialism. For much of the nineteenth and twentieth centuries, Shanghai symbolized for Chinese patriots the loss of their territorial integrity. The British success against the Chinese Imperial forces in the Opium Wars gave Britain Hong Kong and extraterritorial rights in certain towns and cities. Shanghai, on the Whangpoo River, seventeen miles from the Yangtze estuary, where European governments could set up autonomous settlements independent of Chinese law, rapidly grew to accommodate the various Western powers' trading interests. Its position allowed the European colonial powers to control all the river trade up the Yangtze far into China's interior (Seagrave 1985, 2). The International Settlement and the French Concession operated as "two contiguous European areas in Shanghai" (Cook 1985, 16). From the 1920s to the beginning of World War II, Shanghai became a legendary urban center drawing thousands of Russian refugees fleeing from the Russian Revolution, Japanese traders, a host of European and American capitalist adventurers, and millions of rural Chinese attracted to its opportunities. Noted for its extremes of wealth and poverty, the city also became associated with corruption, decadence, and moral decay. "Shanghai had everything. It was a city that could give you everything you wanted, from the highest to the lowest. There were no morals of any sort" (Cook 1985, 17).

This Westernized milieu of Shanghai dominates *The Frontiers of Love.* As Sylvia Chen notes in the novel, "The Shanghai which she knew was circumscribed, uncontaminated by the Chinese section, which she had never even visited" (p. 85). Yet in the novel's self-conscious gaps, its self-reflexive interrogations of its own settings, lies a strict condemnation of Western colonialism and its cultural consequences, the anomie, alienation, deracination, and psychopolitical depredations in the wake of Western imperialism. The Shanghai cosmopolites were "unnamed hybrids," "survivors of a colonialism that was fast becoming as antique as peace" (p. 86). Embedded in Chinese society, colonialist racism "held them apart (from the Chinese) in a trance" (p. 87).

Chang's fictive commentary on the problematic of the colonized is contemporary with Frantz Fanon's study of the colonized in *Black Skin, White Masks* (first published in Paris in 1952): "People were true to nothing in Shanghai; they belonged only to the surface values of both East and West and leaned heavily toward the exoticism of the West. If one did not hold on carefully to one's sense of self, one might wake up one morning looking for one's face, so easily lost" (p. 87). The sentence expresses both nostalgia for a truth, for those deeper values of a culture, whether East or West, that can provide an individual with a sense of unity and coherence, and a consciousness of its unavailability. "Face" here signifies not merely the physicality that functions as a marker of race and thus of cultural identity but more complexly the Chinese notion of self-respect within a society, that is, the specific social positions of individuals. The consciousness of a Chinese majority shut out of the foreground of dramatic action gives the novel its complicating thematics of race and culture.

Shanghai as a metaphor for a historical and political identity reminds us that the boundaries which we think of as defining national, cultural, racial, gender, and other identities are inherently unstable. As political and epistemological construction, Shanghai was both Chinese and Western, native and foreign, liberatory and oppressive, national and international. Like the three major youthful characters (Sylvia, Feng, and Mimi), it literalizes the identity "Eurasian": "Shanghai [was] a Eurasian city" (93). As Feng, the son of a neurasthenic Englishwoman and remote Chinese father, acknowledges, it is Shanghai's duplicity, its Western colonized culture, that contributes to his identity confusion: "Strictly speaking, it could not be called Chinese, though it was inhabited mostly by Chinese — Chinese who were either wealthy, Westernized or prayed to a Christian God" (p. 21). For Feng, questing for ego coherence and unity which he has conceptualized as single-race identity, such cultural doubleness, figured in the material culture of Shanghai, is intolerable.

Thus the novel is not simply a historical novel, although it offers pleasures even on that limited level. In its almost faultless structuring of multiple points of view it plays out obsessive interrogations and reinscriptions of identity that deconstruct the usual notions of national, racial, class, and gender identities into their phenomenological and epistemological brittleness. As policed borders or as cultural and racial expression, the novel represents Shanghai as the site of violent fragmenting identities, of conflicting evolving and contingent futures. The frontiers "of love" delineate the psychosexual and sociopolitical processes, the "imaginings" through which individuals and nations unmake and make themselves.

Both as analogue and as precursor, *The Frontiers of Love* speaks to the most contemporary debates on biculturality and biraciality. Its representations of young "Eurasians" making their difficult way through the minefields of race, class, and nation loyalty and affiliation join these debates to insert into the reified nineteenth-century imperial notions of the stable ego and the superiority of Euro-American civilization a critique of Western colonialism and racism, metropolitan decadence, and Euro-American decline. These thematics were so unexpected in the 1950s that the enthusiastic critics who acclaimed the book's publication chose to ignore them. Instead, they read the novel within the genre of realism as an expression of private and individual lives: "remarkably, [Chang] enters the minds and hearts of her characters, young and old, European and Oriental, reveals them in their strengths and weaknesses, in their moments of self-deception and revelation" (Benjamin Lease, *Chicago Sun-Times*). *The Frontiers of Love*, however, is a modernist novel in which "characters" signify more than their illusions of verisimilitude.

In the maelstrom of identities-formation that the novel dramatizes, the minor European characters are cast as static fragments, unable to change out of their racialized moulds. Feng's mother, Audrey, kept in luxury by her Chinese husband who has otherwise abandoned her, is stranded, "left . . . in a Chinese city" (p. 27). Cut off from her society yet unable to change, she clings to Feng and to her possessions as the only things through which she has her identity. Helen Chen, Sylvia's white mother, however, is aggressively American. Despite her marriage to Liyi, a Chinese intellectual caught in the momentous shift from a Confucianist to a Communist society, and her two children who claim a binational identity, Helen is violently anti-Chinese. Her cruelty to her husband's nephew, Peiyuan, demonstrates a racist irrationality, a dehumanizing of the other through gross prejudices based on fallacies of physical distinctions. To Helen, her "'American-style' home was superior" to her husband's "old homestead in Singkiang . . . [which] seemed foreign and therefore primitive" (p. 79). Her racism is most overtly aroused by Peiyuan's "queer Chinese" presence in her home; she sees him as ugly, a symbol of what has stood in the way of her "going back to the States" (p. 140).

Helen's "contradictions," her love for her Chinese husband and her children, enacted simultaneously with her hatred of the Chinese, echo Robert Bruno's "contradictions." Robert pursues Mimi passionately, declares his love for her, but is unable to overcome his father's prohibition against marrying her because she is "Eurasian." These minor characters—English, white American, and Swiss—represent a range and complexity of Western attitudes toward the Chinese and toward Eurasians. Privileging themselves as racially single and superior, their relations with the racial Other are fraught with exclusion (as with Feng's mother), hatred (as with Helen), and fascination that eroticizes and reduces the Other to a sexual object (as with Robert).

These minor characters, however, are not flat or one-dimensional villains; their race attitudes are not simply evil. As much as the characters they act upon, they suffer from the consequences of their racial positions. Audrey, Helen, and Robert are all "unhappy" characters; their inability to construct new paradigms of relationships that supersede the degradations of race divisions is their problem as well. Thus, Robert is fully aware of the difference between his father's anachronistic position and his own progressivism. He associates his father with colonialism, which he calls "a cruel act"; and foresees a future of liberation for the Chinese people, "great armies of them liberated from original sin and their feudal parents" (p. 40). But his relationship with Mimi reproduces in the field of sexuality that cruel colonization of the Other that mixes "progress with exploitation" which he condemns in his father.

The major characters are neither European nor "Oriental" but are boldly identified as "Eurasian." The term "Eurasian" is an earlier category that anticipates those spun off in late twentieth-century debates on race, ethnicity, and multiculturalism. It does not even appear as a category in the influential *Harvard Encyclopedia of American Ethnic Groups*. The coining of the term "Eurasian" is usually ascribed to the Marquis of Hastings in the seventeenth century, referring to the children of British men and Indian women at the moment of British colonization of the subcontinent. The notion and fear of miscegenation (of mixing "blood" and of consequent generational degeneracy through interracial marriages) did not appear to have been motivating forces during the period of first contact. On the contrary, in 1683, to facilitate the penetration of the East India Company into India, British soldiers and traders were encouraged to marry Indian women so as to produce "a stock of Protestant Mestizees" (Gaikwad 1967, 16). In 1786, because of increasing competition from British subjects coming out for employment into the colonies and the need for greater control of its employees, the East India Company passed repressive measures restricting the economic roles open to the children of these marriages (Gaikwad 1967, 20–21). The term "Eurasian," exploited by popular writers playing on Western prejudices, became associated with negative qualities, and the community in India began using "Anglo-Indian" instead to name itself. However, according to the *Oxford English Dictionary*, by 1869, "Eurasian" was used to refer to the mixed race of Dutch, Portuguese, Hindu, Malay, that is "blood mixed in all degrees."

The notion of "mixed blood" assumes an a priori condition of "pure blood"; it ascribes to a narrow, deterministic, and biologistic view of humans that has been scientifically proven unfeasible but that has remained culturally compelling for many people. Race as a product of the "pure blood" of a people is patently only a social myth, once we acknowledge the specific histories of group immigrations, interactions, and encounters. But it is a myth around which many people organize their belief systems, values, and political structures. While "race" as a social category gives us a means to construct identities of communities (as in the conflation of race with national identity), infusing individual actions with seemingly transcendent histories and meanings, it more problematically operates to exclude, creating classes of "others" that become dehumanized and so open to exploitation and oppression as inferior.

The potential in such categories for violent control is dramatically represented in the scene where the *kempetai* interviews the friends arrested by Japanese soldiers on suspicion of celebrating the news of Japan's surrender to the Allied Forces. He separates the white Russians into a corner with other foreigners; sends Feng, identified as Chinese, to the opposite corner; waves over to the foreigners Mimi who claims her Australian father's identity; and places Larry, the "neutral" Irish, "alone in a third corner" (p. 119). Recognized as a "white Chinese," Sylvia is allowed to stand with Feng. This scene enacts in microcosm the geopolitical divisions of people through arbitrarily applied categories of race and nationality the better to enforce a tyranny of one group that has set itself up as superior, in this case the Japanese military. In this scene, Feng and Sylvia, the "white Chinese" or Eurasians, are separated from everyone else as a group historically seen to operate as an "Other," on a precipice between Europe and Asia.

Mimi, the beautiful daughter of a Chinese socialite and white Australian adventurer, unlike Feng and Sylvia, refuses a "white Chinese" identity. The horror of being named "Eurasian" explains Mimi's psychic and erotic destiny. Courted by the older, wealthy Robert Bruno, the eighteen-year-old Mimi abandons herself to her newly awakened sexuality, only to find herself deserted by him. In one of the novel's central scenes, Mimi's Chinese Aunt Juliet confronts Robert and draws from him the acknowledgment that it is his father's prejudice against Mimi's mixed race origin that has led to his rejection of her niece: "And yet you cannot marry her because . . . your father will not countenance your marrying a Eurasian!" (p. 174). Mimi's terrible hysteria comes at the moment of her aunt's pronouncement of the irreducible nature of her mixed race identity: "Nothing will change the fact of her Eurasianness!" (p. 174). Her tragedy, spinning her from the tender confidences of first love through the masochism of promiscuity (p. 232), repeats the stereotyping of the Eurasian as the subject of conflicting race identities, resulting in self-hatred and sexual confusion and laxity (Wallace 1930; Crabb 1960; Younger 1987). These images of the Eurasian formed the bulwark of analysis, resistance, and representation in academic and literary works up to the 1960s, when the term became displaced in the United States by seemingly less loaded words: "biracial," "Amerasian," "Asian American" and "happa."

Chang's novel tracks the issue of biraciality through the "consciousnesses," of three young characters. Its twenty-six chapters form a layered, polyvocal structure, dominated in turn by the voices, in the third person, of characters whose combined effect is to represent a series of phenomenologically textured discourses on identity. Sylvia Chen's point of view dominates in chapters 1, 4, 8, 10, 12, 14, 17, 21, and 25; Feng Huang's in chapters 2, 5, 9, 19, and 23. Mimi's point of view rules chapters 3, 6, 11, 16, 20, and 24; Chen Liyi's in chapters 7, 15, 26; and Peiyuan's in chapter 13, 18, and 22. These chapter layerings do not so much constitute a neat stitching of the plot and subplots as they suggest a simultaneous ravelling and unravelling of interwoven themes.

The plot itself is a basic form of drama. Waiting out the Japanese Occupation in Shanghai, three young people of white and Asian parents arrive at different resolutions to their identity dilemmas. Mimi turns to promiscuity after her affair with a rich Swiss who will not marry her because his father disapproves of her mixed-race status. Feng rejects his mother's English identity and collaborates with the Communist saboteurs to affirm a Chinese racial identity. His collaboration leads to the brutal murder of

Peiyuan, the Chinese cousin of his lover, Sylvia, herself a child of a Chinese father and American mother, and destroys their relationship.

This bald plot summary, however, misses the entire fabric of the novel's complex themes, which weave psychological renditions, historical narrative, and sociological observations into a finely nuanced mobile play of meditations on the nature of identities. In this metaphysical drama, the novel's language shifts to a different intensity, of syntax, rhythm, and counterpointing of the abstract and the sensuous, that carries the fiction out of the production of prose and into the transcendent mentality of poetry.

In abstracting the novel's themes, therefore, we must account for the way its language operates as multivocal and dialogical discourse, in which subtly and with duplicitous variations a range of social attitudes, values, and classes are uttered. The novel's stylistics, in short, are woof to the fiction's thematic weave, and the novel's poetics and politics are simultaneously produced. Bakhtin points out that, above all genres, the novel "best of all reflects the tendencies of a new world still in the making . . . . it infects [other genres] with its spirit of process and inconclusiveness" (1981, 7). A major feature in Chang's novel is how the tensions between prose and poetry undergird the narrative to represent the thematics of interpenetrating and variegated subjective and historical (objective) realities. The novel, as Bakhtin has theorized it, "can be defined as a diversity of social speech types (sometimes even diversity of languages) and a diversity of individual voices, artistically organized" (1981, 262). In giving voice to multiple points of view, *The Frontiers of Love* illuminates multiple consciousnesses, each with its own ideological "unity." While Sylvia may be said to be the central character, the novel contains not one heroine but several foci, all, in Bakhtin's definition of the novelistic hero, "located in a zone of potential conversation with the author, in a zone of *dialogical contact*" (1981, 45).

Mimi, for all the pathos of her psychosexual disintegration, is the least fully drawn of the three main characters. Her self-absorption reflects the narrow, shallow conscience of an individ-

xiv

ualistic perspective. Privileged by class and beauty, "no laws but attitudes governed" her (p. 34). At the same time, as a deracinated subject, she is figured literally and metaphorically as an "orphan." Robert's appeal is precisely the illusion of power that he confers on her. The sexual politics figured in their coupling forms a dramatic protofeminist critique of the asymmetrical power relations in heterosexuality. Mimi understood "her own worth" (p. 40) through Robert; "his love and need for her . . . gave her a sense of richness and power" (p. 41). In constituting her position as dependent on Robert, she was also surrendering herself to his power: "She wanted also to be of his world. Until him, she had not known she was essentially homeless" (p. 74). Robert's rejection of her therefore, while it is firstly a sexual rejection, is also experienced as a terrifying loss of her identity. Mimi cannot move out of the a priori positioning of her self as a sexual object ontologically grounded in the status of the male subject; so marked by her first lover, she becomes "a willing victim . . . making her body pliant, asking any man to punish her and to find her beautiful" (p. 232).

Feng and Sylvia present more self-reflexive points of view. They recognize themselves as "two white Chinese" (p. 126), a phrase that subverts race distinctions in collapsing and fusing two conventionally raced subjects. But that is as far as their similarities go. Feng Huang, christened "Farthington" by his mother, in rejecting his mother's English "eccentricity" in a Sino-centered country (p. 27), rejects the class and race categories assigned to him by this biological bond. In place of this smothering Western matriarch, he adopts the patriarchal ideology of revolutionary Communism, as seen in his relationship with Tang, the Chinese foreman of the Bruno printing plant and Communist cell leader. Feng's discomfort with his birth identity, resulting in his hollow ego, leads him directly to an authoritarian regime for identity security: "He felt more self-respect when he was in custody, in the uniform of a cause" (p. 32). His ego drive to escape the burden of identity conflict and self-hatred, leading him to seek dependency on a more dominant Other, parallels the process of Mimi's relationship with Robert. Feng's "victimization" by a predatory ideological regime is more masked than Mimi's. His betrayal of Peiyuan, which results in Peiyuan's brutal murder, appears to give him more agency than Mimi; but a close reading demonstrates that like Mimi he suffers a death of the self. Mimi's sexual degradation is equated with Feng's moral death. Leaving Shanghai as commanded by the Party's organizers, Feng perceives his utter loss of "feeling" — "a kind of impotence, the facing of the blank wall of self" (p. 226). In subordinating his "feeling" self to ideology, "a code by which to live," Feng, like Mimi who subordinates her self to the aggression of male sexuality, seeks to "expend this distaste for himself" (p. 226).

In Mimi and Feng, *The Frontiers of Love* critiques how the sociopolitical pressures on individuals to position themselves within a single race or nation or class or political identity result in the destruction of "feeling" selves. The novel's meditations on the nature and construction of being constitute therefore a politics as well as a poetics of feeling. Feeling is not merely aestheticized as beautiful and moralized as good. It becomes the domain of individual action in which what is beautiful and good are decided; an ineluctable necessity for material struggle rather than an expendable luxury built on class privilege. Because knowing, believing, and acting have their origin in individuals' feelings, the danger raised in the exclusionary propensities of any form of identity politics is the suppression of feeling in order to arrive at a fixed identity formation.

Peiyuan's pivotal position asserts the erased centrality of China in the novel's colonized historical moment. As Sylvia's sixteen-year-old country cousin, "an untainted Chinese" (p. 146), Peiyuan represents a new generation, culturally almost untouched by European colonialism, whose energy and ambition promise a different future for China (see chapter 13, pp. 149–52). While Helen finds his "Chineseness," figured through his physical appearance and his use of the language, intolerable, Sylvia envies Peiyuan for his cultural connectedness. Peiyuan's "Chinese house grew inward, but included the outside . . . . It humanized the earth around it" (p. 143). As an idealized figure for a new potential China,

Peiyuan's tragic murder indicts not only the shadowy emergent Maoist forces, portrayed by the foreman Tang, but also Feng's fanatical intellectualism and Liyi's impotent liberalism.

The novel concludes with Sylvia and her father Liyi, who are similar in their distrust of the dangerous tendency toward racist reification and in their urgent need to keep their identities in process. Anguished by her mother's abuse of Peiyuan, Sylvia announces, "I am Chinese!" (p. 140). But this strategic separation from Helen's racism does not cancel Sylvia's "illegitimacy" as Chinese. Sylvia understands that to her "pure-blooded Chinese" neighbors, she is not a Chinese. Ironically these Westernized Chinese, "caught in the vacuum between generations in China, robbed of all values, could yet rob you of what you were" (p. 145). The individual's announcement of an identity is always hostage to others' social constructions.

Sylvia's refusal to foreclose the question of identity confers on her admirable qualities especially suitable for an existentialist heroine: "she could be anything, experiment with any possibility. Living between two worlds had made her sensitive to the nuances, the innuendos of everything between those two, all the variations" (p. 145). But it also signifies certain psychic costs: the fragmentation of identity, its instability and the risks of incoherence: "But where was the crime, and had there been one, except in her own heart? She was so many different people, and she could no longer maintain the balance among them all" (p. 146). In contrast to characters that maintain single fixed identity positions, Sylvia's tentativeness is fragile and vulnerable: "Her mother at least had a point of view, and Sylvia only had an undependable pulse, racing over nothing at all. . . . Sylvia felt threatened, afraid, as though Helen could rob her of herself" (p. 49).

In this effortful process of coming into being, Sylvia like Mimi looks to the male for self affirmation. She sees Feng as "pure and strong and completely free from ambivalence" (p. 182)—qualities that Feng projects as mirrors to an ideological code. These women characters are presented as passive recipients of male power; to Sylvia, Feng "could plunge her into the marketplace of life" (p. 182). Their selves are absences that can only be filled by male subjectivity. Sylvia "felt only like a photographic plate which was less than nothing unless exposed to light. And Feng's love was her illumination" (p. 183).

Unlike Mimi, however, Sylvia is endowed with the grace of intelligence that finally resists this replication of patriarchally inscribed sexuality. And unlike Feng, the difficulties in her position between two cultural sites, China and America, have not hollowed her ego, for unlike Feng, her commitment to China is nonideological. It springs from and is confirmed in her feelings for China, grounded in a childhood in Beijing (formerly called Peiping or Peking) which informs her sensuous and mental consciousness. Among "the hybrids and the cosmopolitans," those who "possessed the subtle authority of the foreigner" (p. 86), Sylvia is a Chinese in her feelings for that material reality called China. In a powerful recitation in which memory is both mixed with and reconstitutes desire, the sensations of a Chinese childhood become rewritten as "concern for the country" — a concern, moreover, "that was simple, feminine, specifically organic to her experience" (p. 55), in contrast to Feng's revolutionary commitment to a Chinese future, which is complicated and masculine and calls for a denial of his life as a "civilian," "a young lawyer and his parents' son" (p. 32). Sylvia's rhetorical exaggeration — "that one's first memories should be of loving and that these should be under the Peiping sky" (p. 57) — underscores the relation between human subjects and place. This thematic, often vulgarized in popular culture in terms such as patriotism, nationality, community, and country, recognizes certain primordial bonds, shaped within the forming ego, to a geocultural site. These memories, the novel argues, "should be and remain and live at the young core of every adult, be the solid unwavering pivot of the unchanging child in every grown person, the point of eternal return, the memory which is the person, beyond which no history can recede" (p. 57).

Memory, feeling, and desire are the operations that secure individuals in the world, but when they function to deny the same operations in others, they become the means by which other subjects are unsecured, "obliterated" as Sylvia fears Helen's rampant Americanism will obliterate her (pp. 47–49). The novel's dramatization of different ontologies points to the need to break the oppositional binaries set up, for example, between East and West, Asia and Europe, Chinese and American, capitalist and labor, male and female. It does not so much posit a distinction between true and false selves as it plays out the tensions between the space of the indeterminate subject—with its claims on feelings, memories, insights, and desires—and identity politics—the contestations of the social construction of the person as sexualized, classed, and raced subject, a social construction that is by its nature overdetermined and fraught with contradictions and material consequences. Sylvia's early insistence on a "true" or "real" self is a form of nostalgia for a fictive coherence recoverable only in memory. At the novel's conclusion, after Peiyuan's funeral, in a complicated epiphany, Sylvia sheds "attachment and dependency" to accept full responsibility for her self. In this paradigmatic shift of the place of the subject, from the "soul" to the body, from the ideal to the material, she takes on the power of agency: "Abruptly, she had no longer felt accidental, but responsible. She was Sylvia Chen, and she would speak out for herself" (p. 237). Interestingly, "accidental" is opposed not to its philosophical antinomy, "essential," but to "responsible." The individual becomes a subject not by a predetermined metaphysical condition, an essence, or by an overdetermined social role, but when she becomes an agent; thus, the identity of the subject is always contingent on the ways in which it chooses to act. Sylvia's entry into agency marks her entry into a different subject position, as if she were taking "her first breath of life" (p. 237).

In its plotting of multiple points of view, the novel can be read as an early rehearsal of the current debates in identity politics, between the essentialists and the social constructionists. We may think of Feng's "resolution" to the debate as that of "strategic essentialism": taking on a raced identity in order to effect desired sociopolitical ends. The cost of such essentialism (that is, of characterizing individuals as corresponding to an essence of race, gender, or other essential category of being) is a loss of feeling for others, an impotency of the self. Sylvia's "resolution," however, is no resolution; it offers instead an enlargement of her feelings. Now Sylvia "felt she was strong enough to be able to help her 'sister' (Mimi) tomorrow" (p. 238). Passing by again the familiar three beggars, now "she knew she inhabited their consciousness as much as they did hers" (p. 239). The novel argues for the place of feeling in the social constructedness of the subject. Know thy self—what the Greeks had sacralized as the first goal of learning—can only be achieved "in her heart" (p. 239). Constituted within the individual's sentient body, therefore, the identity of the subject is always being formed, never finished. Our final sight of Sylvia is of one expectant, still undisclosed: "She expected a new and sudden vision" (p. 240).

But it is Liyi, Sylvia's father, who is given the last word in the novel. Liyi's point of view inserts a different version of identity binaries in the novel. While the narratives concerning Mimi, Feng, and Sylvia contain elements of the *bildungsroman*, the novel of development, whether as regressive or progressive structures, Liyi narrates a generational rupture. Like his daughter, Liyi is uncertain and tentative about his point of view. While Sylvia envies him his grounding in Chinese culture, he understands his own position as less secure, more complexly fragmented. He is a member of that historical cohort of patriotic Chinese intellectuals who received their training in the West: "They had returned from studying abroad, and had been inoculated with Western drive and pragmatism, vaccinated against their Chinese *laissez-faire*" (p. 164). Liyi experiences his own rupture from Chinese society viscerally in his feelings for his children: "He could hardly bear to pronounce the word "Eurasian"; it was as though his seed had produced mavericks, or mutations" (p. 162). At the same time, however, he embraces his children as the agents to a modern China, seeing in Sylvia, for example, "his own daughter, and the very word 'daughter' filled him with warmth and love—she was an extension of him, a miraculous bridge in flesh into the future" (p. 77). Shaped by a conservative China, Liyi is still able to imagine a different future; thus he actively welcomes his displacement by a younger and "foreign" generation: "the young *were* wiser than the old; they had to improvise the future" (p. 78).

In the novel's conclusion, walking through the Chinese countryside, Liyi recovers from his guilt and despair at Peiyuan's death: "The miracle was beginning to happen. He was going to feel again." His love for his children and for Helen lead to a life-affirming consciousness, that "Life was not to be resolved, but to be lived — a constant improvisation" (pp. 244–45). The novel ends on an antinihilist affirmation of the problematic of race: "That had been the bravest thing he had done — to marry Helen and bring two Eurasians into the world." The subjectivity within each individual is itself a familial and communal project: "they were together in this: each would have to explore the humanity in himself." Liyi articulates the novel's "message" on identity positions: "To be Chinese was not enough .... The times were demanding new loyalties, more discriminating, more humanitarian" (pp. 245–46). Substitute "American" for "Chinese," or "white," "black," "Asian," "male," "female," or any single category of identity. In arguing for the operation of feeling in the politics of identity, the novel argues for a displacement of the policed identities of nationalities and races that produced the horrors of the Second World War, and for an imaginable brave new world of feeling subjects all equally constituted within a "culture of consciousness"[†] in which race, nation, class, and gender fixities are rendered as ideologically impossible.

The novel's vision of a society of new, more discriminating loyalties is not utopian; rather it is a necessary project that is already urgently upon us. *The Frontiers of Love* must be read within an Asian American cultural context not on account of a biographical argument — Chang was born in New York of a Chinese father and Eurasian mother and spent some of her childhood in Beijing, before returning to the United States to be educated later

[†]I owe this phrase to Stuart Hall who used it in a talk given at the University of California, Santa Barbara, on April 24, 1993.

at Barnard (Fisher 1980). Rather, it is an eminently Asian American text because, like Jessica Hagedorn's *Dogeaters*, it possesses a narrative sensibility that is capable of passing in and out of Asian and American fields of reference without self-consciousness or awkwardness.

Chang says of herself, "I'm an American whose background is Chinese, but I suspect it's as an American that I sometimes write about the Chinese in me" (pers. com.). How disparate is that self-identification from that implied in Kenneth Rexroth's generous praise: "Of all the novels of the Far East published this season, Miss Chang's book, at least for me, has the most reality" (*Nation* 1956). Indeed, the "Far East" of the novel was a product of both Western colonial and Chinese national cultures. It is a "Far East" that today has set just as unsettling roots in America, in the fluid dynamic ethnoscapes of a Chinatown, Koreatown, or Little Saigon. Or in the plural cultures enacted by Amerasians and Asian Americans to whom the reified signifiers of Kipling's "East is East and West is West, and never the twain shall meet" are patently absurd although still potent with divisive force. The novel's moving meditations on the complicated, terribly serious work of forming one's identity, without foreclosing possibilities, without fixing identity, through the enlargement of one's powers of imagination and feelings for others, speak especially to these Americans whose identities encompass the hitherto dreaded incompatibilities of white and yellow race and culture.

SHIRLEY GEOK-LIN LIM
University of California, Santa Barbara

Appiah, Kwame Anthony, and Henry Louis Gates, Jr. "Editors' Intro-
    duction: Multiplying Identities," *Critical Inquiry*, 18 (Summer 1992):
    625–29.

Bakhtin, M. M. *The Dialogic Imagination*. Trans. Caryl Emerson and
    Michael Holquist. Austin: University of Texas Press, 1981.

Cook, Christopher. *The Lion and the Dragon: British Voices from the China
    Coast*. London: Elm Tree Books, 1985.

Crabb, C. H. *Malaya's Eurasians*. Singapore: D. Moore for Eastern Uni-
    versities Press, 1960.

Durkheim, Emile. *Moral Education*. Trans. Everett K. Wilson and Her-
    man Schnurer, pp. 67–68. New York: The Free Press, 1961.

Fanon, Frantz. *Black Skin, White Masks*. Trans. Charles Lam Markmann.
    New York: Grove Press, 1967.

Fisher, Dexter. *The Third Woman*. Boston: Houghton Mifflin, 1980.

Gaikwad, V. R. *The Anglo-Indians: A Study in the Problems and Processes
    in Emotional and Cultural Integration*. Bombay: Asia Publishing House,
    1967.

Hagedorn, Jessica. *Dogeaters*. New York: Pantheon Books, 1990.

Lease, Benjamin. Review of *The Frontiers of Love*. *Chicago Sun-Times*, 1956.

Rexroth, Kenneth. Review of *The Frontiers of Love*. *Nation*, pp. 271–73,
    Sept. 29, 1956.

Seagrave, Sterling. *The Soong Dynasty*. New York: Harper and Row, 1985.

Thernstrom, Stephen, ed. *Harvard Encyclopedia of American Ethnic Groups*.
    Cambridge, Mass.: Harvard University Press, 1980.

Wallace, Kenneth E. *The Eurasian Problem*. Calcutta, Simla: Thacker
    Spink and Co., 1930.

Younger, Coralie. *Anglo-Indians: Neglected Children of the Raj*. Delhi: B. R.
    Pub. 1987.

The Frontiers of Love

CHAPTER ONE

In Shanghai she could bathe herself three times a day in the summer and still not feel refreshed. Often, Sylvia Chen would not dry herself after stepping out of the tub, but walk back to her bedroom naked and dripping. For a few minutes, as the water evaporated, she felt cool and unencumbered, almost as though she were suddenly transported to a more astringent climate. But the illusion lasted only briefly, and Shanghai's humidity soon settled on her again like an extra suit of clothing.

And so, tonight, she stood absent-mindedly by the window (nothing happened these days to catch the mind and make it spring up alertly) and looked out at the twilight, the small pool of water at her feet turning the floor into a slippery mirror. Carefully she stepped around the rug and lay down on the thin mat on her bed. The fine straw smelled slightly of grass and of the out-of-doors, and kept the bed cool to sleep on. She turned herself every few minutes, lazily enjoying the prospect of going out soon. When she stood up again to go to her dressing table, she was dry and had tiny marks of the straw on her body, as though the twiglike feet of birds had walked on her arms, her breasts, her back and thighs.

She turned and tugged at the curtains, covering the window completely, before she switched on the lamp by the bureau. She looked again to make sure that no light leaked out, and then began to dress carefully. It was a carefulness that was meant only for herself—it would help her mark the event. But later, to her mother, who stared at the "good" dress she wore elbow-shaped pavement between houses, and she still had a fifteen-minute walk down two avenues.

Two years before, the Jastrows had made them all promise to meet in their house the night the war ended. This summer no one even mentioned the possibility of the war ending. Early this summer the Chens had put in a stock of dried beans, rice and other staples against the eventuality of an American siege of the China coast. The outside world seemed farther away than ever. The war grew older, but that peace would make a new beginning seemed beyond anyone's comprehension.

"*My* living room!" Sylvia wanted to exclaim, unreasonably. "I am going to *my* living room!" She was possessive about these evenings at the Jastrows. She wanted so much to be able to invest them with life. She wanted so much to have these evenings inform the doldrums that marked the days between this gathering and the next. She pinned too much hope on them. She knew it, but could not help it. They were all any of them had! Her reason told her she was being overdramatic, ridiculous. But her heart beat a little faster as she climbed the stairs.

The building the Jastrows lived in always reminded Sylvia of Greenwich Village, which she had found a kind of haphazard haven from the squared-off blocks of Manhattan that year she had been in the States. Even squeezing by the refrigerator at the top of the stairs leading into the three rooms of the Jastrow apartment gave her an inexplicable pang—it took her back to Charles and Perry streets, their uneven stoops and tiny irregular rooms where so many people found refuge from the expectations of their parents.

She wished she could brush away the darkness like cobwebs. A great longing and impatience overcame her in the hallway, as she groped her way into the dim room. "I'd be lost if I could walk anywhere unhesitatingly after so many years of semi-darkness!" It seemed the war had conspired to cripple all her natural instincts. At twenty, she seemed both untried and aged, inexperienced and disillusioned, too!

She squinted in the dim and familiar light of the living room. The single lamp was placed on a low coffee table before the divan on which Julie Jastrow lay, waving her thin hands in conversation. Beyond the pink tent of light the other figures appeared like half-draped forms, covered with gloom. Sylvia found herself half smiling, flattered that no one had stopped speaking for a moment to greet her. They were much too good friends for perfunctory greetings. But Julie stretched out a hand over the table and Sylvia thought, as she did each time, what a strong, almost demanding handshake her hostess had.

The Jastrows—and she felt a surge of emotion thinking about them—were the solid center of the group that met, welded to each other, settled and complete. They were the necessary hub, but they were sufficient unto themselves, and seemed to have acquired an invisibility, demonstrated even now by Bill, Julie's husband, who stood by the sideboard unassumingly mixing the drinks. Having a child, the only child of the group, they were committed to reality; the others, and among them Sylvia included herself, were unmarried, with themselves alone to possess, and were committed only to a future escape. The Jastrows, she thought with sudden passion, were excellent, special friends. She would never forget them.

"*My* living room!" she thought again. It offered Sylvia more privacy than her own at home, which was dominated by her mother. Here she felt free, she did not have to account for herself at all; but even as she thought it and set her package on the sideboard, turning away with a glass offered her by Bill Jastrow, she knew it wasn't entirely true. But the impression lasted only a split second, then was lost. She wanted to lose it. She felt a sobering influence in the room, and tried to put off meeting it.

"Miss Chen," a voice said jestingly and slowly, "are you trying to avoid me?" It was Feng Huang, speaking English formally, pretending it was not his *mother's* tongue and that he had difficulty with its construction. Sometimes Sylvia could shake him for his affectations. Sometimes he was a snob in reverse—denying his own uniqueness and trying to force himself into the mold of "the common man."

"Sit here," he commanded, pointing to the empty place on the couch beside him, which Sylvia had noted as soon as she had entered.

"Later, Feng," she said, irritated with herself for making it sound almost like a promise. "I don't want to sit down quite yet," and while anyone else would have felt that her tone compensated for her decision, Sylvia knew Feng Huang was displeased. She moved away, half turning her back to him. He had a way of making her unhappy with herself; and although she was not fully aware of the reason, she put off any encounter with him.

Then she gave a soundless chuckle of delight. Larry Casement and Hasan Kemal, the Turk, were standing by the window, arguing in loud whispers.

"All right, don't listen to me!" she declared, apropos of nothing. They weren't even listening to each other. She plunged into their individual harangues with one of her own (how well she knew point and counterpoint: it was always about nineteenth-century poetry, British poetry, to be sure) and she parodied their whispering. She nodded her head, gesticulated, stamped her foot for emphasis. They put their arms around her, and leaving them resting on her shoulders, continued their strident conversation without a pause.

She smiled over the incongruous two: Larry Casement, blond and Irish (which was the reason he had escaped being interned with other enemy nationals, the Americans, the British and the Dutch), and Hasan Kemal, the dark, wiry Middle Easterner, who, like Larry, had been educated in a British school in Shanghai. "I say, bloke!" Hasan's voice would cry out, not knowing how bizarre the phrase sounded from his lips. His eyes stared at Sylvia now, without really seeing her—round black eyes, whose expression was so innocent as to seem almost blind behind his horn-rimmed glasses. Sylvia laughed to herself, and wanted to kiss him on the tip of his pugnacious nose. But

8

Hasan was even too innocent for that; he would have shrunk back in alarm, and Larry, his inseparable companion, would have enlarged on the comedy and embarrassed them both. Hasan Kemal was gentle and candid; Larry just the opposite, caustic and knowing.

Sylvia turned away from their conversation. It seemed to herself that she was always lurking in other people's doorways, trying to overhear their lives. Looking around now, she saw a not too unfamiliar picture. There were times, in fact, when she had been bored, bored to a kind of agony, because even these evenings provided no variety. Feng Huang was sitting sidesaddle on the couch, listening to Mimi Lambert, who sat on the floor beside him, talking busily, earnestly. She seldom had anything to say to Feng, and he now leaned toward her with an attentiveness Sylvia would not have thought he possessed. The demonstration is meant for me, she realized, because I have slighted him. It made her look at him, as if for the first time. Feng was a large, almost heavy-set young man of twenty-six. His shoulders were thick, as though he had taken up boxing; his neck—where men's strength showed most clearly—was strong and tanned. His face was intent and, unlike the others, pure and focused completely on the outside world. He was a Eurasian who could never reconcile himself to being one. His mother, Sylvia knew, was an Englishwoman now separated from the Chinese lawyer she had married, putting a full stop to the world tour she had been on almost thirty years before. Two years ago Feng had officially dropped the name she had given him, Farthington, and now his name was brief and Chinese, Feng Huang.

Looking up now, Feng said to Mimi, "Robert is here!" He seemed surprised, glancing from Robert to Mimi and back again. His trying to understand made his face especially alive.

Mimi seemed just as untroubled and beautiful as usual, but she answered Feng dully, almost irascibly, "I know," and gave up her pretense at chatter. At the same moment the Jastrows exclaimed over the figure at the door.

"Robert Bruno!" they both cried, as though their loudness might dispel his shyness. "Close that door," they ordered him merrily, "or you'll have the *pao-chia* after us!" The draft had stirred the black curtains; they would be fined if the lamplight reached the sidewalk.

"Oh, Mimi, really!" Sylvia wanted to cry, for Mimi Lambert was gazing assiduously at Robert's feet as he walked into the room, his diffidence making him conspicuous. Mimi sat in a parody of stoniness, and, of course, everyone knew that she and Robert had had a quarrel. "We are all present, then, all accounted for," Sylvia thought of announcing pompously, "all of us who have survived more than four years of meeting at the Jastrows," while Mimi slid herself around on the floor, cruelly ignoring Robert, who sat down on the couch. Her action transfixed them, so that everyone seemed to be struggling within himself to find a way to end the silence.

Then at last Mimi tossed back her dark mass of hair in a theatrical motion, stood up with the awkwardness of a certain petulance she carried with her always, and kicked back one foot slowly, deliberately, in Robert Bruno's direction. Had she been a few inches closer, her heel would have caught him on the cheek, but her movement was clear enough. It released Robert. He leaned forward quickly, but was too late to seize her foot. She had run out of his reach, stumbling into Bill Jastrow's arms. Almost simultaneously, everyone was again talking good-naturedly. The Turk fell to winding up the Jastrows' ancient victrola in a frenzy, while Larry selected dance records, commenting on their rhythms and berating their vintage.

"I wish, I wish, I wish!" Sylvia wanted to fling out her arms and declare her desire. But what was this desire, which made her so restless, while it also made her want to reach out for more dissatisfaction? "Why am I so— Oh, to be someone else, to be different! What makes me feel so old and so new!" She was so susceptible, she could surrender herself to her own intensity. But she was also so reasonable, she was her own cruel, saving monitor. She hated it when she felt like this, sunk inward until she was a dim image in a niche, looking out on, but not participating in, the life of others.

So now, staring at Mimi, whom she had known so long, Sylvia envied her her ability to project herself, to act so freely, so unconsciously. She felt that if she watched Mimi long enough she would learn her secret. She knew that to Mimi, in turn, she herself was "a mystery," a word Mimi pronounced with jealousy, but perhaps that only meant that Mimi labeled what she did not have the urge to define. Mimi had declared she would have liked to have been "a mystery" herself, slight, sensitive, carrying around in her eyes and posture a delicate watchfulness. But Sylvia, even as she was whirled around now to the rusty sounds of old jazz records, in turn by each of the men in the room—with the exception of Robert Bruno, who held in his arms a laughing Mimi—Sylvia thought only how different Mimi and she had turned out. They could have been as similar as sisters. The same racial ingredients had gone into the making of them. Mimi was Mimi Eloise Lambert; her full name was Mimi Eloise Hong Lambert, daughter of an Australian adventurer and Rosalind Hong, that reckless Chinese socialite who had shocked the Peking Hotel populace twenty years before with her décolleté gowns and tennis-playing paramours.

"I am lonely," Sylvia suddenly knew. But why? She was not alone. This lassitude, so shot through with sudden spurts of agonizing desire and hope, this watchfulness that only she seemed to have—as if she must even breathe gingerly lest she scare away the moment when she could come into possession of herself—it was all so tedious, unnecessary. Yet she tended her hopes and fears possessively, learning from them.

She now watched Mimi push Robert Bruno away, and turn to fill up her glass with more of the acidic drink that the Jastrows concocted of whatever their friends were able to contribute. Mimi held her glass with a soft gaucheness, one hand brushing back the mass of hair falling into her eyes. She never carried herself straight, but her slouch followed the aristocratic line of her profile and was part of the unawakened grace of her careless posture. She's unmarried, Sylvia thought, but she marries whomever she turns to, talks to, smiles at. Whomever she dances with, Mimi is all faithful to, until the end of the dance. It was a talent all the men recognized and one which inspired both Robert's love and his anxiety.

But I'm different, Sylvia thought. My posture is straight, like a five-year-old's, the shoulder blades vulnerable-looking. I'm feminine by suggestion; she's lavish. She puts people at their ease because she has no self-consciousness. But everyone acts upon me. Only a certain dry turn of my mind saves me from the danger of being overimpressionable. Mimi asks nothing of herself—she *is*. And I? Perhaps I shall always be trying to be someone.

Sylvia looked at her again. Mimi wore a dress with a voluminous skirt and shoulder straps that needed constant adjusting: she moved a gleaming shoulder forward and replaced a strap and smoothed a lock of her heavy, wavy hair in a single slow movement. She would not have dreamed of wearing a Chinese dress.

"There are enough people in this country who *have* to wear them," she'd say, almost as a witticism, and she included her own mother, when she was alive, in the majority.

Sylvia wore Chinese and foreign clothes alternately, jockeying her dissatisfaction with herself in each. Tonight she had contrived to look classically Chinese, for she kept her hair shiningly clean and deliberately straight, cut at a provocative length, neither long nor short. It blew away from her face, making her seem almost boyish, and then swung back to lick her cheek in a line that was gamin. But she could no more look Chinese than Mimi. Their eyes were brown; their hair, too, and turned reddish in the sunlight. And their exoticness lay in the truth that they seemed to have no racial identity at all.

Sylvia wanted to purse her lips and blow on the room like a candle. She could almost see their husky whispers gutter in the still, airless gloom. Out of habit, they spoke quietly, as though the Japanese were listening outside the windows, as though they themselves were guilty of expressing subversive opinions. Actually, everyone had long ago given up commenting on the progress of the war. They rarely turned on the radio, which broadcast only Domei items—the official Japanese news—and their own apathy alarmed them sometimes. It seemed to Sylvia to indicate more accurately than any other aspect of their lives how estranged they felt, their small individual concerns eddying slowly in a tiny circle, while "out there" the great dramas were being enacted: the war in Europe, which had ended in May, and the one which still held the East embattled. Even the alien nationals who were now being detained by the Japanese in internment camps around Shanghai could be said to be participants, because of their very passive internment, in the sense that the group at the Jastrows was not. Their being "out of things" was the common denominator which held them together—their world carved in one dimension, between the second dimension of the foreign colony and the third of the Chinese matrix, the Chinese lying there like quicksand to swallow the other two. It was a common denominator Sylvia knew none of them dared to examine. Larry Casement was Irish, Hasan Kemal a Turk, Robert Bruno was Swiss, the Jastrows were Jewish, and Feng Huang, Mimi Lambert and Sylvia Chen were Eurasians. No one of them was Chinese. And none of them could be alien in the secure way that an American or a Britisher could be.

Sylvia found herself shrugging imperceptibly. But she could not shrug away the present, and whatever happened later, it would always be part of all of them. She turned back to the conversation. Politics and the war were not topics they avoided; the subjects simply no longer seemed to come up. Instead, they spoke of Dos Passos, Hemingway, Freud, and forgot to leave off whispering. Only Mimi sometimes spoke out in so normal a voice, it seemed she shouted.

"Where *were* you?" Mimi now asked Robert, who sat on the couch and regarded her with the amusement and gratitude of a man who welcomed her breaches of behavior. She was so unself-conscious, she put even him at his ease—he who would always look over the brink of himself, and never be quite able to step out of his inhibitions. Her eyes sparkling, Mimi glanced at Feng, as though she were sharing a secret with him, as though they were somehow in league against Robert. But Feng did not respond. How hard it was for him to share anything with another person, Sylvia thought. There was something isolated about Feng. But still she envied him. His isolation seemed an act of choice; he was positive, though unresilient. She envied Mimi, too: she was incandescent. She saved nothing of herself; she was expending all her charms now in challenging Robert.

Mimi's question was repeated at more length now, and still louder: "Whatever made you arrive so late? Where *were* you?"

As though committed by her tone to speak as loudly as she, Robert replied, so that everyone could hear, "Well now, I don't think it would be quite gallant of me to reveal *all*," and Sylvia wondered if he intended to insinuate that he had been with a woman. But Mimi had already lost her smile—she was really so literal about everything that he seemed to be fearful that she might bring on a scene with which he could not cope. Feng Huang made a sudden gesture of self-defense, for he was sharing the couch with Robert and must have remembered that swift backward kick of Mimi's earlier. He uttered a sound that was intended to indicate laughter, but Sylvia, who now sat on the floor before the couch, saw that Feng was not smiling. He was biting his lip, looking past Mimi, preoccupied with his own tenseness.

Sylvia had seen Feng irritable before, fractious and restless. He was a man of many acts and disguises, she thought, for the first time trying to spread before her the image of his different expressions. There were times that Feng, boyish, open, artless, was almost poetic in his purity; at other times his boyishness turned into a sort of carelessness, his openness into a callousness, his ingenuousness into recklessness, and his poetry into violence. He now did not know what to do with himself, having nothing on which to vent his energy.

The music came to an end; the last record selected by Larry had been played. The new silence had the quality of a drought, Sylvia thought, withering and sterile. She wondered whether to the others it was just an enjoyable lull, whether it was only she who found the pause so destroying. She could not tell from their expressions, but it seemed to her a pause in which each of them wondered why he had so looked forward to the repetition of a not-too-exciting evening, even while not abandoning the hope that the next one would not be too far off.

"The truth is," Robert Bruno was saying, "I was at some entertainment, which," he hastened to add, in a lame effort to allay Mimi's reaction, "was most enjoyable."

"En-ter-tain-ment?" Mimi Lambert drawled, stringing out the syllables in disbelief. "I don't believe a word of it," she declared, not even deigning to look directly at him. But she flounced around voluptuously and fell into the space on the couch between Robert and Feng. Slowly she adjusted her shoulder strap, while Robert contemplated her as though he were measuring the pain she could inflict on him. Feng Huang jigged his foot impatiently, waiting a little apprehensively for the rest of the drama.

"What entertainment?" Mimi asked flatly, relentlessly, and Sylvia again found herself watching her. She could never rid herself of the impression that Mimi's simplicity was of the most complex kind, that her innocence was both chaste and crude, tantalizing and yet probably easily understood. "Are you going to tell me or not?" Mimi smiled, softly and menacingly, enchanted with her own performance.

"I was at"—and Robert sighed, truly reluctant to admit it to the company at large, yet unable to resort to whispering now—"I was at the Chinese opera."

"You sound as if you are ashamed of it!" Feng Huang cried, jarred into sudden life.

"The Chinese opera!" Mimi exclaimed. "Why, who goes

15

to the Chinese opera?" And she laughed at Robert unmercifully. Then, quite deliberately, Sylvia thought, Mimi turned an innocent gaze on Feng. She seemed determined to provoke him into noticing her.

"Who goes to the Chinese opera!" Feng Huang shouted. He uncrossed his legs, and as though a great twitch of anger possessed him, suddenly stood up. "No one—no one here goes to the Chinese opera!" He sounded as though he were strangling; he repeated himself, trying to find the words he wanted to use. "You—you—" and half choked.

He glared at Mimi, hating her because, as Sylvia knew, she epitomized all the superficiality of a Shanghai socialite, hating her for his own inarticulateness. But suddenly, Feng found his voice. "Why, you might get contaminated! You poor creatures living in exile from America, where you have never been!"

Sylvia sat paralyzed on the floor, while Feng paced the room, his movements distorted by his own hostility. Mimi raised her eyebrows and leaned toward Robert, pretending that she needed his protection.

"I've kept it all to myself too long," Feng shouted. "Years and years and years of listening to all of you! You have lived all your lives in China. But do you know it? Do you have an iota of curiosity about the country? I'm not asking you to have feelings about it, but just plain curiosity. All of you have held your noses and yearned for America. You feel besieged by Asians in this—this outpost, this colonial outpost, Shanghai!" He laughed bitterly, and the sound seemed to pierce Sylvia's chest.

"But what brought this up, Feng?" she asked, making her voice as even as possible, as unpatronizing as she could. "All Robert said was that he had attended a Chinese opera!" Her reasonableness seemed directed at placating herself as well, for Robert's confession had started a feeling of guilt moving in her.

Sylvia had reminded Feng of herself by speaking. He bore down on her awkwardly, treading on her shoe.

"*You* know what I mean, so don't pretend you don't. I've watched you for years. You know better, but you let yourself be swamped by these—these"—and he almost spit as he said it—"these old China hands." He pointed at Robert in particular, for Robert's father symbolized a generation of foreigners who had successfully exploited the China market. Sylvia felt shaken, unnerved. She tried to breathe evenly, and caught herself on the intake of a wracking sigh. She wanted to say something pertinent now, something accurate. But, unlike Feng, she felt that she had no point of view.

Robert came to her rescue. "I was just talking to my father today," he brought out smoothly and with the suavity of long training, "and saying that our days are numbered. We, we Westerners have had it here. But"- – he continued, addressing the room at large, in an effort to divert Feng from his violence—"but my father is of a more optimistic generation. He is planning to expand his business interests, not merely maintain a status quo. And I, the errant son," he said with an expression of sadness, "tell him to be satisfied with what we've got—we, as the Bruno family, you know—for once the war ends, we'll find things different in China."

"You certainly will!" Feng cried, with a stubborn, naked jut of his chin, asking for a fight. But before he could go on, Sylvia interrupted, now more afraid of where his anger might take him than of speaking up.

"The expansion your father plans," she asked Robert, for her own father was manager of Bruno Senior's printing plant downtown, "will it affect the press?"

Robert Bruno helped her again, speaking so deliberately now that it was almost impossible for Feng to interject a comment. "As a matter of fact, my father was thinking of buying out the two papers and the Eastern Press—of amalgamating the editorial and the printing departments under one management. It would mean many changes in the operation and the personnel."

"And Mr. Bruno, Senior, will have no more regard for the rights of the employees than the men in ownership now,"

Feng put in quickly. "The printing plant," he repeated, as though making a note of something whose importance no one else suspected. "It would mean many changes . . ." he ended under his breath.

"I think you owe everyone an apology," Mimi said to Feng, in her best social manner, her face halfway between a frown and a plea. She raised her hand to adjust a shoulder strap and then seemed to change her mind. She let it hang and shifted her pose. Her face was impudent and seductive.

Feng, astounded, stared at her and around at the rest of the company. His shoulders lifted, not in a shrug, but as if in a supreme, agonizing effort to adjust his rage to his own body. He does not know how alone he stands, Sylvia thought. His back toward the door, he looked at them and seemed to feel hatred and pity for them. She could hardly bear to see what was written on his face. His eyes seemed to say that he had betrayed himself every time he had come. His body declared in a rejecting movement that he had never belonged in this room. Quickly, not even seeming to want to make his points any more, too upset to be articulate, he declared, "I apologize to no one! I shall never come back here again!" and turned and slammed his way out of the apartment.

"No! No! No!" Sylvia wanted to cry. He was both right and wrong, which made the rest of them both wrong and right. She longed for a single, comforting bias.

None of them tried to stop him from leaving. For a while they were stunned—as much, it seemed, by the brevity of his attack as by the force of his displeasure with them. The latter had obviously been growing steadily but unknown to them; the small spark that Robert and Mimi provided served only to set off a hostility that had been pent up for a long time. Yet they were shaken, for he had been one of them for so long. They felt, Sylvia knew, as though they had harbored a dangerous explosive without knowing it.

But as the evening continued, they decided they had done him an injustice in not asking him to explain himself, in trying

18

to slur over what seemed by its suddenness and aggressiveness only a flare-up of extreme bad temper. "Next time," Hasan Kemal said, "next time, we'll have it out with him," and promising themselves that they felt better, they forgot that Feng Huang had declared there was not going to be another time here for him.

When he had slammed his way out, only Sylvia Chen had moved. Involuntarily, she had got up while he stood at the door, and when he left, she had almost run after him. Embarrassed and perplexed by her own action, she had stopped and leaned against the wall. All at once, her head had begun aching: he had touched a chord in her own anxieties. She was guilty—she was guilty of not knowing who she was. He, at least, had chosen to be Chinese. But she was both as American as her own mother, and as Chinese as her father. She could not deny her own ambivalence. She leaned against the wall, and cried, surprising everyone and herself, "How I wish they'd bomb us tonight!"

The moon was bright outside, a perfect waste of a beautiful night. For her friends, she had defined their loneliness. How well she knew that they ached for some recognition. The Americans were no longer even raiding occupied Shanghai. And her own existence seemed to mean nothing to herself or the world. She felt forsaken.

CHAPTER TWO

Anger never quite completely released Feng Huang, and now, as he walked briskly back to his mother's house, his eyes closed briefly in unspoken eloquence, an eloquence he could not muster into language. The right words never came to him when he needed them. His inarticulateness seemed to sieve out the significance of his arguments and let through only blunt accusations, meaningless because they did not express anything but his frank irritation.

At home, he paced up and down in his room, and picking up a magazine, he slapped it hard against the wall. He was overjoyed, he thought, elated, exuberant that he was at last rid of them—meaning everyone at the Jastrows'. His tension did not lessen. He still felt it manipulating him. He could not settle down to read; he felt hemmed in on all sides, and blocking out his disappointment with himself over his conduct that evening (for he had thought himself impervious to their idiocies), he blamed his feeling of claustrophobia on Shanghai itself. For as long as he could remember, he had sat crouched under the weather and under the almost physical climate of the enemy occupation, waiting. It seemed that as long as he could remember, it had been like this—the weather effecting a siege, a damp, freezing, fuel-less siege in the winter, and a damp, stifling blockade of heat in the summer. All of them (and he could not help but include the Jastrow group) were waiting, trying not to expend too much life now, lest they have less to give to their futures. They took small breaths and husbanded their heartbeats. Some day the weather would lift, the Japanese occupation would shatter and evaporate, releasing them. Each one felt that some day he would come into possession of a heritage—himself. Some day the myth of life would unfurl and send them on voyages of themselves.

This particular district of Shanghai, too, he thought, was responsible for the acuteness of his agony. The French Concession, in which they all lived, was a borough set apart. Strictly speaking, it could not be called Chinese, though it was inhabited mostly by Chinese—Chinese who were either wealthy, Westernized or prayed to a Christian God. In the good old days, before the Japanese occupation, his part of Shanghai had the atmosphere of a suburban area, busy with the comings and goings of foreigners entertaining on their lawns and at the international clubs. It had been a section that had supplied its own aura of well-being. The Chinese and the foreigners had walked around the French Concession in tennis outfits at eleven in the morning, changed into afternoon clothes after "tiffin," and ended their day in tuxedos or lounging pajamas. But whatever costume they graced, they looked martyred, languidly sacrificed upon their fiendishly good fortune.

Shanghai values were not his, he thought vehemently, if the city could be considered to have any at all—any which were not false. He was alone in feeling this, and the impossibility of communicating it to any of his friends, like the impossibility of sharing anything with his mother, seemed to straitjacket him. Still pacing his room now, he heard her calling from upstairs, "Farthington, dear!" She cleared her throat and said self-consciously, "Feng . . . Feng . . . Feng . . ." pronouncing his name as though it were a strange Yorkshire syllable.

"Caught between this," he muttered to himself, thinking of her voice as a demon that filled the house, "and those friends of mine!" Oh, what chains and nets and webs the years contrived to imprison one with! Oh, he had not been wrong to take the step he had taken six months ago.

"Feng, dear!" The rebellion had actually started four years

ago when he had slammed his way out of her house (it was ironic that to hold his own ground he had always had to run away), this Englishwoman's house, dark as an Elizabethan tavern, the walls lined with somber wood. He couldn't believe this woman was his mother, but it was so, it was undeniably so. It said so on his birth certificate, on his father's marriage license, on their divorce papers. It had been confirmed a million times in his own memory. His father was no longer her husband, but she had borne Feng. She was still his mother, and *her* son would always be Farthington. Feng even looked like her, his father's Chinese features modified by her sharp nose and her coloring. She had red hair and no freckles, but Feng had brown hair and freckles on his olive skin.

"Oh, Feng, dear," she pleaded, her charm teetering on a whimper. Four years ago he had decided he could wait no longer. But though he had slammed his way out of her house, he had come back, cajoled by her voice. Her voice could reduce him to water. It could convert his resolve into water that sloshed back and forth, up and down, in his room which seemed now to be a bright cell. He had come back four years ago on the condition that she transform one part of the downstairs of her house into a self-contained apartment for himself.

"But, of course," she had said and looked at him as at an unreasonable child who would presently come back to his senses. She had had a better grip on herself in those days. "Your own little bachelor hideout. But why not, my dearest? Did you think for one moment I wouldn't agree? I don't know . . ." she had trailed off, shaking her head. Her hair was fine and still the brilliant red that had attracted his father. It was dressed in a high and loosely piled pompadour that always was on its way down. It descended with little sighs and ended in wisps about her face. Fine gold hairpins jutted out precariously from behind an ear, hanging by a single hair; they sat on her shoulders, they caught in her lace bodices; they left a trail wherever she had been.

"I don't know . . ." she had complained three nights ago

22

from the top of the stairs. I don't know, she had told him when he was ten; I just don't know why your father doesn't want us any more. He could see her put her finger tips against her mouth and look around her, bewildered. And now she was calling him again: "Farthington!" She would come knocking at his door, he thought, if he didn't answer her soon.

He picked up the magazine that he had sent flying across the room, and smoothed the pages. His father's study and what used to be an almost baronial dining room had been converted into his "hideout." He had two rooms that were his own —and he had insisted that the paneling be torn down. The walls were plastered and painted white throughout. The sunshine streamed into the bedroom in the morning, and at night the bright lamps cast a salubrious glow. Both rooms had the air of the sun deck of a sanatorium. Here, he felt, he could convalesce from the effects of his mother's voice.

"Are you there or not?" she asked flatly, as though talking to space. "Speak up if you are," as though he were a ghost in his own apartment. He put down the magazine and walked to the door that led to the hall and the stairs.

Feng stood outside his solarium, on the thick rug. He could see his own reflection in the ornate hat and umbrella stand, designed by some cabinetmaker in London. "By appointment of the King" was stamped in its expression of solidity and craftsmanship. His father gave them everything that money could buy. He not only paid Audrey a handsome monthly allotment, but he also denied them their self-respect on each holiday and birthday by sending lavish and insolent gifts. Last year he had ordered that the house be completely redecorated. Another year, when he had planned to send them both on a world tour, the war had broken out. He had not set foot in the house since Feng was ten—sixteen years ago. But ever since he had grown up, Feng saw his father from time to time downtown for lunch.

Audrey was hesitating on the stairs, like a limp stalk.

"What is it?" he asked. What had she mislaid now? What

could he get her from the kitchen—for after nine in the evening she would not disturb the servants. It was not *comme il faut*. Perhaps a window sash had got stuck? A drawer needed prying open? A trunk needed lifting?

"Feng, my dear, I'm so glad you're home."

"I'm earlier than I thought I'd be," he said, thinking that if he had managed things better at the Jastrows' he could have avoided this. "What is it, Mother?"

"You do seem to have a lot of friends," she answered vaguely.

"I do?" he said, snorting a little. But she need not complain; he was home most of the time. Where was there to go? However, she really did not chastise him unduly over his movements, God knew. It wasn't what she said; it was her voice, so charged with dependency. "But you called me," he reminded her.

"It's just . . ." she said. "Oh, it's really nothing at all. I could have waited till morning. But I thought you might be interested in it. Yes. It wasn't just my own curiosity about it, you know. I think it just might interest you."

"A mouse? A cockroach? Some animal you can't identify?"

She moved her eyebrows, like an actress portraying the deepest hurt, but then, seeming to think he might have meant to be playful, she quickly adjusted her face and said, "Nothing quite so amusing, I'm afraid. Come along and tell me what it's all about." She turned on the stairs, kicking back her long thin robe and flicking her mules gingerly. He followed her up, resisting a compulsion to pick up the two hairpins that lay on the carpeting.

Her rooms—her bedroom, boudoir and writing room—were all pink and silver against the brown of the walls.

"Sit, dear," she said, waving at the pink love seat in her writing room. On her desk, inlaid with mother-of-pearl and trimmed with silver, were bills and notices spilling out of a pink cardboard box.

"I was just going over some things," she said, "and how my affairs do need tidying. I seem to go from one year's end to

24

another collecting things. I said to myself this morning that what had to be done, had to be done. I simply had to sort these things once and for all." She turned and looked coyly into his face. "How about a cool drink first? I've some juice in the thermos and biscuits, too." But he did not have to refuse. His mother couldn't concentrate on anything for long, and now she was looking for the hairbrush to push back the mass that was slipping over her forehead.

"Do you think I need another perm?" she asked, examining a strand of hair. "I hate what they do to the ends."

"What do they do to the ends?" He was surprised that he had even responded; he was aware only of the sensation that he was slipping from himself, that the chocolate and pink room was an elevator sinking fast.

"The ends . . . look," and she bent over him, casting a veil of scent over his mind. "They get dry and almost split."

"Mother," he said abruptly, "what is it you want me to look at?" She moved around, flicking her mules and waving her fingers as though they had a separate life of their own.

"Oh, yes, yes," she said, hovering over the desk. "Now where did I put it? Ah . . . there we are," and she handed him a bill in Chinese. "Perhaps you can tell me what that says. It may be quite important."

"It's a bill," he answered.

"Oh, I know that, dear."

"It's a bill for a bracelet you ordered. Coral and pearl, apparently. Pink coral to be set in silver."

"But—" she hesitated. "I have ordered no such thing."

"Not recently, perhaps," he said, "but then this bill is quite old."

"It is?" she exclaimed with false surprise. "How peculiar! Indeed, how peculiar!"

"It's ten years old," he said. "And you've owned the bracelet for just that length of time. Father paid for it ten years ago, and this bill should have been torn up then."

"It's that old, is it?" she repeated, picking at her hair again.

She laughed. "Oh, I suppose I should have disposed of it. Yes, dear, you're quite right." She blinked and put her fingers to her lips.

Feng went up to the desk, a frail and delicate piece of furniture desecrated by the rude bills littering it. On the top of the box had been penciled in his mother's handwriting: "1935 —Bills Paid." She never threw anything out. He felt she must still have his baby fingernail cuttings stored away between pink satin.

My mother, he thought. She had to resort to trickery and lying to annoy him. She was always doing things like that, and then standing there, stricken, like a backward child.

"I'm naughty," Audrey said. "I'm sorry I'm naughty. Forgive me, Feng." She put out her hand, while her hair settled to a lower position.

Feng stood in the middle of the room, refusing to give any ground. As it was, he felt he would have to climb out of the room, it had sunk so deeply into the night. He would be sucked in by the lace and the frills, the bejeweled room of her femininity.

"Sit awhile, dear," she said. "I'm very lonely." She tried to smile for his sake. "I know I'm not supposed to say that," she quavered, and he knew she referred to his past indictments. ("Don't plead!" he had often cried in irascibility and despair. "Fight! But don't plead with me!" And her resigned and passive answer returned to haunt him, "But you see, I—I can't help it. I can't help being myself.")

"Feng, dearest, do be kind." She now touched his arm. "Feng, dearest, are you listening to your mother?" Her voice trailed away, but had a naked staying power in its faintness. She was alone, he knew, and he was the only living thing she could hope to claim. Her voice tried to persuade him to desert himself and settle down to being her son only. Her soft influence made him feel violent.

"I'm busy," he said curtly, and turned and left the room. Something Robert Bruno had said at the Jastrows' about the printing plant gave him the gift of purpose. When in doubt, don't think. He remembered that he had told himself this many times. When in doubt, act.

He pushed the thought of his mother out of his mind. He could see her sit down now after he left, and stare, sitting stiff and stony, all her wavering bewilderment gone for the moment. Her hands would be still as she stared into her emptiness. Her Chinese husband had left her alone in a Chinese city. Feng knew that sometimes she felt herself quite unfocused and yet clever. Cunningly, she contrived to make him visit her rooms. And of course she kept bills. Of course she kept things. When you couldn't keep people, you kept things. But Feng had long since learned to harden himself against her tragedy.

He had not intended telling them that night; he had been told to lie low until they could give him a new assignment. But he liked action: it had a double effect. It freed you from yourself and it committed you to reality. He walked quickly, for he had been on his way for an hour, on foot most of the time from the upper reaches of the French Concession to his destination downtown in the International Settlement.

Feng had had to wind in and out of back streets to avoid the Japanese patrol, and to hang back in doorways when stray pedestrians crossed his path. They had special passes which allowed them to walk abroad after the curfew, whereas he had only a Chinese identity card and an ambiguous nationality apparent on his face. He had found a solitary pedicab in an alley and the driver had pedaled him part of the way.

"Let me off at the next corner," he had finally said, and paid the man when he stopped. Then he had walked down two blocks and turned onto Avenue Edward the Seventh. How different everything looked at night. It wasn't just that familiar streets were dark and completely deserted. They were lunar and sterile and somehow foreshortened, as though it took people, masses of humanity, to give the landscape its correct perspective. He felt he should have overcome the feeling of unfamiliarity, for until recently he had been making night visits regularly. Not to this particular part of town, but then not so far from here either. And it was around here that he worked five days a week, a junior partner in a law firm run by a college friend of his father's. The night visits he had been making had been like going to midnight mass in celebration of his conversion. Those visits—and he had begun to miss them—were perhaps his *raison d'être* for the present, and they were candles burned on the altar to his future.

After turning off the main avenue, he seemed to walk into a wall of darkness. The high forms of storage houses and godowns leaned over him. At the end of the street was the looming structure of the printing plant. He went up to it, feeling the walls and the main entrance set in from the sidewalk. Then he walked along to the right until he saw the shape of the side door. He knocked three short knocks and two long ones. When no one answered he knocked again, and looked at his watch with its luminous hands. It was almost two in the morning. The men had not left yet. He knew their habits. They worked from midnight to three-thirty, and then the five men walked out of the plant separately. Tang left first, for he had to be back at the plant by nine in the morning, since by day he was foreman of the linotype workers.

Feng wondered if he should call. But his voice might reach a watchman or the police. He knocked again and pressed his ear to the door. Hearing a rustle behind it, he whispered loudly, "It's Kuo. It's me, Kuo." The door, still on its chain, opened slowly and Tang's face peered through. He closed it again partially, releasing the chain, and let Feng in.

It was almost pitch black inside. The low ceiling dipped in places, squares of tin roofing hung down where the nails had rusted and loosened; a mass of pipes, ropes and the legs of old furniture lay in the corridor. Feng bent his head, and gingerly followed Tang, stepping over the debris. He had never been in the plant before, but he knew this was just part of the improvised shelters that led into the main building.

28

Directly ahead of them, light shone under a door, but they turned left and entered a closetlike room where a naked bulb hung from a hook on the wall.

Turning around, Tang looked at him, his Chinese eyes saying nothing at all. "Well, Kuo?" he asked at last. He continued to stare at Feng, taking in his well-tailored suit—Feng's oldest and least well pressed, his comfortable moccasins and his well-fed air.

"I've something to tell you," Feng said, wondering why Tang always disconcerted him, making him feel guilty of a vague crime. Tang made him feel less Chinese than he was.

"I've something to tell you, too." Tang turned on him. "Wait," and he put up his hand. "You were told to keep out of things for a while, weren't you? He," he said, and he always referred to this "he" as though he were a mysterious patriarch, "he has plans for you. You were told not to contact us. You were told to lie low for a while, but apparently Kuo likes to take things in his own hands."

"What I have to tell you is important," Feng put in quickly. He recognized the element of truth in what Tang said. That was why he had this power over him. But Feng had decided to come, and since he had, he would justify himself.

"Old man Bruno may be revamping the operations here, buying over and amalgamating the Eastern Press and the papers with the printing concern. It means, among other things, of course, changes in personnel." He looked at Tang meaningfully. Of the five who ran up their leaflets at night, Tang was the only one who also worked at the plant itself; it was he who had a key to the place.

Tang's body jerked in his soft Chinese gown as though his muscles were knotted on hinges. In a tense flickering motion that Feng could never get used to, his tongue came out and licked his upper lip, while the strings in his neck stood out in a spasm. "I suppose this amalgamation is taking place at nine in the morning," he said sarcastically. "I suppose you heard this piece of news at one of your foreign cocktail parties. Maybe in English and over a drink things sound more urgent.

But I doubt it. You showed poor judgment coming here tonight."

Perhaps he was right, Feng admitted, but only to himself. Tang had had it in for him, even from the start. In this world, where he was known as Kuo, Feng would allow none of his reasonableness, none of his equivocations to show. Stubbornly, he argued, "I wanted you to know as soon as possible. As for foreign cocktail parties—"

"Okay," Tang said unexpectedly in high-school English. "Okay," and he went back to Chinese, "don't explain everything. Must you always explain, explain." He switched to another gear. "Who told you this piece of news? Some little debutante mixing rumors with flirtation?"

"Bruno's son," Feng said, glad to see the flash of disappointment on Tang's face. Tang could hardly deny that he was a reliable source of information. "Bruno's son—who is opposed to his father's plan. His son, who is perspicacious, suspects a new era may be dawning in China once the war is over." He laughed.

Tang did not waste time responding. His tongue flickered again, a strong muscle, but his eyes bored into Feng's, and Feng knew what he was thinking. Chen Liyi was the manager of the plant, the Chinese major-domo under Robert Bruno, Senior; he was responsible not only to Bruno, but also to the over-all Japanese supervisors, the sons of Shinto and kings of the occupation.

"No," Tang said, after brief consideration, "Chen Liyi probably knows nothing about it. He's one of those extant liberals who recoils from asking any questions, or asks every question of himself and none of anyone else." He spat with a deftness that was Chinese.

"Just as well," Feng replied, or perhaps Chen Liyi would have known what Tang was. If Chen Liyi were more directly inquisitive, less apolitical, they might not be using the plant at night for their own purposes.

"Still," Tang said, "he has to do with the hiring and firing.

If . . ." But one of the men had entered the room—a Chinese with a clean pate and bright, glistening teeth, wearing the clothes of a workman and rope-soled shoes. Feng had never seen him before.

He handed Tang a long galley, damp from the press. It smelled of metal and oil and ink, and Feng suddenly was reminded of how close to the waterfront they were. It was as though the galley had soaked up the odor of the docks, the outside world.

Tang glanced over the paper, held it before Feng and laughed unaccountably. In the early morning, the leaflets, freshly printed, would be distributed among the party workers. "We are waiting now," one item read, "for the American Navy and Air Force to defeat the Japanese in the Pacific." Unequivocally, the column stated that the Nationalist forces were being allowed to expend themselves, while "we" await "our" opportunity to take over the Yangtze Valley.

Feng read it in a glance, his eyes jumping over the small Chinese type, the subheads. Tang said, "Okay," again, and the man left. The press would be rolling in a minute.

"Well?" Tang asked him again, partially dismissing him.

"I know Chen Liyi's daughter," Feng said, almost involuntarily. He wanted Tang to find him valuable. Tang filled him with a sense of inadequacy.

"Chen Liyi's daughter?" Tang asked him superciliously.

"Sylvia Chen," Feng said. And the idea was born whole. He had not even seen it until he came upon it now like a path on a dark plain. I shall cultivate Sylvia, he thought. Yes. Through her, he could find out what her father, Liyi, knew. And through her, he could prove to Tang how indispensable he was.

"I see," Tang answered flatly. He didn't seem impressed, but Feng thought his expression might be deliberate—to rob him of confidence—and did not allow himself to become discouraged.

"It might be a good idea," Tang added, patronizingly. "You

have yourself an assignment," and he turned to go. "But don't come here again, unless you're directed to."

Then Feng said, "Okay," and, though he was perspiring from the heat in the windowless room, he felt better. He felt the way he had during those night visits, when he had been a courier. Assignments gave him a discipline, put him in custody. He had never felt comfortable being himself, just Feng Huang; somehow he recognized that a civilian status made him feel inadequate, as though his suits were too loose, and he felt shy, was embarrassed by the freedom. As a civilian, he was just a young lawyer and his parents' son. He felt more self-respect when he was in custody, in the uniform of a cause.

Now he had a role in an issue larger than himself, just because he believed. And he would make Tang believe in him—Tang, who made him ache to justify himself. He knew they needed him. Not for the reasons he would have liked, perhaps. He was Kuo here. The disguise was necessary in Shanghai. Some day (in Yenan even now) they could go by their real names. But they needed him because he was well heeled and didn't look quite Chinese. As a Eurasian, he could pass as anything, including a playboy. Eurasians and playboys in Shanghai were suspected of everything, and because of that they were suspected of nothing. He was needed, and he felt secure in that.

CHAPTER THREE

"You're a baby," Robert Bruno would say, making Mimi Lambert angry, for it robbed her of even a retort like, "I am not!" That would only have proved her infantilism.

No one else had the ability to confuse her, and she took great pains not to let him see her discomfiture, for until Robert Bruno had come along, no one had ever affected her so. Sometimes Mimi even resented him, but only to love him the more. Sometimes he seemed to rob her of everything that she was, and this was true despite his admission of his own deficiency. "You put me in touch with life," he had once said to her. For a brief while after that, his five-feet-eleven seemed manageable to her, his unaccountable "departures" from her (which he could effect even when he was sitting next to her) seemed less portentous. But it was true that he periodically robbed her of her assurance. Without undue egotism, Mimi Lambert had always known she was "a beauty," had always recognized her own assets. Long ago, when she was twelve, she had studied herself in the mirror and decided how to toss her hair back, how to cross her impeccable legs, how to look into a boy's eyes for the maximum results. Having mastered her own personality, she was almost able to forget it—at least, to forget it enough so that even that forgetfulness added to her charm. She was carelessly beautiful, lazily feminine, casually flirtatious.

But Robert made her feel—and for weeks she had searched for the word—he made her feel *young* and she hated it. He made her say the most foolish things, she cringed in retrospect.

He made her an absolute schoolgirl, and then either smiled at the infant he had created or tolerated it with a weary adultness.

"Pray, what do you take me for?" she had asked prissily the first time he had tried to make love to her. Afterwards, she could have bitten off her tongue. She wondered secretly how her aunt would have taken it, had she overheard. She was sure Aunt Juliet would have shaken her fashionable head in shame. Mimi had unconsciously imbibed from her mother's sister the values of a cosmopolitan and snobbish society. No laws, but attitudes governed their lives.

"I take you for a woman," Robert had answered simply, so simply that Mimi had looked at him to make sure he was not condemning her for not being one. He subtly undermined her ego; she could no longer deny the realization to herself, but it was too complex a thing for her to think through. At another time he held her hand so tightly as they drove or walked or sat in a theater that she protested, and he said, "I need to feel you actually here. You seem to keep your finger on an artery of mine that bleeds slowly." In two sentences he again restored to her her whole personality. For half a week she was once more her buoyant self. She was so much herself that she did not examine Robert's need. His handsome sullenness, his refinement of feeling, his ever- and over-active conscience —her awareness of these qualities became blunted through her own good health. She saw his pain (and even his drinking) as enhancements to his character. She was right in feeling he made her young and unsure, but it never occurred to her that he found refreshment in her innocence or comfort and strength in her unawareness.

Mimi was not analytical, and even though Robert did and said inexplicable things which made her happy or sad (she, for instance, would not have described these states as "secure" or "anxious"), she carried around with her only a single impression of the man she loved. Robert—and all other impressions were momentary aberrations—was to her tender, civilized, tall and sometimes husky-looking, adult (she took a personal pride in the fact that he was thirty-four, as though he had attained that maturity for her sake alone) and intriguing. His intriguing-ness came as much from a physical property (he could look both elegant and bohemian at once) as from his inaccessibility.

"Will you love me forever?" Mimi had asked often, whenever an unexpected intensity asserted itself through her kittenishness. She'd stand behind him as he sat in his huge living room, and threaten to strangle him with her bare hands if he didn't say yes.

Unhurriedly, almost carefully, it seemed to her, Robert would answer, "Not forever, but long enough," and try to capture her hands. She had to decide that he was teasing her, for his reservations did not go with his demands. He became increasingly dependent and angry, as she put off his insistence that they make love, that they "play at being grownups." Very simply, regally, "No," she said. He would laugh then, retorting, "Is it your Chinese propriety or your Australian puritanism showing?" She knew he had her marked as "his," but Mimi wanted to capitulate only when *she* really wanted to. It would happen one day, she promised herself, but she would be the only one to determine when. She would know when. Her instincts would tell her. As her Aunt Juliet would say, reverting to Chinese suddenly, "*Teng hao shih chen.*" The stars and the weather would have to be propitious.

The evening after the gathering at the Jastrows', Robert drove to her home to pick her up. As she came down the stairs she could hear Aunt Juliet saying, for she was on her way out, too, "Forgive me," stressing the words like a French woman. "I must hurry for I am late. Forgive me," she repeated musically. "Mimi will be down in a moment." The precise clicks of Aunt Juliet's high heels marched out of the living room and onto the polished floor of the hallway. Her Chinese aunt was tiny and brisk, pettable as a miniature poodle.

A moment later the house was quiet. Mimi found Robert sitting in an easy chair. She leaped off the last step of the stairs, ran across the room and jumped sideways onto his lap.

"My hoyden," he called her, adjusting his legs under her weight. "You're much too big a girl to do that," and he referred not to her age, but to her size.

"I am not!" she protested, before she could help it. Again he had forced her into childishness.

"No, not too big," he said, smiling down at her. "Really quite well rounded and yet trim." And as though his own description had made her more vivid to him, he bent his head to kiss her on her throat. Mimi had thrown back her head, her hair hung over the arm of the chair. Upside down, she watched the *amah* pretend not to see her as she returned from ushering her aunt out of the door. Ever since Mimi had been a child, the servants had always found her an interesting topic of conversation. Sometimes she created scenes so as not to disappoint them. Now she got up suddenly, as though wounded, and said loudly in Chinese, translating it into English for Robert, "You love me only because of my body." Then she began to laugh, certain she had provided a morsel for the company in the kitchen. They would explain everything away by reminding themselves that she was as good—or as bad— as a foreigner.

But Robert protested sententiously, "I love you because you are real. You don't know how real and how lovely you are. I feel ghostly except when I am with you." She did not understand him, and no longer made even a perfunctory attempt. She allowed him this kind of privacy, for she was too indolent to follow the strange clues to his personality. All she did now was to stop laughing and grant him a sad look for two or three moments. It seemed to satisfy him. She wanted him to be happy. She did not like him to be unreasonably deep—as she termed it. It seemed unnecessary to her.

They left the house and he helped her into the car. She sat with her thigh against his, as he swung the car out of the driveway and onto the road. She lay back, turning to look at him, knowing her red blouse of thin silk was becoming. The large

36

puffs of its sleeves stood out transparent and stiff from her sloping shoulders. Her hair had been pulled back on the side that faced him and was held by a large dull gold flower.

They sped through the cardboard city; most of the shutters were up. Mimi felt herself lulled, as though in a luxurious projectile that carried them past everything, that purred under their own passivity. Before the war, Avenue Joffre in the French Concession had been a kind of White Russian Piccadilly, but now any life at all took place inside isolated *boîtes*. Robert was one of the few people who could still afford such evenings—it was part of the atmosphere he carried with him and which she enjoyed as though she had somehow earned it.

"I wish this moment would last forever," she said. Robert put his arm about her, holding her close.

"Always evoking eternity. It's a dangerous concept," he admonished, and she only felt more feline. "Didi's" she had murmured earlier, and she wanted to pout, not from peevishness, but out of contentment. He seemed to have abdicated his will to hers. She wanted to spend the rest of the evening with him in her favorite night club, Didi's, spend the hours like a fortune of money, a landfall from a lottery.

They entered Didi's; the amorousness of the place rubbed against them like smoke. Outside, it looked to Mimi like a boarded-up guest house, but the inside was lined and satiny as a powder box. Every woman felt dramatic as she walked in, and Mimi now turned her eyes—she could feel framed by her own loosely waved hair, she could feel the stares of the men—toward the spotlight on the tiny dance floor. It shifted jerkily, in a sliding movement, in preparation for the early show. The band seemed to insinuate licentiousness into its music.

First they walked to the bar, because Robert wanted to, and Mimi lent her presence without quite participating. Every now and then she cast a veiled but sweeping glance about the room, as if denying to herself what she was doing, denying the satisfaction she received from the attention she attracted. Robert nodded at the Sikhs and the Japanese who stood at the bar, drinking silently. "You know everyone," Mimi wanted to say, and this, like his age, was something that he seemed to have achieved only in order to make her prouder. She felt artistic and perverse, so that when she saw Hasan Kemal walk in, looking strikingly dark in his white Palm Beach suit and followed by a party of eight or nine Chinese men, she said quickly, adamantly, "Why, we must join them! Robert, let's do!" and in a few moments they stood by Hasan's table. Two extra chairs appeared out of the air; as they were introduced, all the Chinese stood up and sat down one by one like soldiers falling gradually out of formation. She presided—between Robert, Hasan and the floor show—over a table of almost a dozen men. She felt very much as if she had herself in tow, was managing her own fate with ease and poise.

Had she been asked to describe her own sensations, she might have said she felt drowsy; part of Mimi was always half dozing within her—it was her way of avoiding responsibility. She wanted to ride with waves of experience. In her partial drowsiness now, she heard the men talking.

One of the Chinese leaned over to say to Hasan Kemal, "Look, he wears a girdle!" Mimi stared at the entertainer, a nervous man, good-looking as a riding master at a third-rate academy might be, or a dancing teacher at a resort. He always did the same imitation of a repulsive female; she knew it quite by heart.

"A good joker," another Chinese said. His English was incongruously poor, for he was dressed as collegiately as any undergraduate in America.

"He means it's funny," Hasan explained, acting the host. The Turk expressed only courtesy and consideration with every one of his gestures. She had never seen his eyes so round and dilated. He was the only one at the table who knew all of them, and he seemed both childishly delighted that this was "his party" and serious because of his responsibilities to them all. He put his arms around Mimi, on his right, and Robert, on his left.

"He is a good friend?" another Chinese asked Hasan blandly,

pointing to Robert with his chin, in a typically Chinese motion, indicating no ill-breeding, but a rather civil skepticism.

"Very good friends," Hasan answered, with a lifting of his own chin. His simple pride made him look fatuous.

"The best," Robert said, smiling into his drink and then looking up and declaiming, while Mimi listened like a wife who knew her husband would not disappoint her, "Hasan and I are brothers. One from Zurich, the other from Ankara. We are friars of the same order. We have skiied since childhood on the slopes of Big Business."

"Are you speaking in English?" the collegiate Chinese asked, while Mimi smiled a little superciliously to herself. She would not have known whether she smiled because only she knew that Robert was preparing himself to get pleasantly drunk, or because the Chinese seemed so impossibly unsophisticated, but asked his question with a kind of humorless Chinese arrogance.

"I am speaking in rhetoric," Robert continued, out to bedevil him. "Mr. Kemal understands. We recognize each other as brothers of the same fraternity of mercantilism. Our days are numbered—equally. *Fini*, as they say in Switzerland. *Kaput*, as they also say in Switzerland. The Chinese won't tolerate us much longer."

A quietness fell over the table, and again she could not tell if it was because they did not understand him, or that they were impressed that Robert's frame of reference—a foreigner's —allowed for self-criticism. Suddenly, however, she could not bear the Chinese faces, so neutral in their carefulness not to make an error, so unanimated, so unimaginative somehow. She was glad her Aunt Juliet was different, a maverick; she wanted to do something herself now to break through their traditional inhibitions.

"Hasan," she announced, "I'm going to dance with every one of your friends. And don't you dare stop me. I always get my own way in the end." She protested heatedly and prettily, but Hasan only looked complimented that she was going to help to make his party a success.

She danced with them, with each of them in a row going

39

down one side of the table. She was so carried away by her own impetuosity, it was not until she had danced with almost the last man that she noticed that the Chinese all danced the same way, correctly and anonymously. Each one told her she was most gracious, most beautiful, most charming and most youthful. It was the last adjective that she could not forgive them. At nineteen, she didn't feel youthful. She was young—as young as Robert had a talent for making her feel. And she refused to help them out as they spoke stammeringly in English. She refused to let them know that her Chinese was almost as perfect as her mother's had been.

When she returned to the table, Robert was saying to silent admirers, for now they were all listening with deference, "No exploitation without vexation," and he repeated it twice, tasting it on his lips. "My father," he continued disjointedly and pedantically, "will finally understand. His crystal ball reflects only the early rites of the twentieth century. It is out-of-date, useless, blind to the future. Colonialism is a cruel act; it mixes progress with exploitation. Missionaries," he said, "American missionaries brought Bibles, medicine and outdoor sports. Yes, they brought Jesus and basketball. The children of the Middle Kingdom now wear halos and sneakers. Sneakers," he said, pointing at them all, "sneakers have a great deal to do with the future. I see Chinese marching in T-shirts and sneakers, great armies of them liberated from original sin and their feudal parents."

Their silence was applause. A surge of pride went through Mimi. Her Robert had them in the palm of his hand, and he was expending nothing of himself except a little alcohol and verbosity. The Chinese were not so inhibited as not to show they were in awe of him, who sat among them with the simple prestige of a foreigner enhanced now by his erudition. Yet this man, to whom they all deferred, as only Chinese could with unspoken ceremony, depended on her for his happiness. Suddenly, Mimi understood—she felt—her own worth, and she wanted to spend it on Robert with largesse.

It was a moment from which there was no returning. His love and need for her seemed to cover her like a mantle. It clothed her very being and gave her a sense of richness and power. The realization had overwhelmed her. . . .

Later, as they lay in bed in his house (the house was a microcosm alone in space), she let him pick a speck off her breast. There was no going back from that moment on. She did not want to go back, but the irrevocability of the decision (once done, nothing in this world could be undone) was here in the weight of Robert's presence, his body lying naked beside hers in the dark.

Mimi felt profoundly serious—an unfamiliar sensation—and her sigh seemed almost like a sob, so much so that Robert stopped kissing her to stare at her closely. She laughed suddenly, wickedly, making him look rueful and wounded, and let herself be crushed against the pillows. She couldn't bear feeling so much in love—and Robert's ruefulness seemed to increase her burden of emotion. Her own intensity surprised her.

"You're a little hoyden," he said for the second time that evening, and his hands made her laugh.

"You're not ticklish!" he exclaimed. "You're not the ticklish kind. You can't be."

"Yes, I am," Mimi answered, and added irrelevantly, "but you are perfect."

"Ah," Robert said, "you will please realize that I am not. You will be bitterly disappointed if you think I am. I have many weaknesses. This wholeness you bequeath me is a terrible responsibility."

But she had covered his mouth with her fingers, and he kissed them and her as though in an agony. She did not let herself wonder at his occasional pedantry, if she would have even called it that. Quietly, with devotion to their purpose, they began to press against each other, while to her the house seemed to expand into an infinite place.

CHAPTER FOUR

The night before, Sylvia Chen had dreamed heavily, and awakened reluctantly in the morning. Later that day, she thought, she would probably have proof again that her dreams were often reversed in time—they did not always come after the event which might have caused them but often before, as though they were forecasts of the weather ahead.

"Come in," Sylvia said a few hours after waking and, as she said it, it sounded familiar, a cue that would lead her forward into that Saturday, and illuminate what she had dreamed. Though she had not heard a sound, she knew her father was standing by the door of her room. His hesitancy could reach her no matter how occupied she was; it traveled along her nerves and stammered in her senses.

"Come in, do," she insisted, but ungenerously did not turn around from her book.

The afternoon had just begun, taking the city in its lap. Her father now stood at her window, looking over the wall that hedged in the open garden of their neighbor's property. He cleared his throat, and she could see him leaning on the sill, turning his head to the right where another apartment house, a duplicate of their own, stood casting its shadow into their courtyard. The Chinese families who lived there took long siestas on the narrow balconies. Only the servants moved around below, soundlessly, in white jackets and black trousers, straightening the wash or taking in the deliveries. To Sylvia the after-lunch quiet seemed to give the scene the quality of a fable. Beyond, on the near horizon, the intersection of streets was quiet. Bicycles, rickshaws and pedestrians moved slowly in the simmering heat.

She could feel her father struggling within himself to speak, to appeal to her. Stubbornly, she did not want to help him.

"Sylvia," he brought out at last, almost plaintively and without looking at her, "your mother is mad at me."

She turned to stare at the back of his head, forcing her eyes to be noncommittal. It always shocked her to hear him utter in his Chinese accent such colloquial phrases as "mad at me" or "sore at them." He had a long face for a Chinese and a high, receding forehead; these expressions were wholly out of keeping with this fine and tailored face, and his rather remote air.

"But that's not so serious, is it?" Sylvia asked, and regretted her tone immediately. He had often confessed to her that before his children he felt half-relic, half-contemporary. Of course, he often pointed out, children were one's equals in modern China, but today she felt he was prepared to reverse that—he was almost equal to his daughter.

"Couldn't you—couldn't you just go in and say a word to her?" he asked. He turned around, smiling; his smile always grew in proportion to his distress. "It's so much easier for you, you see."

She knew he would let himself say no more. His strict code of dignity would not allow it, and already she was beginning to yield, to do his bidding, as she always did, for no one but her mother could stand up to his soft insistence. Because he so feared direct encounters, Sylvia had never dared to question anything he did or said. Even to have remarked, "But I think it is wrong for me to arbitrate every time," would have seemed a frontal attack on his delicate ego. They were prisoners of their shyness with each other.

But Sylvia couldn't resist saying in a grudging tone. "But of course, for this is the land of the go-between," and as an unwilling one, got up and walked into the living room. A barricade of static hung between it and the bedroom where Helen, her mother, was sitting. She was probably traveling around the world on the impetus of her anger.

"Mother," Sylvia ordered, as soon as she reached the bedroom door. "Mother, stop sulking at once!"

Helen looked up from her nails, which she was filing by the open window. Sylvia could see her blue-eyed stare in the mirror. Her back was turned to her, like a cat's, deaf to everything except her own willfulness.

"Helen Ames Chen," she cajoled, for with her mother Sylvia was not at all shy. "Mother," she said again, but only half-heartedly. Her parents' quarrels were like beds that had to be made up every morning, only to be disordered again. In the end, Liyi would come into the bedroom, feeling that the situation had been changed by his daughter's ineffectual words, and Helen would shed a few tears and they would seem to rediscover each other. They would seem bride and groom again. Helen might go into peals of senseless laughter and Liyi would stand beside her, plaiting her long blond hair, proud and pleased as a new husband.

"Oh, for pity's sake, Mother!" Sylvia said, for Helen refused to respond. Her mock wail made her sound adolescent to herself. At home, she thought, as she stood in the doorway, not knowing what to do next, you had to discount five years from your age. At home, no child could act adult without feeling he was disinheriting his parents. They made you feel guilty that years affected you at all. Relationships were like pressures that pushed you in thirty-six directions of the compass. But, as in a crowded streetcar, if you learned how to maintain your balance against all the weights, you might arrive at yourself.

"Mother," Sylvia said with a sigh, feeling her father moving nervously in the living room. "Let's go for a walk, Mother. Just you and I, and we'll splurge and have ice cream somewhere. Just like sisters."

Helen stirred at that, as easily mollified and distracted as a child, and before she could make a show of reluctance, Sylvia continued, "I'll get dressed and be right back," and left. Out of the corner of her eye, she caught her father's delighted wink. But she did not acknowledge it. Each of her parents had a way of wanting to make her an accomplice.

"You look pretty, my dear," Helen said a little later, "all dressed up to go out with me. And I shall get dressed up to go out with my daughter," and she came up and kissed Sylvia behind her ear, "my one and only daughter." And then Helen was off, tossing her dress and bag and slip and hat and veil on the bed. One by one she put them on, her gaiety contagious, and patted herself and Sylvia with *eau de cologne,* spanking fresh as a morning at the beach. The spontaneity felt familiar, like a phrase of music that cannot be placed, but which recurs at different times until several moods have accrued to it. Such good spirits could not last, Sylvia knew, but put her doubts away. After all, nothing lasted, but no one was insecure about the ephemeralness that was a part of misery, too.

"Where shall we go?" Sylvia asked, when they were at the gate downstairs, and it seemed to her they had the vistas of all the summer resorts they had ever been to, the boulevards of Tsingtao, looking naval and Mediterranean on Sunday, the bright, bleak edges of Hulutao, the terraces and hotels of Chefoo and Hongkong on the bay—all the vistas seemed laid before them again.

"Let's be really crazy," Helen said, emphasizing the word "crazy," as though putting it within inverted commas, for unless she was beside herself with anger, she rarely stooped to expressions that might be considered colloquial. "Let's be really mad and—and go to Bubbling Well Road."

They laughed and practically skipped down the street arm in arm.

Walk, turn left; walk and walk, turn right. More walking. And still Sylvia did not feel tired, for the air was fresh after the morning storm, the trees stirred, sprinkling them with rain; all the trees and all the houses, and all the little people on all the little streets—everything was small and clear and manageable. She could be happy because she was small, too; her life was little, complete, defined. In a sudden, brief glimpse she saw what life was—quite beautiful and quite manageable. The storm had left, and now they seemed to be going up some steps leading into the afternoon.

No one, Sylvia thought, could do anything more outrageous in Shanghai than take a walk on Bubbling Well Road in the International Settlement and have ice cream. The ice cream was an anachronism in the mouth, sliding down like a memory from her tongue to her stomach, as she let the cream and the luxury absorb her. There wasn't much ice cream in Shanghai these days; only infants and the very ill were able to get rations of milk, for the Japanese had killed most of the cows at the beginning of the war. Sylvia could see rows of brown, white and speckled cows standing in the fields and dairies, standing at ease on three legs and munching, waiting to be machine-gunned by the conquerors to provide meat for their troops.

Sylvia looked at her mother now with new eyes—familiarity had an unfortunate way of breeding a perspicacity which almost denied a mother an independent identity. As though the sparkling light of the afternoon illuminated Helen, Sylvia had a strange sense of "remembering" her against the background of Shanghai, a city barricaded for so long. Americans like her mother had been allowed to stay out of the internment camps because of their Chinese husbands; instead they were required to wear red arm bands with numbers printed on them. She was conspicuous—as Sylvia had always found her mother conspicuous—and to any Japanese gendarme who wanted to stop her and inspect her identity card, Helen was number 123.

They continued down the avenue, while Helen said, "Now if we were back in New York," but Sylvia was not listening. She had caught sight of *Yiao ching*, the schizophrenic Chinese girl who had bleached her hair platinum. *Yiao ching* had turned the corner with the air of someone avoiding an unwanted admirer, vulnerable, petulant and egocentric, but she could not avoid the eyes that followed her strange figure. Sylvia wondered how anyone so brainless could be so neurotic, how so much mental aberration was linked to so little gray matter.

But Miss Chu is most consistent, Sylvia said to herself—this girl who always matched her Hollywood coiffure to wedge shoes, and used hatboxes for handbags, slung a trophy of dead fur around her neck. Sylvia had run into her innumerable times and knew the small, bewildered Chinese face, the leaf-shaped eyes which peered from under the platinum mop, as she sidled in and out of shops, signing checks with her Parker 51 pen.

That Parker pen saved her, as did her Ronson lighter, these American gadgets that every Chinese who called himself modern coveted and obtained by illegal means, on the black market, if the proper channels did not yield their precious cargoes. By owning these, Sylvia thought, *Yiao ching* still operated as a Chinese, a Lana Turner whose real image, if only she would probe deep enough, would always be Yang Kwei-fei, the Tang Dynasty beauty.

"Now if we were back in New York," Helen repeated and went on, "we could take in a Broadway show or spend a week-end in Connecticut. We could go up to the Cloisters, or the Frick Museum, have dinner in the Tavern on the Green, and then take a long, long drive on those highways they have in America. You remember them, dear. You must remember the traffic and the signs everywhere, the small towns and wayside places, busy gas stations and certified rest rooms." Sylvia's breath caught slightly as she looked at her mother striding purposefully down the sidewalk, making a bit of Philadelphia here in Shanghai because of her sturdy oxfords and the aggressive swing of her legs. Mother was homesick. Helen was homesick for America, and Sylvia felt green and tender for her.

"I'm so sorry," Sylvia said, for her mother was very far from home.

"Are you really?" Helen asked sharply, for she could not sustain dreaminess for long. "Sorry because we ever came back? But you wanted to." It was true; Sylvia had hated America

47

that year. "Sorry because out here we're just decaying, out here in the middle of nowhere." "Out here" was the vocabulary of extraterritoriality and colonialism, and Helen meant it literally, in the Rudyard Kipling sense, white man's burden and all. Out here in the jungle, out here in the desert, out here among the savages, out here in the leper colony. And the Chinese to her were part savage, part leprous and totally mysterious.

But it's natural for her to think this way, Sylvia reminded herself, tamping down the pulse that had begun to beat too fast. So many things could set off this sensation of wanting to run, or wanting to stay and fight it out until the true meaning behind everyone's words could be determined. But this was her own mother, this woman was part of her, and surely her mother had the right to be terribly homesick.

"And you and Paul had wanted so much to go to America. Do you remember? You were practically babies then and you wanted so much to go to America because I had told you about the hot cross buns, and shopping in Rogers Peet, and sodas and sundaes in Schrafft's, and putting nickels in the Automat slots, and the sightseeing tours everywhere, and New Year's Eve in Chinatown.

"You were so eager to leave China that year—of course, there were the air raids—that you even said (and the young can be so hard)—that you even said it was all right to leave Daddy in Shanghai, that you simply must go to America. Paul, you and I must go to America, just until the 'incident,' the war, blew over. And on the *Empress of Japan* you didn't seem to miss your Daddy at all, but ate everything on that menu, and it was quite a menu.

"I don't understand you," her mother continued. "First you wanted to go so badly, then you hated it, and now I just don't know what you feel. I just couldn't venture a guess at all."

She stopped suddenly in exclamation over a cart of flowers that had spilled half its load on the sidewalk. She must buy

48

some from the poor vendor, and she set to picking, comparing and bargaining.

It was all wrong. But it was her mother's truth, and maybe her mother was right. Her mother at least had a point of view, and Sylvia had only an undependable pulse, racing over nothing at all, quibbling over such unspecific things. But she couldn't, she couldn't accept her mother's version of things. Sylvia felt threatened, afraid, as though Helen could rob her of herself—as though Helen, in her vigor, could obliterate Sylvia's very existence.

Sylvia and her brother Paul had not been babies in 1937, but they had been young, only twelve and seven, and of course they had thought it was a great lark to go to America, the America Helen had told them about for all of their lives. Maybe it was because the trip coincided with the beginning of Sylvia's adolescence, but everything was less wonderful than expected; everything was a disappointment. The hot cross buns were bought in a crowded Hanscom's bakery, not (as it had been in Helen's childhood) in a dimly lit, romantic little store. And the hot cross buns were bought in the glare of daylight and on aluminum counters (America's face was aluminum as China's was ceramic), and not after the opera, as Sylvia had somehow imagined it, the satin and cloaked night people pouring out of the Alhambra of music and song, each clutching sweet hot cross buns in their gloved hands. And Rogers Peet was only a store for men's furnishings. When the carton boxes arrived in Nanking with Rogers Peet written on them, it seemed that the store was a combination of bazaar and treasure house, something foreign and mysterious as a hoard in Egypt. And Schrafft's was a pretension for the dull-minded, and the Automat was a mess hall for prisoners of desolation and loneliness. And as for Chinatown, Sylvia could not even bear to think of it to this day, that ghetto begging tourists to inspect its shame. And, of course, there were other things, bigger things, more important things that unhinged her, because she had walked out of her childhood the same year

49

she discovered that her mother's America was an illusion and was, for her at least, untrue. How terrible it was that she had given the first twelve years of her imagination to such a lie.

She would walk down Third Avenue and stare unseeing at all the antique stores, just to be near something ancient—a small ruin of candelabra, a small heap of moldering beauty, something old and patina-ed to remind her of China, something old and intimate and taking up room for no other reason than for its own inefficient self.

She had been homesick then, but she had also been an adolescent, and thought not always of home, but also of the air, or the thing that could not be seen, touched or found on land or sea. She wanted the day to be special, not only for herself, but for everyone, and she wanted this thing, this thing that no one had ever seen, heard of or dreamed of before, to be waiting for her as she left the front stoop. It must behave in a way true to itself, but it must behave magnificently. And the thing and she would know, would simply recognize each other, and there! she and the thing—which was air, man, earth and idea, all wrapped up into one unity—would recognize each other, and that would be the beginning, the end and the middle of her life. Of course, needless to say, it never happened; nothing was waiting at the front stoop, and her disappointment, the name she gave to her disappointment was America.

Sylvia laughed at herself, laughed at the memory of herself as a twelve-year-old who was now, after all, only wrapped up in eight more years of foolishness. But this foolishness was called growing up. No wonder her poor mother did not understand her. Who would (for Sylvia thought of adolescence as a somewhat psychotic period of one's life), and who wanted to achieve perfect understanding with insanity?

Her mother now laughed, too, echoing Sylvia, and handed her a bunch of roses and some young bulbs. "Aren't they exquisite, my darling? They're American Beauty roses; they look just like the ones I had in the garden in Nanking. And

50

the bulbs. You know how your father loves narcissi. They are so delicate and Chinese. And I'll carry these," and the vendor filled her arms with two dozen gladioli of assorted colors. They were still stiff with freshness, hard flowers unfurling from the ungiving stems. They stood away from each other, even wrapped in the funnel-shaped paper, and as a bunch they had to be held like a brittle package.

I'm like those gladioli, Sylvia thought, young, hard and ungiving still. I must learn to relax, to resist less. My mother shouldn't threaten my existence; she doesn't mean to; it all lies in me. And the tether seemed to give way, and even the leavings of their conversation did not disturb her on the rest of the way home, not even when her mother said, "It was the biggest mistake of my life, returning to China in thirty-eight." And Sylvia knew she didn't mean that the mistake had anything to do with Liyi. Helen loved Liyi and would always love him. But she didn't love China (why should she?), and she did not recognize the conflict, an inheritance she did not even know that she had given her children.

But the afternoon's aura seemed to have been left at the front gate as they climbed the stairs.

"Those bulbs," Helen said, as she tossed her hat on the bed. "Give me those bulbs right away. No, no, not like that; you'll hurt them, silly. There, now, you take care of these gladioli and I'll pop these roses in here." The roses were for her bedroom, hers and Liyi's; the gladioli Sylvia arranged in two cut-glass vases (purchased one extravagant day at Jensen's) in the living room. Helen moved in quick, energetic strides up and back, left and right, the bulbs held in one hand, and soon the flowers were arranged with the greatest efficiency, while Sylvia held her breath.

Her father had been reading in the living room, waiting for his girls to return, and now rose, standing in absent-minded admiration of the surfeit of flowers. In China, flowers were not purchased only at the florist, but even at market places, next to garlic and pigs' feet, at corners and bazaars, and they seemed to flourish in dirt and manure, in flood and drought.

"Oh." He suddenly recovered his senses. "Let me take care of the bulbs. I know just what to do with them."

"Certainly not," Helen flashed. "I'm taking care of them. I bought them, didn't I? For you. But I bought them and I'm taking care of them and you keep out of this!"

"Yes, yes, yes," and he smiled at Sylvia. "Yes, Helen, yes." Her father knew when to shunt onto a sidetrack, to bide his time. For when Helen got charged up, she was dangerous, ready to plow down anything that stood in the way of her goal.

"But," he ventured placatingly, "may I bring you a dish to put them in? Allow me to do just that much for my wife."

"Allow you nothing," Helen retorted. "I'm doing this. Stop interfering, for heaven's sake. Can't you see I'm thinking!"

There was no doubt that she was thinking, Sylvia thought, watching her eyes roam the room under the pleated brows. Until she had discharged this energy, completed the task, they would have to try not to exist, try to be invisible. If anything lay on her track before she slowed down, the accident would tear a rent in their lives.

"Out of my way," she said to Sylvia, who stood transfixed before the cabinet. "Can't you see your mother wants to get something," and she gave her a jab with her elbow. "What is the matter with you, can't you move?" She rattled the door of the cabinet, which she had locked with housewifely possessiveness just the day before.

"Get the key! Get the key!" She stamped her foot. "Do you hear me, get the key!" And Sylvia resisted an involuntary desire to jump, to run, to oblige—anything but to stand there, grinding down her nerves.

"What key?" Sylvia asked slowly, deliberately. "And where is it?"

"In the bedroom, naturally. On the bureau, with that other bunch. Hurry, my hand is getting into a cramp, holding these fool bulbs." Helen was practicing forbearance, marking time and controlling her temper with great effort.

There were seven keys entangled in paper clips and rubber bands. Sylvia told her so, raising her voice a little so it would carry into the living room. "Shall I bring them all?"

"Oh, for heaven's sake. Bring the whole bureau, but bring something quick. I can't stand here forever because of you!"

Sylvia spread the keys out on her palm and held up the palm for her mother's inspection. Helen picked one and tried to jam it into the cabinet, but it wouldn't go in. Besides, she had to use her left hand, since her right was tightly clasped about the bulbs, dripping mud and threadlike roots.

Her mouth clenched tight, she tried another and a third. "Why don't you," she cried, glaring at Sylvia, "know which key it is? You take no interest in your own home." Her vengeance reached out into the future. "You'll be sorry one day. You'll be very sorry." She turned on her heel and collided with Liyi, who held a plate in his hand. She recovered very quickly, very angrily, and said, "Give it to me quick, and don't try to be funny," snatching the dish out of his hand and clapping the bulbs onto it. Sylvia stood like a camera, receptive but incapable of moving.

Then she could see that Helen was thinking again, her eyes darting; she strode away, staring furiously at her right hand, so soiled and uncomfortable with dirt. Her whole body was contorted with rage. She strode into Paul's room—he was out riding his bicycle after the morning of rain—to put the dish on the window sill, as they always did, for Paul's room was the sunniest, his window lined with cacti and flowerpots.

Sylvia heard a strange noise, a moan perhaps, a tortured sound, and Helen stepped back into the living room. Her task had not been completed, for the dish was still in her hands. Her eyes were filmed over and fixed in anger, frustration and confusion. Her mouth still hung open after uttering the ugly cry.

"He's sleeping in there!" she said. "Sleeping, sleeping in my house!" She flung the dish and the bulbs at Liyi. They crashed messily at his feet. "Your stupid nephew sleeping in my house. Oh, I tell you I can't stand it. I can't stand it another second." So Peiyuan, Sylvia thought, Peiyuan who now shared her brother's room, had been sleeping after his day of job-hunting. And Helen had not been able to reach the window sill beyond his bed.

"I can't stand him," she said on the point of tears, "sleeping with his big teeth showing! My house isn't my own, with him around!"

And there was Peiyuan now—not quite fully awake, standing in the doorway, understanding every word of it. He was a rustic with an uncanny capacity for understanding anything in English that referred to him. What would her father do about this? Sylvia was afraid for him.

She was afraid, and although she knew it was a craven thing to do, she left the room and slammed her bedroom door behind her. The scene outside her window had changed. It was dusk now, but she did not notice. She was breathing in long, controlled gasps, angrily and despairingly.

Helen's explosion would resolve itself, Sylvia knew. But the thought brought her no comfort. She felt shattered, both agitated and enervated. Her mind was frozen on a single incident.

The day Peiyuan had arrived, Helen had come into the living room and stood apart. Then she had acted as though she had to invite herself to sit down. Sylvia and her brother Paul had not been able to look at her staring at Peiyuan. They knew what she saw, and knowing had made them Judases. She stared at an intruder, an unhandsome Chinese boy, disheveled from his journey, a bumpkin. Wait till she sees his bed roll, Sylvia had thought. He wasn't a city boy, and so he had worn a coarse and faded long gown, and a pair of denims under it. His feet had been dusty in canvas crepe-rubber shoes, and his cheap watch was as large as a clock on his wrist. He had the features that Helen found so antagonizing on some Chinese. Such small eyes (What's the matter with you Chinese, having such small black eyes?), the kind of Chinese nose that looked stuffed and adenoidal, and such large, uneven white teeth. The cowlick made him look unkempt, indolent, unmannered as only the Chinese could be, what with their spitting out of tramcars, picking their ears at movies, belching at meals. His whole appearance was slack, except for the activity of his eyes, bright and eager (but they were small, tight-lidded, like Korean eyes), and the mobility of his mouth (hardly ever closing upon those teeth).

Sylvia had not had to give Paul a sign to know. Their hearts had contracted slowly, and they breathed as though in secret. They could never explain their cousin Peiyuan to Helen. Even in a starched shirt and tie, he would not be transformed. He was not an idealized Chinese whom Helen might approach understanding, accepting. He was real and their apartment had suddenly become too small.

Helen made Sylvia defensive about China. Now Sylvia remembered—in her dream last night she had been haunted by her father's eyes. They seemed to whisper as he carefully stared, carefully examined nothing at the middle distance; he was Chinese, so Chinese, she often envied him: he could afford to forget that he was. Emotions had spoken across her dream as though she were a telephone exchange; emotions turned into faces. She had been an umbrella under which they stood: Liyi and Helen. But the umbrella of herself closed in slow motion. She had then stood between Liyi and Peiyuan. She grew specific and plain. She had felt rather than seen danger among them. Morning came, and she had awakened reluctantly.

Her concern for the country reiterated itself in the daylight, a concern that was simple, feminine, specifically organic to her experience. Memory was a miniature locomotive, making a small intimate trail into the lamenting Chinese landscape. The land she had seen as a child was populated with the resigned living and the limitless dead; the mud houses of the peasants and the dirt mounds of the buried; the farmer looking up as the train passed like a slow planet through his fields; the village folk crowding against the train windows, offering wares and services, hot tea and steamed cakes, roast ducks, eggs, bird cages, cricket crockery, toys made of glass, paper, split bamboo. But her mother never bought anything, except tangerines perhaps, for they had had their picnic box packed at home with sandwiches and fried chicken, enough to last a day and a night, if the journey was to be a long one. Only Yennai, the *amah*, sometimes leaned out of the window and argued with the vendors, bargaining with dignity and shrewdness and retiring to her corner of the compartment with triumph and a pot of tea.

It could not be that summers in Peitaiho had really existed, that Chefoo and Tsingtao were not figments of an imagination that had stepped out of its healthy limits. Where were those whitewashed stones which guided one's way in the moonlight to a house by the sea, trickling in finger-high waves at Baby Beach? She was six, clutching the reins of a donkey, her straw coolie hat trailing on the sand, while behind the hedge her brother sat sucking his thumb in a bed of flaming marigolds.

All things were blue and white, the sea and the sails, the sky and the sheets blowing on the clothesline. Where were the Bartlett kids now, those blond children who stole an ear of corn in the field one day and ran and ran and ran, certain they were pursued by the police, and hid with her in the stone jar half filled with rain water? Then there was Johnny who gave her a flower and was a true lover at seven. He was American, too, and even in her memory their blondness made her uneasy. It was as though a bird repeated his call, reminding her and making it overcast in the weather of her reminiscences. And she could still taste Chefoo and smell the raw silk they brought in bolts to the hotel, letting the yards fall in wide folds on the terrace amid their tea and butter creams. There was refuse floating in the harbor and great American Navy ships anchored in the distance and a feeling of rain and geese coming down from the north. When she was ten, they spent three months in

56

Tsingtao, clopping down the drives in carriages, eating succulent noodles out of a bowl in the restaurant on the beach, tracing the formality of the pebbled walk around the Aquarium. In Laoshan behind the bay, topsy-turvy Chinese tea houses were perched over waterfalls and her mother was caught bathing nude by a sedan-carrier, and screamed and ran out of sight. Sylvia wondered if any of this had really existed at all, had any of it really been?

Those were the yellow days of childhood, and white and blue seemed always to be the colors of discovery. She slid back several years, looking for herself in another city, the incantations of longing making her thoughts as large and formal as prayers. . . .

Peiping, the old walled city, was her first home. Sylvia remembered a medieval incandescence flaring in all its seasons. Life there, between walls that divided and secluded and marked off in patterns of regular and irregular squares, was as fully *now* as the warm grasp of a hand, as quilts tucked thickly under the chin, as minutes spent coin by coin by an old man in the sun. She remembered childhood and hot cereal and soft-boiled eggs. She thought, tasting these again, that one's first memories should be of loving and that these should be under the Peiping sky; that one's early eyes should grow deep with looking upon that northern largeness; that one's proportions might embrace both the utter intricacy of the new moon— the thinnest shining lunar prophecy of a crescent suspended over the spring mud—and the boldness, the lustiness, the full-blown wonder of solid sunlight and blackest artesian depths —that these should be and remain and live at the young core of every adult, be the solid unwavering pivot of the unchanging child in every grown person, the point of eternal return, the memory which is the person, beyond which no history can recede!

In the northern spring, the New Year began with celebrations and red lace paper pasted on doorways and clanging of gongs, a chilly beginning in loud noises and bright colors, then warming, softening, destroying the winter stoniness of earth with March dust from the Gobi. Sand-blinded, the rickshaws wore khaki hoods buttoned like upright sleeping bags, and the rain fell from heaven straight down into the foot-thick dust like closely packed nails of liquid under the hammering of thunder.

Then, the kites! Offerings to wind and sky! Octagonal or triangular, airy as a skeleton with feathery fins, or fancy as a fiery dragon with scarflike tails undulating in the wind. Fish swimming sturdily, star shapes, circles linked with tinkling wires, humble homemade rag and sticks, an unsteady clown climbing, a disembodied strip of brilliance wriggling up the sky, a shape, a form, a color—all looked into the stratosphere. When still earthbound, they were awkward, stumbling across the walls amid shouts and laughter. Then they gathered strength, pulling, tugging to be free, bursting into the upper sunshine, high above the city wall, floating, sliding, resting on a shadowless reef, anchored to a small boy, an animated dot below, or an aspiring blue-trousered man sprinting across a square, or an old pipe-smoker squatting on his haunches; they linked—by a thin disappearing line of silver, an intangible linear thought, a wire shimmering between the infinite and a dark head in an encamped town—a kite, a thread, a spool, a hand.

In summer, the trees bloomed, acacias, lilacs, mimosas, and the bushes producing giant peonies bent over with their burdens. The house was cool, green, with shades letting in only a fragrance as distracting as a stealthy kiss. Mornings were lemon-colored, afternoons gold, the heat dry and virile, hitting one at the front door like the sound of drums. Down the streets, people hugged the shade, as though the sunlight might efface them, so deep and intensely it shone. The imperial parks and lakes were busy with families in rowboats, arrested in jungles of lotus plants; students found love in small pergolas, tourists examined the white balustrades, the marble and tile, the walls encrusted with dragons, the windows cut out like peaches and

58

pears. Cameras snapped their eyelids, making a harvest of permanent reflections, to be leafed through in other times, in other worlds.

If she had been a good girl all month, one night Sylvia would be taken to the Tsengs', to a garden party in a huge palace-like home. Evenings were uncharted continents for grownups only. The lanterns glowed mysteriously both indoors and out, the house sprawled like a large latticelike cage, gleaming with dark Chinese furniture and porous places where the porch seemed to hang askew from the left wing. Musicians squeaked away on instruments, emitting a tart sound, sliding off into tones both raw and sweet. Then a crashing of cymbals and the shadow play was on, the white cloth screen flickering with the colored puppets jigging around like noisy little deities. Much running back and forth with dishes and cups, the grown-ups chattering in shrill voices. There were hectic exclamations when a gust of wind almost blew down the screen and the lanterns shuddered and tore loose, to be pursued in the rock garden. A prelude of autumn chilled the party, and the ladies were estranged in their flimsy dresses and thin jade bracelets. "Indoors, indoors," someone ordered with hospitable truculence, "and more wine before midnight!" The musicians shrugged and the puppeteers took advantage of the commotion to test their chopsticks in the forty dishes on the lawn.

The autumn moon was the most glorious, prodding desolation, leading as it did into the dark of the year. October lingered, clear as the blue-white of a child's eye; it rested in an open movement, flowing over and above the walls. The rancid human smell of the alleyways was washed clean, and heaven blew cool, agate colors into the leaves. The heart was released and longed for a mooring, for the sun of the year was leaving on a tide of time, and winter was wide spaces between the northern cities.

Snow on Peiping! In her thoughts, object and emotion melted into each other—the dusty plodding of camels' feet felt like the cushioning of fatigue against the long winter night. Her

59

bedroom was a nest at the end of the long corridor of home. The Chinese seemed to have learned the art of quilt-making from the falling seams of snow blanketing a familiar nature. Hush, there was no sharpness here! Whiteness was a presence like large words written in the sky: purchase spring with minted snow! The child-in-her had thought this must be God descending in myriad white miracles. Oh, dream me, dream me, Sylvia raved as a talisman against the present. Let there be silence; the dazzling shadow of the infinite fell on those pines, those tiled roofs, that rocky earth, winter hardening, selfishly unyielding, turning its back upon the chilly human orphans and hungry dogs trotting quickly on icy feet. In wintry aspirations the spirit strengthened, under sterile moonlight were human intimacies born. So went Peiping into spring, breaking fearfully like girlhood into love, so went hamlet, village, town, city, all the explored and seminal land, peopled for so long by so many dark heads. . . .

Sylvia did not know how long she had been standing before her bedroom window. It was almost completely dark outside. The apartment was quiet, another Shanghai evening rubbing warmly against its walls.

CHAPTER FIVE

For a purpose, Feng Huang knew he could be pleasant and entertaining. Purpose was something he had looked for all his life—a pole that would help him vault over the endless little quagmires of a personal centerlessness. It had never been enough for him to live and just have a job. He had always sought something more, and until fairly recently had not been able to define exactly what it was he wanted.

"Would they be able to understand this?" he thought even as he spoke to Sylvia's parents, and shrugged inwardly. He wanted understanding, but had never received any. Now he did not care if he was understood or not. He had always been alone, and he saw himself operating through life like a car through traffic. It had ceased to occur to him to lament over his condition. He had traded self-pity for a weapon, and had lost little in the transaction, he felt, except introspection. Anyway, in China introspection was redundant. The country was populated by millions of introspective souls. What was needed was "out-trospection."

For an hour he tossed the ball of conversation between Helen and Chen Liyi with only half his mind on what they were saying. He told them he had just been walking by and had "decided to drop in," saying it with a polite lilt in his voice, and half believing his own pretense at nonchalance. Actually, Feng had considered the event for several days. The thought of phoning first made him suddenly shy—he had never called Sylvia before and, of course, his calling her up would be noted and discussed. How he hated the small bourgeois constructions that were automatically and unrelentingly assigned to everything one did—the laws of society were more predatory even than those of nature.

From under his knotted brow, he now stared at Mrs. Chen, who had executed a number of gyrations when Sylvia had ushered him into their living room. Sylvia had masked her surprise almost before it had registered; at least, one made contact with her on the second level immediately: you felt you were accepted for yourself, and he suspected that Sylvia's range could encompass almost any motivation. (The thought excited him.) But Helen Chen had quickly shaken out her party manners, like a perfumed handkerchief tucked down her bosom, and now it seemed to him she was waving it before his nose. Her formality rustled like taffeta—she was ready to preside. Feng felt a resistance travel up his spine; it made him feel gauche, fidgety and superior all at once.

"We must have some tea," Helen had said, and under his close scrutiny—he could have willed her to elaborate her folly —it seemed she was about to lean back on her throne and pull a velvet tassel. He felt witty, and wanted to say that, unfortunately, this was an apartment house, compact, designed for modern living, but in the end less functional than palaces, even though they had a reputation for being draughty. Helen moved quickly—the rest of the family seemed mesmerized by her, too—and traveled down the steps in the hallway. She raised her voice slightly.

"Tea," she ordered, "Chinese tea." A concession to the majority? He smiled to himself. Or a practical measure? For Chinese tea was easier to get these days than the foreign brands. It also did not require cream and sugar.

"Tea, weak or strong? Shall I let it brew a bit?" Helen asked him a few minutes later, but he did not answer, did not even take one step in the pattern of her social gavotte.

To Sylvia it must have seemed that his attention was straying, hanging somewhere between the floor and the ceiling, held up perhaps by his raised eyebrows, for she began to act as interpreter: "Mother could like to know whether—"

"It's a good thing I didn't phone first," he found himself saying, and felt their bewilderment, but didn't explain that if he had given them any notice at all, the damask tablecloth might have been laid. "Doesn't matter. I like any kind of tea," he supplied brusquely, thinking that his visit had been twisted out of its original purpose. He had wanted to see Liyi and Sylvia. He had seen his move as a direct line, but he would have to expend his energy dodging Helen.

"Medium, it'll be, for all of us," Helen declared, and started handing around the cups.

All of a sudden he was filled with hatred. Families were all the same, he thought. Sylvia's parents filled him with the same anxiety that his own did. Sometimes he thought he could never escape it—the hatred, which was like a routing of enemies, and part of his identity as Feng Huang. It propelled him. He would almost be afraid to lose it, and his unhappiness with it, for he would be robbed of himself.

"Do have some," Helen said to him, "You must," she insisted. "Mr. Huang, don't stand on ceremony."

Sylvia took a piece of ginger, as though to shame him, for he had refused to be gracious enough to accept a sweetmeat. She chewed it conspicuously, and he felt his own eyes close in irritation. When he opened them, Chen Liyi became the next victim of his misanthropy. He suffers from a sense of original sin, Feng thought triumphantly, forgetting how Tang could manipulate his own guilt. He saw Liyi look furtively at the time; he seemed to be worried about the nine o'clock news.

"Turn it on," Feng said, and wanted to add, "Don't hesitate." Liyi looked at him smilingly, stretching out a supple hand. The introduction of a fifth voice, one that had its speeches prepared, would surely ease the strain.

Liyi had turned the radio on low, Station XMHA, and pulled his chair near it, withdrawing from the others. It was an act of consideration, Feng knew: in thus giving his attention to the

63

news, Liyi was according "the young ones" some privacy. But Feng chose to pretend to misunderstand his kindness.

"Don't turn your back on me," he declared flatly, and Liyi seemed to jump, just as Feng had wanted him to. Liyi now leaned back in his chair, a smile playing on his face, his leg shaking up and down in an old Chinese gesture. He started to apologize, to justify himself, and Feng wanted to submit both of them coldly to the torture of an explanation. But just then the radio announcer, his words splintered by static, said something about Wang Ching-wei.

"Why don't you make it louder?" As he demanded more volume, Feng saw Sylvia watching him with an expression of distrust and modulated astonishment. Or was it faint amusement, an air of judgment suspended? That was what he disliked most about her: he could not pin her down. And as for Helen, at the teapot—she looked petulant, on the edge of a tantrum of disapproval.

"That opportunist!" he exclaimed brusquely, since the family seemed to wait for him to supply more fuel for their condemnation. He wanted to review Wang Ching-wei's history for them, especially the story of his role in the Communist party in the twenties. When Wang Ching-wei decided to head the Japanese puppet government in Nanking, he had gone back on one of the three principles, that of nationalism. The communists, Feng thought, not the Kuomintang, had been betrayed.

"When the war is over, the collaborationists will get their due," Feng continued. "They'll be harried out of their hiding places and exterminated, all of them."

"There'll be lots to do once the war is over," Liyi said, surprisingly briskly. "Taking care of the puppets is only one small aspect of it. Vengeance, anyway, is not an important part of the Chinese make-up."

"No, compromise—compromise is a more important part. We'll be compromised out of existence."

"But people have always compromised," Liyi replied. And Feng could hear him telling his daughter later, "Your friend

64

Feng is peculiar." Feng wondered if that would prove to her that fathers were always out-of-date. It amused him to think that perhaps Sylvia would stand up for his opinions, if not for his behavior. "Sun Yat-sen compromised," Liyi continued. "The Kuomintang compromised. The warlords compromised. The Communists have compromised, haven't they? I mean, they have been known to accept a temporary setback."

"There are two ways to clear up any mess," Feng retorted, "the scientific way and the traditional way. The only trouble is that the traditional way has been tried and found wanting. It's been tried for centuries and has failed for just that long."

"What is the scientific way?" Sylvia asked, too coyly. She seemed to want to add, "I'm just a girl, I have to have things explained to me."

He did not attempt to disguise his disdain. "In a nutshell, a capsule, or do you want the whole treatment this evening?"

"Nutshell, please," she replied, looking at her nails. "That'll be all I can absorb."

"You're not serious. I'm not going to waste my breath on you." He found himself sighing as though despairingly. He was sorry, in a way, that he so despised her. Like himself some time ago, she seemed totally immersed in her own tragedy. People, he thought, did not differ from one another very much. Each was unique—but they were also so much alike, each one essentially blind, afraid, alone. And his thinking this reminded him of his old self, the Feng who allowed himself to feel, to indulge in the why and how of each individual soul. He looked directly at Sylvia now, her complexion pink with the heat, and he resented her. Then his old self winked out, a weakly burning cinder. He had trained himself to give up dredging through his emotions—his own cynicism had frightened him. He was interested only in the state of men's futures—their futures not as souls, but as social beings. He wanted no more questions, no more mysteries. He was interested only in answers now. He not only had a point of view; he *was* his own point of view. . . .

Just as he thought, Liyi knew nothing about Robert Bruno

65

Senior's plans for the printing plant, and was not disturbed to hear the news second-hand.

"As a matter of fact," Liyi said, barely interested, it seemed, but wrinkling his high forehead, "Sylvia mentioned this the other night. She seems to think"—and he smiled a little—"that it may mean bigger things for me, though I don't quite see how—if the war continues."

"You'll be manager over more people," Feng said, feeling that he was drawing diagrams for the simple-minded. "The character of the two newspapers" (they were two English-language papers of very small circulation) "can be determined by the personnel you hire. It's something to bear in mind." He would keep his finger on Chen Liyi's pulse. If through his friendship with him, he heard of one or two openings before it became general knowledge, if he and Tang could get one or two of their own men in as editors or reporters, this "cultivation" of the Chens would have been worthwhile.

"You know that I am a professor of journalism," Liyi said, "and could possibly go in for the editorial side of things my-self until such time as I can get back to teaching. But one's hands are kept cleaner in the administrative end. You do what the boss and the Japanese supervisor think best, and you compromise on the lowest level only. I would not want to take directives on the level of editorial policy. That's why I am not unhappy doing what I'm doing—for the time being," and he waved his hand disparagingly.

"For the time being," Feng wanted to remind him, was now stretching into its sixth year. People covered up their own inadequacies with layer upon layer of rationalization. They called some self-destructive obsessions love; they called the lack of courage wisdom. Feng felt unashamedly complacent that he had sacrificed his own personal doubts in the sweep of a large movement.

"You forget," he said, "that Shanghai is atypical. People like you sit and wait for something to happen. You must make it happen, as it is happening outside this Japanese-dominated

66

area. The future is being made out there, while you are treading water here. You play safe, and make a livelihood. That is not enough. It has never been enough."

"And one's family?" Liyi asked, speaking more to himself than to Feng. "Livelihood is one of the three principles," he added facetiously.

"You're a Nationalist?" Feng asked. The Three Principles of the People had been set up by Sun Yat-sen, and both the Nationalists and the Communists used them. But Chen Liyi could only be a Chungking man.

"I'm a Chinese," Liyi said, bored—the only kind of aggression he could be provoked into, Feng thought. "I do not play it safe from choice, as though life is a game that one can play recklessly or carefully. I have a family. I could not go to Chungking because Helen is an American. You know the Japanese still keep tabs on her, checking every two months or so. I not only lost my job, I lost my university. One has to eat, war or no war. So . . . Bruno came along."

"I'm not a Nationalist," Feng said, not having heard a word of Liyi's defense. He had heard only the quality of Liyi's voice—that lack of passion that made Feng reckless, that underlying fatigue that seemed to be the result of a thousand inner harangues. Feng couldn't tell them what he was. He was a lover who could not breathe the name of the loved one in Shanghai, but he skirted danger, hinting at his romance. "The Nationalists," Feng went on, "are bringing up the country on outdated economic theories, nineteenth-century theories. They hold the country before a mirror of the West, and then bind it down with Fascism, a blatant totalitarianism with war lords as impresarios." He spoke furiously, as though he might be interrupted.

"Look here," Liyi interrupted, and Feng could see the stupendous effort even the beginning of such a mild defense cost him in nervous energy, "let's begin at the beginning—"

But Feng was already interrupting him. "Who's that talking in the next room?" he asked, listening.

"My nephew, Peiyuan," Liyi said, seeming relieved that the subject was slipping away from them. "Peiyuan, my brother's child, is staying with us," and he looked at his wife, who closed her eyes briefly and moved testily into their bedroom.

Through the closed doorway, they could hear very little, except when Peiyuan raised his voice. "Smuggled through the lines," they heard; "reconstruction" and the "era of peace" and "the youth movement." The word "duty" punctuated the end of every paragraph.

Liyi smiled. "He's sixteen," he explained, "and is not talking to the furniture. My son—Paul is fifteen—is listening breathlessly. His Chinese cousin is bringing him up on the ideology of the new China."

"There are two kinds of liberals," Feng said. "There are those who will wait and see what the Nationalists will do after the war ends, and there are those who will wait and see what the Communists will do after the war ends. They have one thing in common—the 'wait and see.' Which kind of liberal are you?" he asked, especially rudely.

"Well," Liyi began, and Feng knew that he was bewildered by such crudity. "I suppose—"

"Liberals!" Feng thought and said, "Liberals can only muddle the issue—in that, they do have a purpose. But in themselves, they are less than nothing, mere dilettantes in politics."

"I am a liberal," Liyi replied stubbornly. "I will wait and see what both the Nationalists and the Communists will do after the war is over. I am not pro either one; I'm pro-Chinese. It leaves us open to many doubts. But it leaves me *open*, and that is the important thing, my young man."

"Pro-Chinese!" Feng exclaimed. "What does pro-Chinese mean? How will you be pro-Chinese? It's not the sentiment that counts; it's the implementation. But that—that you liberals don't understand. That's what's going to defeat you. That's the difference between you and—that's the difference," but he checked himself with an ungracious grinding of brakes.

"As a liberal I know that Chungking is fascistic, but not fascistic enough to rule strongly, only fascistic enough to allow for certain abuses; and I know that the Communists are progressive, too progressive to want a united China, too progressive to fight the Japanese in this common struggle. The more reverses the Nationalists suffer, the better for them in the long run. We liberals have too many eyes and no hands. That's the tragedy."

"Liberals may have a certain amount of awareness, a decadent awareness, but they have no goal, no purpose." Feng then lied flatly: it was necessary. "The Communists *are* fighting the Japanese on all fronts. Do you think the coalition efforts mean nothing?" But he remembered the item he had read that night at the printing plant. The Communists were marking time in the northern provinces, fending off the Nationalists with "peace within the house" efforts, while America was asking Chungking to join with the Reds in exchange for aid.

They had raised their voices. Suddenly the door to Paul's room, which had been ajar, was flung open, and a Chinese boy stepped out, grinning. "You're speaking Chinese!" he exclaimed.

"Why not?" Feng asked, as Liyi introduced Peiyuan to him. But the boy refrained from answering after seeing Feng, for after all (and Feng knew it well), Feng hardly looked Chinese. It amused him to see how his hair, brown like Paul's, and his freckles—which no Chinese had—nonplused the boy.

"I hear you're working on your cousin," Feng interjected, and both Peiyuan and Paul grinned the foolish grins of self-conscious adolescents. Peiyuan reminded him of someone, he couldn't remember who.

"Well . . ." Feng said, suddenly wanting to be able to come again soon, "I've got to be going," and only the boys seemed to be sorry. Helen appeared, ready to make a gracious but expeditious farewell, while not attempting to hide her opinion of his abrupt departure. It must have appeared to her even less seemly than his having dropped in on them so unexpectedly. Liyi looked drained, as though many hours had passed instead of just a little more than one.

Sylvia seemed to want to follow him into the hallway. He said good-by to them all, and walked ahead of her onto the landing at the head of the stairs. She closed the door behind them.

He waited for her to say something, to reproach him. He walked down two steps, and turned, to find himself looking up at her. In the shadowy light, nothing showed but her bright, almost astounded eyes, and one smooth, slight arm, hanging fluidly by her side. He did not smile or say anything, but was suddenly overcome by the boorishness of his behavior all evening. He no longer felt driven by his hate. He felt washed clean, and suddenly extended his hand, and taking her wrist, held it while he said, as though reassuring himself, "I shall phone you in a day or two. I shall call you, Sylvia," and turned quickly to go down the stairs.

He felt strangely light-hearted as he walked away from their gate, as though the humidity had lifted and the wind was coming down from the north. Then he remembered whom Peiyuan reminded him of. He had enjoyed his delighted "You're speaking Chinese!" The boy had been disappointed when he had left. But Feng had wanted to end it then. Another five minutes, and he would not have been welcome soon again.

Peiyuan had reminded Feng of himself. He would have liked to have been that boy. In his own mind, except for lapses into pessimism, he was that boy—fresh, believing (and he was certain they believed in the same things) and totally Chinese.

CHAPTER SIX

Before Robert, Mimi had never been even remotely touched by any other experience. Unhurt, unawakened, she had been a virgin even in the matter of her parents' dying. She had not understood her loss or their passing from life, or the miracle and agony of survival. Mimi had been a happy child.

She remembered being reckless—at least, Sylvia had always called her reckless—and she had wondered what she meant. "Why, you're practically a tomboy!" Sylvia had explained once when she was nine, staring at her, as though she had just realized that it wasn't quite accurate, and repeating, "Well, practically." It was true Mimi's knees were always patched with iodine, her hair always in her eyes, her skin tanned by the sun. As a child, she stayed outdoors as much as possible and her vividest experiences had been of climbing.

"I can fly!" Mimi had cried, lifting her arms and running on the spine of a tiled roof in *Peihai*, the imperial park, in Peiping. "Watch me!" she screamed, feeling she was pursued by the four other children, but she had left them behind on a lower roof. Fearlessly, she ran, and climbed onto another tier of yellow tiles. Years later she could not remember what they, picnicking with a schoolteacher, were doing on a roof, nor could she remember the building. It seemed a jumble of walls, beginning low where the ground rose abruptly and then leading to the peaks of an elaborate pavilion. Below her, the schoolteacher, a freckled American lady, was slapping her hands together to gather in her flock. Mimi remembered sighing dramatically, but there was no one to overhear her, no Chinese princesses of the turn of the century walking through the royal park with a graceful inclination of their bodies.

Partly out of pity for the teacher, Mimi had turned around, run and jumped down, run and jumped down again until she reached the lowest roof. Before her, across the shimmering lake, blazed the sun, beginning to set. The tiles were on fire, a golden mosaic of mirror and flame. Blinded, she slipped, sliding down the side of the roof, smiling. There was so much freedom in letting go. "Good-by, sky!" she had wanted to sing, hearing the screams below her. Then the sun seemed to die. She went out of existence, and when she came back everyone was bending over her and her broken leg. But the leg healed, and she was almost memoryless about the event. She only remembered the sensation of having been sharply alive that day.

Another time she was sitting on the branch of a small tree, watching Sylvia and a friend climbing other trees on either side. The other girl—and for some reason she could not remember her name—was two years older, eleven, and was saying in a hoarse voice, "I could tell you a secret, but I won't."

"You don't have to," Mimi replied dreamily. It was a little cool in the tree; she edged over to where the leaves let in more sun, feeling the roughness of the branch under her legs.

"Wouldn't you like to know—" the girl teased. Her voice was always deep, as though she had a cold, and when she laughed she hardly made any sound at all.

"Sure, I'd like to know," Mimi found herself saying. She really hadn't been paying much attention at all.

She remembered only the beginning of what the girl had to say, "Boys are different from girls. I'll tell you how they are different. And they do things to girls." Mimi remembered her heart going fast, as though in fright—but she did not understand why she should be frightened—and how vivid the grass beneath the tree seemed, coarse tufts imbedded in the earth, and the loud rustling wings, as if everything were suddenly too close and alive for comfort. Everything seemed to

72

be growing around her; she could almost hear the tree's pulse. She faintly disliked the girl later. But soon the whole incident was forgotten.

When she was a child and tanned, her thoughtlessness made her tomboyish. But at thirteen, she had suddenly filled out, grown aware of her femininity. And now her thoughtlessness might be called "abandon." But she who had always seemed to herself merely voluptuous, though small-boned and dainty (for hadn't she studied and defined her own physical assets carefully long ago?), found out how ravenous she was beneath her softness. She wanted Robert—she wanted him in several senses of the word. She was hungry for him physically; he had awakened a latent directness in her. What had formerly seemed laziness in her personality, lethargy, had become (she could feel it herself) a dead seriousness. That lethargy had colored all her behavior. She never took trouble over social trivia. She was too lazy to shake hands, when a spoken farewell would do. When she was not interested in a conversation, she made no effort to hide the fact, or to contribute toward making the talk more interesting. She merely gazed into space —not sullen, but completely bland. Yet, if she was enjoying herself, no one was more deeply engaged in the moment. She never went against her own will (like doing unnecessary chores, seeing people or attending parties she only half wanted to) and therefore she never complained either. It was almost as though she had no preferences, no prejudices, just because she instinctively asked herself to meet no standard of consistency. She was almost conscienceless. Her own single-mindedness now surprised her. She wanted to waste little time in playing the game of love. It was too much bother—a ceremony for the untried or jaded. She gave directly, entirely, without bargaining.

She wanted Robert "that way"—her term for carnality. His sexuality—his purging himself of his tensions through her— matched her passion exactly. In the act of love, there were moments of such intensity, she felt maddened as though with hate. Since he was so elusive most of the time, she was satisfied only then, deeply appeased, almost as though she had killed him, and so had him forever. As soon as it was over, she returned to ease and affection, no longer clung or lashed him to her. Relaxed, she could smile, while they said foolish, meaningful things to each other.

Other times, she dared him, provoked him to a male chauvinism, so that he would conquer her, so that she would "die" beneath his arrogance. "Do what you will with me!" she had cried one afternoon, not hearing how melodramatic the words were, how challenging the tone. She had closed her eyes as he approached, as she imagined his teeth clenched, his grim and speechless determination. He had taken her violently—as she had so intensely willed and yet so passively received. Her utter capitulation had felt like her greatest triumph, and she knew that it was Robert, the victor, who had been lovingly used. Her passion surprised her, but not her improvisations. Instinctively, she knew all things were possible in people.

But she also wanted him in other ways. She wanted to be his companion throughout life—his playmate and helpmate. She dreamed that they could share everything—she who had never really shared anything with her parents, when they were alive, nor realized that she had missed, since their death, such a thing as sharing. But she wanted to see everything through Robert's eyes as well as her own.

She wanted also to be of his world. Until him, she had not known she was essentially homeless. Now she knew that by loving him and being loved by him, she was assured of status for herself and a "society" to which to belong. For this reason she wanted everyone to know they were in love. She wanted the announcement of their engagement and marriage to take place soon. She wanted their relationship, already established in private, to be given public manifestation. She wasn't interested in keeping some of the mysteries of courtship and love to herself. An experience kept secret did not enrich her; it only seemed to rob her of half its pleasure. She wanted Robert and wanted everyone to know it.

Mimi felt that Robert savored her intensity, but at the same time was a little intimidated by it. One evening he playfully suggested that they take a bath together. Giggling, she got into the tub with him. They emerged ten minutes later, the water much cooler, and most of it on the floor. She had suddenly reverted to her childish wildness and spent the time splashing him unmercifully. Later, she stalked him, while he feigned (she thought) a helplessness. "You've got me where you want me!" she hoped he would declare. Instead, he merely pretended to protect himself when she pursued him with speechless embraces. She initiated what he later carried out with devotion. She delighted in her lack of shyness, her fearlessness, her utter confidence in his love for her. She gloried in being Mimi Lambert in love.

CHAPTER SEVEN

Chen Liyi closed the door on himself quietly and resolved to shut out all the points of view that seemed to have the power to disintegrate him.

"There goes an opinionated young man," Helen had said, after Feng Huang had left. "He is so ill-mannered, you'd think he hadn't had all the advantages I know he's had. His mother must be terribly disappointed in him."

Liyi had found himself coming to Feng's defense, though he, too, had been put at a disadvanatage by the young man's methods. There was always an element of hitting-below-the-belt in the lack of civility. The only way to meet it was to stoop to equally pernicious ways, but one was never quite willing to sacrifice one's taste for a valueless victory. He had answered, "Feng Huang is an idealist, I'm afraid. You don't understand idealism."

"I understand bad manners," Helen had insisted, and Liyi had laughed. She was matter-of-fact, literal and essentially correct.

Then Peiyuan had said, "A Confucian gentleman would not have made an idealist, or vice versa. And some esthetes forget to brush their teeth in the mornings, they are so pre-occupied with purity."

Helen had merely *humphed*. Peiyuan had spoken in Chinese and she did not understand all of it. But Liyi knew she did not like Peiyuan's talent for epigrams—she found them incongruous with the boy's blatant puberty, his ungainly enthusiasms.

But to return to the subject of Feng Huang, as Liyi reminded himself, he had been depressed by his visit. Feng was so much out of Liyi's range that he was almost another kind of being, reminding him of a robot, where energy replaced spirit and reactions took the place of understanding. What really frightened him was the realization that he had nothing in common with Feng's generation. It made him wonder about his own daughter, Sylvia, and made him realize again that children did not belong to their parents. They belonged to their times and to themselves. One could not save them from life or from themselves, and under the large square tent of reality, it was hard to know who was parent and who was child. Both Sylvia and Feng seemed much more cynical than he had been at their age—he had not been cynical at all—but they also seemed much more vulnerable, vulnerable to problems and pressures that *his* generation had created for them. Now, as he thought of them, and watched Sylvia (his own daughter, and the very word "daughter" filled him with warmth and love—she was an extension of him, a miraculous bridge in flesh into the future), he knew that he was the child, groping to understand her world. He had produced two children who were "foreign" to him on two levels. Physically, they were of another race— a small minority of Eurasians; and psychically, they seemed shyer of him than he remembered that he had been with his own father.

Liyi thought of his own generation as "romantic," the word seeming to him entirely flattering. But it made Sylvia cringe a little, as at the fairly recently out-of-date, like the evening capes and spats of the elegant thirties. It had been stylish to be romantic in the years following World War I, when he had attended the University of Missouri. And especially daring and reckless—and he had been so reticent, so demure, except in his fantasies—for a Chinese to be romantic. *His* father would not have understood the meaning of the word, unless it had been applied to wooing. His father would not have understood the anguish of it. Romanticism was like defying destiny (and all Chinese sought destiny like a banister in the dark). But defiance was destiny, too; it made for individual fates. And he thought suddenly, whatever happened to that romantic girl, the first Chinese girl to cut her hair short? She had been the first Chinese girl to dispense with a chauffeur, and she had driven her own car into her own swimming pool. The older generation had laughed, vindicated, but the younger generation was always right. It was an iconoclastic thought in China, and Liyi felt secretly flattered that he was capable of it. But the young *were* wiser than the old. They were directly engaged with the present; they had to improvise the future.

"I am going to look for work in Shanghai and send money home every month," Peiyuan had said five weeks before. His nephew Peiyuan was half an orphan, for his father had died in Chungking. "I'm going to prove that I'm old enough to be independent, self-reliant and responsible." And Liyi envied him for being young enough to understand what every one of those adjectives meant. "Father died," Peiyuan had kept on saying—in Helen's direction—as though sensing her resistance. He had had to come this way—out of the blue. He had had to come without warning, or he would not have had the courage to follow through.

"For love of family and for the reconstruction of China, he died," Peiyuan had said in several different ways, and the repetition of the particular phrase reminded Liyi how much he missed speaking Chinese. Because of Helen, they used only English at home.

And now, after Feng Huang's departure, Peiyuan spoke up, stimulated by what he had heard of their conversation. "I want to go to Chungking. I could get smuggled through the lines." He flapped his soft sleeves, for he still wore his cotton Chinese gowns. "But I'm head of the family, and I have my responsibilities. After the children are grown up"—he had

78

already assigned his sister and brother to childhood, from which he had only recently taken his leave—"then I'll be able to do something for my country. But meanwhile, work, work, and more work." Oddly, Liyi thought, Peiyuan had smiled, enjoying himself. "Someone has to shoulder the responsibility. I cannot fail my father's trust. Duty calls and I answer." It was too charming to be childish and too Chinese to be pompous. But Liyi was surprised that his own conscience bothered him.

"You simply must get him a job soon," Helen had begun after Peiyuan had been with them less than a week. "It's not good for a young boy to be idle."

"But he has just arrived," Liyi had protested mildly. "We should give him some time to adjust. After all, just being in Shanghai is a drastic change for him."

"I should think so," Helen retorted between her teeth, and Liyi knew what she was thinking. The old homestead in Sunkiang, which she had visited once, had seemed foreign and therefore primitive to her. She had failed to see the intricacy and liveliness of life in a large Chinese family. All she had seen were its strangeness and inconveniences. "I should think he *would* find life in this house different," she repeated, and Liyi just sailed over her implication that their "American-style" home was superior.

"Why don't you give the boy a job at the printing plant!" she had exclaimed. "Why, that's a good idea!" she went on, delighted with herself. "You can create a place for him. You're in charge; you can put in anyone you like."

"No, I can't," he had said, and now as he looked at Peiyuan's hopeful face, inspired by Feng Huang's visit, he wanted to repeat it, so that the boy could not miss understanding. "No. I will not put my nephew into the plant. That would be nepotism," and he said it in Chinese for the boy's benefit. It was a big word for what would have been the execution of a small, a petty sin (Peiyuan would only have qualified to be an apprentice linotypist perhaps), but he had stuck to his guns.

"You see, Helen, it's the principle of the thing. I won't indulge in our national sin. In the new China"—and he winked at Peiyuan—"there isn't going to be any of that, nor graft, nor corruption, nor spitting in the streets. If Peiyuan has anything to do with it, once the war is over, we'll be transformed into Utopia, with lots of sidewalks and no germs, no bribes, no overpopulation."

But still, Liyi's conscience had not been put to rest, and now it plagued him again. He could not get away from the feeling that he had refused to help the boy. He had thought he was uneasy because of Helen, so he had hastened to reassure her, "Don't push me, my dear. I know what I'm doing. Peiyuan and I, we Chinese, will put our heads together and find him a job."

But five weeks had passed now, and Peiyuan had found nothing. First he thought he'd be a bank clerk, but there were no openings; then a postal employee, but one had to take all kinds of tests and wait six months to a year; then a tutor of young children.

"All of which," Helen had said, "proves he doesn't know his own mind, and should go back to school. To enter college, that is, if he can qualify." But she did not suggest how he should finance his education—certainly his own mother, a widow now, had no reserve funds, and the Chens could not take on another child with inflation the way it was. A pair of shoes cost half a million CRB dollars. Eggs were a thousand dollars apiece. But Helen could not let "Albert" alone, and Liyi felt guilty when he sometimes thought that giving Peiyuan an English name was just her way of making him more accessible, easier to nag at.

He would help him, though; he would think of a way. It occurred to him Feng Huang would know what to do; so might Sylvia. Their generation was bolder. And he allowed himself to think it might be because of their very youth, for he felt crowded in by accumulations of leftover emotions, recollections, private arguments, dull recriminations. It seemed to him that he could dispel them all if only he could throw open the windows. It had been over ninety all day, but the thick winter curtains had to be drawn to keep in the light of the two lamps. The brownout gave the city a strange morbidity. The apartment seemed surrounded by acres of darkness. His own history hung heavily in the air, an inseparable part of an interminable Shanghai summer. He felt anything but reckless, defiant and romantic. He avoided looking at Peiyuan, who seemed to be waiting for him to say something, and he excused himself as he and Helen walked out of the room.

Peiyuan thought of himself as having a natural audacity. At least, his mother had always half congratulated him on his outgoingness—congratulated him impersonally, that is, crediting his generation with what he felt to be his own talent for expressing himself easily. His parents' generation was very much obsessed with remarking on the merits and demerits of "the younger generation." They were certain a new race was being formed in the public school system (the old tutorial one had been displaced), by the youth movement, by the present war.

But when he was with his Uncle Liyi, he felt all his traditional inhibitions rise to straitjacket him. And it surprised him. . . . It had surprised him acutely the first week he spent with them. Somehow—because he had seen Uncle Liyi last when he had been only eight, too young to form an opinion —he expected the somewhat controversial member of the family (after all, he had gone and married an American!) to be audacious himself, very much in command of any situation he was in, and entirely "modern." As Peiyuan thought the word "modern," he quickly erased it from his mind. He would like the day to come when "modernism" in itself was not a goal for China, but part of the general context of living. Asked to define the word, he would have hesitated. It was as much an attitude—which Peiyuan carried in his "modern" straight athletic stance (in the old China you were willowy, stooped and scholarly)—as it was gleaming railroads, suspension bridges, industrial towns, the breakdown of feudal ways and morals.

But Uncle Liyi was just a man in a strange situation, a bizarre situation. Peiyuan could not forget what he had heard issuing from the servants' quarters that first week. Yennai, the *amah*, was having a discussion in the kitchen. "I stay with the Chens for the master's sake. He is a gentleman, but he should never have gone abroad to study." She hesitated and then added, "His parents must have been horrified!"

Another servant laughed. "At what he brought home?"

As he thought about it, a simple truth became apparent. Uncle Liyi's generation had wanted to get Westernized at breakneck speed. But there were hazards in that. Modernity—and there was that word again—was *not* synonymous with Westernization. That was what his own generation knew. It was a pretty obvious observation, but he felt he had broken through to an important discovery and wanted to share it. He walked out of the living room where Uncle Liyi had left him, and sought his cousin Paul. But even as he entered their bedroom, he knew he could not communicate it to him. Paul still needed working on.

If his Uncle Liyi had surprised him, his cousins Sylvia and Paul had shocked him. They were total "foreigners" with a Chinese surname. And it wasn't entirely Helen's doing. It was also Uncle Liyi's lack of doing—his not asserting himself in the family. Peiyuan decided that he had a mission, one which he could start on right away, a small task of reconstruction before he undertook the large one he had in mind for himself when he was grown-up. He had literally taken over Paul's room, dictating the rule that they were to speak only Chinese in it. "I'll try to speak English in the living room," Peiyuan had said, "because your mother" (he couldn't bring himself to say "my aunt") "doesn't speak Chinese. But your Chinese is so poor"—he almost rejoiced that he could be brutally frank (a part of his natural audacity), though blandly Chinese —"from lack of practice, that you might just as well benefit from my company."

"Sit down," he had said the first time, and had found Paul malleable, "and I'll drill you in syntax." On their common bureau, he had hung a long sheet of paper on which he wrote new phrases every day.

"You cannot rely on just 'picking up' Chinese," he had lectured. "As you know, every ideograph, every word, has to be memorized (and an educated man knows at least fifteen thousand separate ones), indelibly impressed upon the tongue, the eye and the hand. There is very little possibility of inferring from one ideograph to another, to build upon as with your Western alphabets."

"I know *that* much," Paul had interjected, impatient.

But Peiyuan ploughed on. He believed in starting from the beginning, laying the groundwork. "You know, but I must insist on your realizing how far behind you are. If you don't know a Chinese word, don't recognize it, and know the sound and the meaning assigned to it, either alone or in a phrase, you can do nothing with it. I would say that you forgot at least two school grades' worth of words the year you were in the States. And attending these foreign schools has not helped. You are fifteen, but you have the reading and writing vocabulary of a ten-year-old." He watched Paul wince, but would not allow himself to spare him. Reality was difficult to take, but without facing it, one could make no progress. A bit of pessimism, too, might serve as the necessary goad.

He introduced the art of peroration, so typically Chinese, and sat on his narrow bed, arms in his sleeves, nodding his head as Paul struggled with the topics he assigned: The Role of the Family in Chinese Society; The Evils of the Black Market; British Imperialism and the Opium War; the Outlawing of Bound Feet; China's Place in the Twentieth Century; The Challenge of Democracy in a Feudal Society; The Uses of

83

the Soya Bean; Why Industrialism?; Love—Freedom Versus Marriage.

He took pride in his pupil's progress. The pleasure it gave him made up for the moments of discouragement he had about not being able to get a job. Everything, he told himself, was going to be easier from now on—not that it had been so difficult for him up till then. After all, he told himself reasonably, "I am only sixteen." But then again, impatience swarmed in his breast and irritated him like a rash. But hope kept him exhilarated.

"You are beginning to think in Chinese!" he cried to Paul. Reconstruction did begin in small ways, and always at home.

CHAPTER EIGHT

The Shanghai which Sylvia knew was circumscribed, uncontaminated by the Chinese section, which she had never even visited. There was nothing in the Chinese city except narrow crowded streets, a jumble of traffic and, Sylvia thought, probably some of those incredible ruins of a stone altar, a part of a temple wall, a bronze urn, standing in the midst of a space of ground somehow untenanted. She had seen them in the heart of squalor in Peiping, the aura of the past holding its ground, so that no one, not even a beggar with a lean-to, dared trespass within twenty paces of the hallowed survivors. The tiny gray ruins seemed always to stand in rain; but, of course, it did not rain always in Shanghai, nor was it always overcast. So on sunny days the stone altars must have broken the light on the ground, must have reflected their halfway position between clear heaven and brown earth. The cosmopolitan Shanghai she knew also did not include Nantao, the wicked gambling section, nor Hongkew, in the center of which the Jewish refugees had built a Vienna of a few side streets, not even Chapei, Lunghwa or Hungjao, which she had visited, and which carried the fables of the beginning of the Japanese incident, the bombings and scars of 1937, and the sentiments and guilts which tied them now with the International Settlement. For American, British and Dutch citizens were interned in camps in Chapei and Lunghwa, and somehow one's heart was touched by them, rather than by the thousands—how could you feel for thousands—of Chinese who had been displaced by the war. There were too many Chinese; yes, she felt that to be true; and it was so easy to claim distinction, to be ennobled—as though one had somehow achieved it through conscious effort—just by speaking English and looking, not even Aryan, but just non-Chinese.

Downtown was one constellation of her world, the east end of it running horizontally along the river, the Whangpoo, lined by the Bund, the open, commercial boulevard boasting a skyline of office buildings and hotels. In the midst of the cosmopolitan web were the race track, an open oval in the very heart of the city, Bubbling Well Road and Avenue Foch, private gardens and public parks, but after all was realized, and though the International Settlement spilled into the French Concession, the web held them in with steel bands. Barricades of barbed wire fences guarded the entrances and exits of the city.

Sylvia's world was bounded by St. John's University, beyond Jessfield Park (where not so long before dogs and Chinese were not allowed), and by the Shihs, who lived now—after gracing so many Chinese consulates all over the world—in a plain stucco house, divided into two flats.

She could name them all: the Chens, the Brunos, the Kemals, the Villiers, the Shihs, the Lamberts, the Jastrows, the Huangs, and all the unnamed hybrids. They seemed a whole community, yet they were only the survivors of a large international society eaten away by war and wormwood, survivors of a colonialism that was fast becoming as antique as peace.

All the hybrids and the cosmopolitans, all that were left in China, all that were not in internment camps, still moved, she knew, with the subtle authority of foreigners. Colonialism was still a perfume behind their ears, still the wicks of their unconscious spirits. They moved among the Chinese and left blondness in their wakes, even when they were brunettes. They did not live among the Chinese, but felt superimposed on them like a montage, as though they displaced another dimension in the city, as though the Chinese were somehow invisible.

86

They did not seem to occupy the same space; they were held apart by a trance that would not last much longer. Mimi Hong Lambert had said, secretly pleased, "They can't make out what I am: French, Spanish, Gypsy, even Creole." "They," of course, referred to the Chinese; she forgot she was half Hong. Sylvia felt a violence in herself, for she, too, could be so easily pleased, so cheaply flattered; it was so tempting to give way to narcissism, when the other side of the issue filled one with such dread, such a feeling of impending disaster. People were true to nothing in Shanghai: they belonged only to the surface values of both East and West, and leaned heavily toward the exoticism of the West. If one did not hold on carefully to one's sense of self, one might wake up some morning looking for one's own face, so easily lost.

In other people's houses, Sylvia felt more real, her face was given back to herself. Other people's homes did not seem like jails to her, the way her own sometimes seemed. But when she thought of her friends as single individuals, each alone in his own home, she realized that none of them was different from herself. Each one thought of the others as having more existence than himself. The thing was: you didn't present a framed picture of yourself *to* yourself. But other people were framed and delimited and more real because you could look at them, adjust the frame a little to the right or to the left, and look at them again. But to himself, every individual was an eye, an eye as large and as limitless as everything it could take in.

Yes, after all, everyone's home was a prison. Mimi's didn't seem a prison now only because Sylvia herself was in it—a visitor who made it expand into a market place with the exchange of "girl talk."

Sylvia knew Mimi's Aunt Juliet. The first time she had met her had been as a child in Peiping years before. Mimi's parents had been alive then. For a short period the Lamberts lived in an apartment in the Legation Quarters, a "flat," as they called it, giving it the aura of fashionableness.

"You live in a house and we live in a flat," Mimi Lambert had piped at the age of seven. Eight-year-old Sylvia had not accepted this piece of information matter-of-factly. It had hurt her deeply. She had at once got the idea: houses were no good, flats were much to be preferred to them. To this day, she could not be certain Mimi herself had expressed some sort of snobbery. Probably Mimi at seven had merely been stating a fact. Children made facts seem uncontroversial, like good fortune or doom, unalterable. Now Mimi and her aunt, Miss Juliet Hong, lived in a house and the Chens lived in a "flat." It no longer seemed to Sylvia that apartments were to be preferred to houses. She hardly thought anything was better than anything else. Different, yes, but not better or worse.

Mimi was sprawled on the living-room couch (a stiff, elaborate, horsehair relic from the past), painting her toenails. The room was a study in incongruity. The floor was covered with an enormous Peking rug, deep blue with a dragon design in the middle. A handsome "foreign" console stood against one wall; by the opposite wall was the bar, with sliding glass doors, on which stood several bottles and turned-down tumblers. A fireplace was flanked by six erect, narrow Chinese ghost chairs, ornamental pieces not meant for sitting on. An ornate gold lantern hung from the ceiling over the dragon on the floor, but by the horsehair sofa, and by each of the overstuffed chairs that seemed to have been placed with no pattern in mind, stood functional lamps in aluminum. Chinese embroidered hangings covered most of the walls, and served as runners on the mantelpiece and the occasional tables. The bric-à-brac included a porcelain Madonna, colonial glassware from the States, a jade paper weight, ivory elephants of graduated sizes, Mimi's baby booties preserved in silver, examples of Chinese pottery, a Kuan Yin, and two tennis rackets displayed for some forgotten reason on the low coffee table before the sofa. A door behind the sofa led into the sunporch, but

88

bird cages overflowed into the living room. Some were hung on brackets, others stood on their own stands, but from each of them came a bird cheep or call of a different variety.

"We'll go to my room soon," Mimi said, as though she had sensed Sylvia's appraisal of the parlor. "It's nicer in there."

"Don't see why you can't paint your nails there anyway," Sylvia said, rather more irritably than she felt.

"Can't stand the smell of this acetone. I do everything in here anyway. Keeps my own room neat. Neater, that is."

Sylvia thought it over with admiration. Mimi had a formula and practiced it; so did this aunt of hers, the *laissez-faire* Miss Hong. Most people who were compulsively neat about their property, like her own mother, for instance, went about the house untidily in their ill-fitting underwear. But Mimi and Aunt Juliet, who were always personally neat, made the downstairs of this house a repository for everything they did not need and could just as well have discarded. The sunporch, for instance, was a storeroom for birds, empty cages, extra furniture, Mimi's discarded school books, large Chinese jars, Miss Hong's victrolas, dating back to the first one she had bought in 1919, old jazz records, and boxes filled with the dresser sets—the matching jewel boxes, brushes, combs, cosmetic trays—that each of her lovers had given her. Only their large dining room was spare and consistent. But it was also dreary and forbidding. The black mahogany table that could seat sixteen, the stiff carved scrolls, all of these were so unreceptive to the presence of the soft and tawny Mimi and her tiny, vivacious aunt, that the ladies usually took their meals in their rooms, served by a cook in the kitchen and two *amahs* dressed like dolls. They generally ate at different times, so that six sets of meals were served each day, and more, if snacks were counted. Mimi was very Chinese in her eating habits. She could nibble all day long.

Sylvia was cracking melon seeds, spitting the shells into her hand and transferring them onto a dish in front of her. Mimi put down her paint brush, extended her legs and admired the red toenails. She helped herself to the seeds and spat directly into the cuspidor on her left.

"Use it while you can," she said. "No cuspidors in my room," and tried to blow on her toes.

"We don't own a solitary one."

"I don't own these." Mimi bristled. "They're my aunt's."

"But you know how to use them."

"Any fool knows how to use a spittoon." She had wiped off the top of her nail-polish bottle. "Don't be shy, try it."

"Thank you," Sylvia said, but continued to spit the shells into her palm. Then she switched to the stuffed dates, to avoid further controversy. "Finished?" Sylvia asked, seeing Mimi apply paint to the last nail. They enjoyed each other chiefly because they could always regress to an artlessness when they were together. They had known each other for twelve years.

"No, indeed. Got to have a second coat so it stays on." She handed the melon seeds to Sylvia. "Take one and spit. You've got to learn how to spit. Never heard of anyone not knowing how to. Spit!"

Sylvia grimaced, cracked a seed expertly between her teeth, and spat. She missed the spittoon, as she knew she would, and the shell ended up several yards away.

"It takes practice. Here's another."

The second one dropped drearily on the arm of the couch itself. Ruefully, Sylvia retrieved both of them, to Mimi's protests.

"Oh, leave them. They'll be picked up tomorrow when the room is cleaned."

"It's obvious," Sylvia said, "that you don't live in my house," and suddenly she wanted to throw off her shoes and fling herself happily about this careless, abandoned household. Mimi did exactly what she pleased. Even when her parents were alive, she had had to submit to no discipline, no small *do's* and *don't's*. Sylvia remembered Mimi's coming into the Lambert living room after sitting in the wading pool they had in their formal Chinese courtyard in Peiping (just before they moved into the "flat" to satisfy a whim of Mimi's mother, who felt an apartment had a transient quality that seemed chic to her at the moment). She had plopped herself down, dripping wet, on the very couch on which they were now sitting. Mimi had picked up a doll and started to force chocolates into its closed mouth. Sylvia's eyes had grown large; she had looked nervously at Mr. Lambert, who was concentrating on tightening the strings of his tennis racket—the very one that she was looking at now—and seemed not to take any notice. Mimi's mother had exclaimed, "Mimi!" but instead of scolding—Sylvia had held herself tense against what was coming—she had cried "What a *drôlette* way of keeping cool!" Mr. Lambert, having satisfied himself as to the tautness of the gut, swung his racket back and forth, his beefy face and steel-blue eyes oblivious of them all.

Mimi's mother, Rosalind, was the more serious of the Hong sisters, everyone said. True, she had married an Australian adventurer, but she had married him, and he wasn't a bad sort. Mark Lambert had not been unaware that the Hongs were quite wealthy, but he had not married Rosalind for her money. He had made some himself on coal mines up in Manchuria. But after marrying Rosalind, he had invested both her money and his, and he had always made it pay handsomely. Thinking about Mimi's parents, Sylvia realized that theirs had been a successful marriage. They had had everything in common—a realistic interest in their financial partnership, a devotion (and no intensity, for society people were not intense about anything, she now realized) to tea and dinner dances, club functions, excursions to picturesque places in the provinces, sports (which Mark kept up to control his weight, and Rosalind enjoyed for the aura of emancipation which they gave her) and a good game of bridge. As for a deeper level, well, it just wasn't missed. Mark, Sylvia now realized, was an adventurer who had wandered into an exotic garden and found its walls not too restricting; Rosalind Hong had enjoyed all the privileges and freedoms that befitted the daughter of an enlightened warlord gone respectable—during the girls' coming-of-age Hong Wen-wei had been quietly instrumental in helping Chiang Kai-shek unite the northern provinces under the Nationalist flag. Rosalind and Juliet had had a liberal education, been sent abroad to French finishing schools, learned how to dance and smoke and participate in what might be termed the gamesmanship of Westernized living.

Rosalind Hong did not feel she had married beneath her when she became Mark Lambert's wife. She had picked up concepts of democracy in Paris along with a French bob and a taste for cinzano. But Rosalind must have been lonely, without knowing it. Her friends, Sylvia knew, could be divided into two or three categories. There were the Chinese social butterflies who had not gone abroad, and who, she felt, were provincial, though they were convinced they were not only sophisticated but also daring. There were the feminists of her generation, who had bobbed hair, but alas, also serious consciences—they had no time for her; they were doctors, lawyers, journalists, fighting for the right to work and the right to work for the rights of their sex. And then there were the other Chinese. This group included all the rest she knew or had heard of. It included Chinese who were educated but hopelessly old-fashioned, or conservative and unapproachable, or emancipated but somehow undependable.

Rosalind Hong was like none of them; she was quite stranded. In the nineteen-forties, Sylvia thought, she would have been more at home, but in the early nineteen-twenties both Rosalind and Juliet were conspicuous lost debutantes. Rosalind must have been the lazier of the two. She found refuge from more effort in marrying Mark Lambert. Her friends thought she was courageous, flaunting his foreignness in their faces. Only she knew that she could relax with him—he was really quite simple, forthright and undemanding. Everything they did together was fascinating just because he was a Westerner, and so she had satisfied her friends' expectations of her. Had she settled for a Chinese husband, she would really have had to justify her choice to them and prove to him wherein she was different by virtue of having been abroad.

In the middle nineteen-thirties, Mark Lambert had become restless. He wanted them to move down to Shanghai, a Eurasian city. Rosalind did not mind. Everyone was moving down to Shanghai or Nanking, where the capital was established. Aunt Juliet joined them just before the war broke out in 1937. Both Rosalind and Mark were killed in downtown Shanghai during the worst of the bombing. They had been shopping and walking past the Great World which was demolished by Japanese planes that came in waves over Chapei, Lunghwa and the Bund.

"Nothing serious, lovekins," Mark had said to his daughter that very morning. Mimi had later told Sylvia that he had added, "They're always shooting in this part of the world. Keeps folks from getting bored." And so Mimi had been an orphan at the age of eleven. . . .

Sylvia had been dancing around the living room, waiting for Mimi to perfect her toenails. Mimi had always seemed untouched. Suddenly, Sylvia stopped and looked at her with new eyes. She rarely thought of Mimi as having been affected by anything. Sylvia stared at her now in disbelief.

"Mimi," she said, and wanted to hug her, kiss her, comfort her. Mimi had been affected more than any of them. She had lost her parents because of the war.

"Just a second, impatient!" Mimi said, misunderstanding. "They've simply got to dry, you know."

Sylvia shook her head, thinking. She continued to whirl, though she did not feel like it any more. She danced behind the couch, where the bird cages hung. She ducked under a low one and planted a kiss on Mimi's head. Then she swung out the door, heading for the dining room, but almost fell into Juliet's arms as she came in, laden with packages and a Chinese lute.

"How are *les soeurs*?" Aunt Juliet asked, flinging the things on the coffee table. "*Je suis epuisée!*" and collapsed into an armchair. She had always thought of them as sisters, "my little nieces," when they were just children up north. Her eyes took in Sylvia, flushed and exuberant. And Sylvia felt her bright glance go over her in unsentimental appraisal. "How is Miss Chen?"

"Just fine," Sylvia said in English, tempted to examine Miss Hong the way she had been examined. But instead, she softened her gaze. She knew how Aunt Juliet looked—small-boned, narrow-eyed, full of a verve that Sylvia found in very few young people. She and Mimi did not have it, for instance. Older men and women had it, the ones who got things done and lived from day to day doing it. "Are you taking lessons?" she asked, pointing toward the lute with her chin.

"You're growing up, Sylvia," Aunt Juliet said, pursuing her own thoughts; her eyes went over Sylvia again, like a hard brush flicking her hair, her eyes, her shoulders, her breasts, her legs. "So it isn't only our Mimi who is reaching—ah, *comment dit-on*—ah, womanhood. I forget sometimes—or I do not keep in the foreground—the fact that there are women in the world besides me." She laughed to herself, sitting in the living room like a shopper who had merely put down her things in order to consider another purchase at the counter.

"Can you sing to the lute?" Sylvia asked again, as a maid came in and placed a cup of tea on the table beside her mistress, a cup with a porcelain lid, with which Aunt Juliet now toyed absent-mindedly.

"I think I resent your growing up," she said without answering. "But it's only because it's hot today. I hardly consider either one of you competition." Sylvia could not be certain she was saying it musingly—there was almost a bit of triumph in her tone. "I'm Chinese, you are not. I've *presque* more than twenty years' experience behind me, and am still going strong." She undid the top button of her Chinese collar and made a gesture as though to fan herself. (She must be warm, Sylvia thought, for Miss Hong never let casualness spoil the utter sleekness of her dress.) She swung her legs forward, her ankles chiseled and neat in the French heels, and lifted the front panel of her dress over her knee. "Yes, I'm taking lessons in the

94

opera," and she pitched her voice high, and seemed to gargle on a falsetto note.

Mimi laughed, "Drink your tea, *yi-ma*," she said. "You're excited and tired." She handed her the dates and the melon seeds and tentatively plucked at the lute. "Sylvia is staying over tonight—for a change. It'll be fun."

Aunt Juliet intercepted Sylvia's quick look at Mimi, but only leaned back and kicked off her shoes. "Yes, I'm taking opera lessons, dancing lessons (Chinese folk dance) and reading the Analects." She laughed again and said softly, "You've been nice, Sylvia, to entertain Mimi so often recently."

"Robert Bruno would love you," Sylvia said, puzzled by her last remark, but somehow wary of asking for an explanation. "He is the only foreigner I know who takes the trouble to look into Chinese things. I mean the only one who does it just because he wants to, not necessarily because it's in any way tied up with his work." There weren't many of those professional sinophiles around any more, the language teachers, connoisseurs of *objets d'art*, the writers of books on "Chinese Poetry, Its Theory and Its Practice," or "Two Weeks in Jehol." But Mimi had suddenly coughed and declared that her toenails were done at last.

"Let's go to my room now," she said sternly, and was already on her way.

Aunt Juliet waved them on hospitably as she said, "That Robert Bruno fancies himself a great liberal. I thought only Chinese liberals were like that—liberal about everything in general and nothing much in particular. Like me, *par exemple*. But Mimi takes after her mother—she likes foreigners," and she picked herself up to retire to her own bedroom.

"I wish," Mimi said when they were alone in her room, "you hadn't mentioned Robert. I'm having enough trouble as it is." She set down her bottles and nail file, and took off her dress. Whisking a dressing gown off the bed, she put it on with a flourish.

"Oh?" Sylvia replied. "And what's this about my staying over tonight? You might have asked me first."

"Well, will you? Can you? I would so like you to." She waved toward the divan in the corner of her room. "I've—I've lots to—well, to tell you."

"Does my staying over have anything to do with Robert?"

"In a way." Mimi hesitated and then plunged on. "On a couple of occasions I've told *yi-ma* that I've stayed over at your place. That's all. I thought it was time I reciprocated. Or she'd get suspicious. You see, I've got to do it this way. Do you see what I mean, Sylvia?"

"No, I guess I don't quite understand. I mean, I understand about you and Robert," and sitting on Mimi's bed, she looked up at her, watching a secret smile flicker over her face. Mimi seemed suddenly a stranger, with a life of her own, a life she couldn't even put into words for Sylvia, who had known her twelve years. "But I thought Aunt Juliet was—was new-fashioned."

"About herself," Mimi said. "But not about me. I'm her big responsibility. She doesn't quite approve of Bobby. She has some crazy notion that foreigners who have been in China too long get will-less, get corrupt, get no good. I don't know what—but she's making it difficult."

"She stays out a lot herself, doesn't she?" Sylvia mused, remembering all the things she knew about Juliet Hong, whose activities were a permanent scandal in certain quarters. Mimi had told her a great deal, too.

"But that's different; oh, that's very different," Mimi said drily.

"I suppose she's right in a way."

"She is not. I hate her." Mimi slammed down a cushion. Sylvia had never seen Mimi irritated and so tense. "I hate her."

"She's right because you are not like her. For example, you're in love with Robert, and that makes all the difference. You're serious, you're in love. She's never been so serious or so in love. She knows it's much more important and much more dangerous for you."

Mimi sat cross-legged on the bed, slamming the cushion down, picking it up again and slamming it down. She blinked, thinking, while Sylvia spoke; she seemed to be listening. But when Sylvia finished, all she said was, "Oh, Robert, Robert. Oh, how I love him," and buried her face in her hands. "Sylvia, you don't know what it's like to be in love, really in love, and to make love. It's the most wonderful thing in the whole wide world. Really it is. Really and truly it is."

"I believe you," Sylvia said briskly. "You talk as though you've got to convince me."

The phone rang, Mimi's private one. Sylvia had always envied her the possession of her own phone, her own number. It must be Robert, they both thought, and Mimi reached eagerly for the receiver.

"Hello?" Mimi said, her voice unexpectedly shaky though still lax and slow. "Oh," she said, disappointed. It was not Bobby, but Sylvia's mother. "Sylvia's staying over tonight," she announced. "I'd like her to spend the night, Auntie Helen. You don't mind, do you?" Then Helen spoke, and Mimi merely nodded her head, handing the receiver over to Sylvia.

"That Feng boy called," Helen said. "He was quite insistent. Wants to take you out tonight. I reminded him it was rather short notice, to say the least, but he insisted that I have you call him back at home. Is he getting interested in you, my dear? I rather suspect it, but hope not. It's not only short notice; it's no notice at all. But you call him back and tell him you're staying at Mimi's. You call him back and show him you've been properly brought up. But you're busy, you see, which is a fact. You're spending the night at Mimi's."

"Yes, I'll call him," Sylvia said, and I'll see him, too, she wanted to add. Just because her mother always tried to tell her exactly what to do—just precisely because of that, she'd see him tonight. They said good-by and she hung up, and then began to dial the number she had been given.

"Feng?" she asked, and it was he who answered. He wanted to take her to dinner and then a recital. Someone had given him two tickets; he wanted to use them, he said, sounding both

97

ungracious and determined. Sylvia had to smile. Yes, she said. Yes, he could pick her up at home at seven. She had three hours to get back and dressed. She was almost laughing as she hung up the receiver. He had sounded so relieved and so businesslike, too.

She turned and found Mimi looking up at her anxiously. "Are you leaving? You are staying the night, aren't you?"

"I'm going out with Feng Huang."

"Are you coming back later?"

"I don't know," Sylvia said, feeling unremorseful. Mimi hadn't even asked her properly to stay. She had just announced it, and was really only using her. "I might be quite late."

"But I want you to stay over tonight," Mimi insisted.

"I can stay over tomorrow night. That'll satisfy *yi-ma*."

"But I want you to stay over tonight," Mimi insisted again. Suddenly her mouth trembled and her eyes filled with tears. "Tonight!" she repeated, and burst into sobs. She buried her face in the pillows and cried like a child.

"Mimi!" Sylvia sat down beside her. "What's the matter? Tell me. What is the matter?" Mimi was sobbing so hard that she could hardly speak, so Sylvia kept murmuring. "You haven't told me everything, have you? You must tell me what the trouble is. Is it about Robert?"

Mimi raised herself from her bed and nodded. "It's about Bobby and me. I know I'm a fool to worry. But supposing I am—pregnant?" And having said the word, she dried her tears and turned to face Sylvia. "I'm overdue," she declared. "I've been overdue a week and it's making me so tense and nervous I can hardly stand it."

"Does Robert know?"

"No," Mimi said, "but that's not what I'm worried about. He loves me. So that's not it. He really loves me very much. But I don't want *yi-ma* to know. Not yet, anyway. But how can I make sure?"

"It's too soon to worry yet," Sylvia said. "Seven days is nothing.

98

"I think I got pregnant practically right away," Mimi said, and suddenly her tension gave way to laughter. She leaned back against the bed post and giggled until she lay limp, and finally staggered up to wash her face. She flung the towel in the air and embraced Sylvia. "Oh, it's so wonderful," she said. "You don't know how wonderful it is!" and buried her face in Sylvia's neck.

She made Sylvia feel like a much older sister. Sylvia patted her shoulder and put her aside gently. "I'm going out with that Feng boy on short notice," she said, imitating her mother. "But I'll come back and spend the night with you."

"Okay," Mimi said. "I'll be here. And I'll be all right to-morrow. I'm seeing him tomorrow night—just briefly, but I'm staying at *your* place on Saturday." She began to sort things out on her bureau. She sat down and brushed her hair, her mouth parting the way Aunt Juliet's did when she put finishing touches to her make-up in the front lobby, waiting for the car to be drawn up outside. When Aunt Juliet parted her lips and smoothed her hair, moving her neck the way she did, Sylvia had always had to look away quickly. It was a private act, not meant to be overseen. But when Mimi did it, she seemed only a passionate and innocent child. Sylvia felt suddenly that she should be warning her, but what she should be counseling her against she was not at all certain.

"Thank you for agreeing to stay overnight," Mimi said. "I'm lonely. And thank you very much, Sylvia, for the evenings I've been staying with you."

"*Il n'y a pas de quoi*," Sylvia answered in her atrocious French, "*ma petite.*" Her heart gave a twinge, as when contemplating something beautiful and premature. When the moon shone on the mid-afternoons of cold winter days, she felt this way too.

CHAPTER NINE

He felt defrauded by the way the evening was going. Snagged on himself, he seemed unable to release either himself or Sylvia from the rhythm they had involuntarily established. He felt torn between concern and indifference—but after all, what had he expected? *Nothing* was the answer. And she apparently had come expecting him to set the tone of their first date together (then, part of him *was* planning to extend this into the future!). She sat in passive receptiveness, awaiting his mood. He realized that he was afraid of this watching quality of hers. It disconcerted him, as any nicety did—and he had to admit that Sylvia's spirit was both refined and full. But he would have appreciated a little roughness now, a few unfinished edges, something to get a grip on, rather than this smoothness and ease. She inhibited him with her delicacy, instead of relaxing him. He could be released only by a lack of civility and finesse.

Feng had chosen Sun Ya's for dinner, and she had picked a booth divided from the main dining room by a curtained door. The occupants of the next two cubicles were playing *tsai chuan*, the finger game, shouting and exclaiming as they won or lost. He could almost see them flinging out the fingers of their right hands in a splaying motion. Each of the players cried out the sum of the fingers he extended and the number he thought his opponent was about to throw out: *liang hsiang hao, chi chiao, san hsing chao*. They seemed to be indulging in an elaborate ritual of cursing at each other, yet they were uttering words almost ceremonious, not bald numbers, but "two lovers" for the number two, "seventh night of the seventh moon" for seven and "three stars shine" for three. The loser had to drink cup after cup of warmed wine, the winner graciously accompanying him, to take the edge off his penalty. At least, the Chinese on either side of them seemed to be having a lusty good time.

He felt a sudden sense of loss, which made him short-tempered. He looked at Sylvia and saw only someone protected and spoiled.

"When did you stop going to school?" he asked, as though they were new acquaintances.

"What's that?" The din was excruciating. The waiters yelled out their orders above the sound of parties. Not a quiet intimacy, but *ruhnaoness*, a "warm and noisy" atmosphere was what made Sun Ya's popular with the Chinese.

"When did you quit St. John's?"

"You know when," she said, but her tone was not fractious. "Last year. The School of Journalism moved into the interior and everything started falling apart three or four years ago."

Then she went on, and he could not tell whether she was just trying to fill in an uncomfortable pause or trying to justify herself. He continued to help himself to the food before him, but did not take his eyes off her face. It was expressive and attentive and soft. Through the softness gleamed something so steady and bright that it made his gaze falter.

"But I had a job," she was saying, "until a couple of months ago. Then the Japanese supervisor took a liking to me. And—and my father doesn't really want me to work anyway." He remembered that she had been a fledgling copywriter (Larry Casement, the Irishman, had got her the job) for a Sino-Japanese advertising agency.

"Emotionally, your father is quite old-fashioned, no matter what he thinks. How long did you work there?"

She answered him, but he was not listening. He only thought: this is not the first time she has mentioned her father tonight. He, however, had left his parents behind. He had carved himself out of the dead tree of their lives—he had been able to do it the moment he had decided to leave his state of passivity. The day he had committed himself (it had seemed sudden, but he realized it had actually taken years), it was as though he had met himself coming around a corner. His dividedness had met and from then on had walked down the street in one body.

"Does your father keep you up-to-date on his work?"

"At the printing plant?" She smiled slightly. "If you mean does he present a daily oral report at dinner, no."

"You should take more interest in what goes on around you. You're not getting any younger, you know."

She stared at him and seemed to waver on amusement.

"Feng, let's just be people tonight. Let's just have fun, so let me be, will you?"

"You go out with Larry Casement sometimes, don't you?" he found himself saying unexpectedly.

"Uh-huh," she answered, not interested.

"Don't you think he's wasting his time, too?"

"Meaning that I am, I suppose," she countered immediately, but not sharply. "He hasn't been as fortunate as you. Has that ever occurred to you?"

"What's the matter with you?" he asked tensely, feeling out of control. *She* was the spoiled one, he had been thinking. She participated in nothing, really. But all she could see in him was the fact of his father's wealth. His father who had set him up in a friend's law practice, and who provided for his mother— and for himself when he was younger—with such insolent lavishness.

"You don't understand," he said, realizing acutely how imprisoned everyone was in his own self. They had known each other for years, but he could communicate nothing to her. He had been thinking of other girls, ones who fought for everything that a girl like Sylvia took for granted and sloughed off with ennui if not indifference.

He didn't care if he had not prepared the ground for his

words now. He was happiest when he was talking *about* something. He plunged on, setting his face against the feeling of impotence that words gave him. But how else could you convey anything?

"Action is the only thing that makes a person. You don't even know the girls of your generation. The war broke out when you were twelve, and since then you've been living in a know-nothing family, and have not had the curiosity to find out about the world on your own."

He had found his eloquence. "Just take a small-town Chinese girl," he said in a rush. "Say she's in her twenties now. Say she came from a middle-class, fairly well-to-do family. In her childhood she was educated the traditional way—a tutor came to her home and taught her to memorize the old texts; she was brought up thinking that her horizons were the four walls of the old family home; perhaps her betrothed had already been selected. Sometime in her teens, though, she discovered this was not necessarily the only life for her. In the big cities— in Peiping, Nanking, Shanghai, Canton—girls were already leading independent lives. They were studying in co-ed universities, making their own livings, choosing their own husbands. She determines to go to middle school. After much defiance and wrangling, wasting perhaps two years, she is allowed by her father to step out of the home and go all the way to—middle school, which happens to be across the street. She has won a victory, not only for herself, but for her sisters, her cousins, all the girls of her generation, not only in her family, but perhaps in families she has not even heard of.

"She thinks of college then. Mind you, Sylvia, this all took place only ten or fifteen years ago. By now her parents are both proud and fearful for her. Proud, because she has distinguished herself. Fearful, because she no longer fits into their pattern of life; she no longer belongs to them. She goes on to a university in Chengtu. Somewhere in between, the war has ravaged her home town. Her parents can no longer help her; she finds herself penniless. This girl, who a few years before would not have lifted her eyes in the presence of a man, this girl joins the army! She isn't sure what her functions are—nurse, stretcher bearer or file clerk—but she acquits herself well. Somehow, a few years later, she finds herself studying again. Studying Western literature, for she wants to be a teacher. She reads translations of Gide and Walt Whitman, taking notes in the penmanship her original tutor taught her. Accidentally, she is wounded by a grenade thrown by the secret police. She was not terribly aware politically, but her boy friend was, and she lost him. Suddenly she was catapulted into the nation's life. Suddenly she has given of herself, and taken life in return!"

"You're awfully romantic!"

"Romantic!"

"You have the strongest sense of self of anyone I know," she said, "but you want to fling yourself away bodily. You just can't bear being human and torn and imperfect—like everyone else."

He almost shouted, "You've missed the whole point!"

He moved his head, and seemed to be shaking with a passion that he controlled only with a fierce effort. "I was talking about a girl. A typical girl. I was telling you how in ten or fifteen years that girl bridged several generations of social evolution through sheer will and determination and guts. She's Chinese. She's Chinese and good—good, do you hear me? She's not one of your Shanghai Chinese, corrupt, irresponsible, selfish, ignorant. She's the new heart of this nation. She is the future. She got things done. She went out and acted on reality to suit her own purposes. She's my pride and my goal. Peiyuan," he couldn't keep from adding, "your Peiyuan would know what I'm talking about."

"I don't think Peiyuan would, quite. And you think my father is emotionally old-fashioned! Do you think my father's story is any different from your girl's story? He went from a queue and classical examinations to a tuxedo for a University of Missouri prom and differential calculus. My father has bridged eons in less than thirty adult years. No wonder," she continued, "no wonder he's filled with doubt and rationalizations and is emotionally old-fashioned sometimes—"

"I'm talking about people and the things they get done. It's about time things got done in this country." But it was useless. She really did not understand.

"I'm talking about people, too, and what they are."

The brightness of her face had become unbearable. It constricted his breathing.

"What they are!" he scoffed. "You sound like a goddam Taoist!"

"I'm not a goddam Taoist!" she protested heatedly. "You're a goddam—" She couldn't find the word and laughed instead.

Dinner was practically over anyway. The evening had been a fiasco. He couldn't resist a final dig. Besides, the boy had been on his mind for days.

"What does Peiyuan think of your life?"

"If you ask me one more question, I'm walking out of here!"

He stopped. His destructiveness had been assuaged.

"Do we have to go to that recital?" she asked.

It was clear she was only waiting until he could take her back to Mimi Lambert's house, where she was spending the night. In her eyes had hovered the question, "Why, why did he ask me out?" Now she did not even seem to care.

He felt totally bereaved—and it was all his own doing. They left the restaurant and rode back to Mimi's in a pedicab, sitting next to each other woodenly, like store-window mannequins. Everyone was alone, he thought, but he was really only thinking of his own loneliness. He had been born into the world alone, and would leave it alone. Under the large bowl of the weather, everyone was alone. But this time his dialectics failed to comfort him. Words were talismans he could hardly finger when he most needed comforting.

At Mimi's gate, Sylvia said, "But I'm neither my father nor the Chinese girl you described. Neither are you."

She looked into his face, as if she had more to say. But the gate opened and she was gone. He walked away briskly, pretending he had somewhere to go, something specific to accomplish. The aimless summer air would be his destruction.

CHAPTER TEN

It was almost eleven-thirty on the night of August fourth when the phone rang. Sylvia looked up from her book, surprise not unmixed with alarm in her mind. It couldn't mean anything good. Paul answered it, speaking very low, so as not to annoy their mother.

"It's Feng Huang," he whispered, suddenly at her door.

"Who is it?" they heard Helen ask from her bedroom. Liyi and she had already retired for the night.

"He ought to know better than to call me at this hour," Sylvia muttered, "if he has to call at all." But she went to the phone in the living room, feeling her way in the dark. The curtains had been drawn apart.

"Who is it?" Helen asked again.

"Feng. Feng Huang."

A formidable silence greeted this, while Sylvia said, "Hello, this is a fine time to phone," but he stopped her on the other end.

"Listen," Feng said, his voice thin with tension. "Are you listening?"

"Yes," but all she heard was an incoherent rumble in a foreign language.

"Did you hear that?"

"What's going on?"

"It's the Soviet Station," he said, as though that answered her question.

"Will you make it brief?" Helen demanded.

"The war is over!" Feng exclaimed into Sylvia's ear. "The war is over!" he repeated. "You and I are going over to the Jastrows' right now."

"The war is over?" she repeated, but it meant nothing at all. "What do you mean, it's over?"

Paul snatched the receiver from her hand and said, "Are you sure? Are you absolutely sure?"

"It's just a rumor, but the Allies are negotiating terms. Terms!"

"We're coming over," Paul said. "We'll be at the Jastrows'," and he dropped the phone and ground a fist into the palm of his other hand. "Come on," he said fiercely, jamming his fist into his hand again.

"Where do you two think you're going?" Helen asked.

Liyi said from his bed, "Don't believe any rumors."

"This is it," Paul declared. "This is it."

"You'd be wise to stay home on a night like this. If it's true, the Japs will be running wild." Liyi didn't seem to believe any of it at all. "Go back to bed now."

"All right," they said and returned to their rooms. But after five minutes Sylvia met Paul and Peiyuan in the living room.

"I want to talk to you," she whispered. The three of them had already dressed: nothing could stop them from going to the Jastrows'. It was something Sylvia and her friends had planned for years—to meet the night the war ended.

"By the way, no one asked you two to tag along." But she laughed as she said it. The three of them tiptoed out the door. Sylvia knew her parents would not even miss them until morning.

Julie Jastrow stood by their living-room door like a wraith in a pink dressing gown. She greeted Sylvia with a wide-eyed stare and kissed her, saying nothing. She took Paul's hand and shook it earnestly, and smiled in her sensitive, tentative way at Peiyuan. Bill was right behind her; he kissed both Sylvia and

Paul, and said something in Chinese, making Peiyuan laugh. Larry embraced Sylvia, and indicated where she should sit on the couch. But she was too tense to relax and stood staring vacantly at Hasan Kemal, who approached her and suddenly smacked her wetly on the mouth. He turned in embarrassment and pounded Paul on his back. Mimi Lambert, who had just arrived and passed the receiving line of the Jastrow kisses, said, "I'm dying. I ran all the way." She collapsed in the largest, most broken-down armchair.

Her voice seemed to grate on their nerves, until Bill Jastrow said weakly, "Let's see—we'll make a couple of drinks," but was at a loss where to begin. Sylvia sat down and watched everyone bite his lips, eyes shining with dry fever.

Feng Huang strode in, looking almost dewy with expectation. "Let's turn on the radio," he said, breathing heavily as he switched it on. But XMHA was dead and the Soviet Station was playing its usual Tschaikovsky selections. He turned it off disgustedly and sat down by Larry.

"You act," Larry said, "as though you won the war single-handed."

"Well, didn't I?" Feng countered good-humoredly.

Everyone stopped his lip-biting to smile briefly. No one referred to the last time Feng had been here or how he had left them, never to return. Sylvia felt their friendship for him was too deep to be affected by one incident. She watched Feng's face. He seemed to have completely forgotten his rage against them.

They sat and seemed to look past one another. Sylvia knew very little more than that her own fearful hopes were rising. None of them had any facts. For months they had heard the Allies were being defeated on all fronts. Now they heard that the Allies had won, and they could hardly believe it. They sat with clenched fists, as though concentrating all the years of waiting into an extraordinary exercise of tautness.

Hasan suddenly stretched his legs, bounded off his chair and pronounced, "Hellish good! Tonight I should be allowed my

Gilbert and Sullivan," and made for the victrola. It was a signal to fall upon the Turk. They dragged him around the room, kissing him and laughing. He in turn tried to stand Larry on his head. They knocked over a table and crashed into a closet. Julie finally said feebly, "You'll wake Jimmy. Remember the baby?" but no one paid any attention. Everyone was dancing except Mimi Lambert.

"Does anyone know where Robert is?" she asked, but she had to repeat it twice before they heard her. "He's not home," she said, when they were all attentive. "His caretaker said he might be at his father's, but no one answers there."

"We'll go find him," Larry announced. "Can't leave out good old Robert!"

"You, me and the two girls," Feng said. "We'll go get him. Come on, Mimi," and before Sylvia knew it, they were running down the stairs.

"Come back soon," Bill said. "Your drinks are ready."

"What about me?" Paul asked Sylvia, but Hasan seemed to have adopted him and Peiyuan as younger brothers for the evening. "We'll get hellish tight together," she heard him saying. When she got downstairs and outside, she looked up. Bill and Julie had flung open the windows. They let the light blaze onto the street. None of them cared. They had been suffocating for years.

Their quarter was ominously quiet and as dark as ever. The little tents of glare cast by the dimmed street lights had disappeared with curfew at eleven. They walked very close together, looking for a couple of pedicabs, but there seemed to be none abroad on Rue Prosper Paris, at the extreme limits of the French Concession. Sylvia and Mimi walked between the two men; Sylvia saw that Mimi was suddenly shivering despite the heat.

"Let's go to Bobby's own place first," Mimi suggested. "Maybe he's home by now. Anyhow, it's on the way." Twenty minutes later they awakened the gatekeeper, who said, "Master not home," curtly, looking at them with disapproval. He knew Miss Lambert, but her companions did not look quite like Mr. Bruno's kind. Mr. Bruno's kind wore ties, for instance, no matter how hot it was. Chinese servants, Sylvia thought, were always even less tolerant than their masters.

They left and walked on, reaching Avenue de Boissezon. It was twelve-thirty; nothing was on the streets except a few stray dogs, mongrels that growled from behind garbage cans and in black passageways. They continued up Avenue Joffre and turned into a side street. The gatekeeper at Mr. Bruno Senior's residence let them in when they said they were looking for the young master. He ushered them down the long garden path to the house, summoning the head boy, who came into the living room sleepily and turned on a lamp.

"Is the young master in?" Feng asked pointedly in Shanghai dialect, though the boy spoke pidgin-English and Sylvia knew he would be proud of it.

"The young master is not to be disturbed," he answered.

"Would you please tell him Miss Lambert is here," Mimi said in English.

"Mr. Bruno has made orders."

"But I know he wants to see me. I tried phoning first. Tell him I'm here."

"After eleven master not allow answer phone," he said. "I cannot help this."

They heard a scuffling of slippers above them, then the clearing of a throat, and the head boy seemed to jump visibly. He hurried softly to the front lobby and went halfway up the stairs. When he returned, he said, "Mr. Bruno not see anybody tonight."

"The young or the old master?"

"I have only one master."

"We want to see young master," Larry said in pidgin-English. "Young man, not old man. We young mans and young womans, too, see? Miss Lambert friend only of handsome young mans."

"Did you tell him Miss Lambert is here?" Sylvia put in.

"He say he do not know Miss Lambert. Please, you go now? My master angry you come."

"We angry not see young master," Larry said.

"Let's go," Feng declared.

"But I want Bobby with us tonight."

"Sorry, Miss Lambert. My master make orders, however."

"What's that got to do with Bobby?" she said more to herself than to any of them.

"Is Mr. Bruno ill?" Feng asked. "The young Mr. Bruno?"

"Yes, ill," the boy answered laconically, edging them toward the door.

"What kind of illness?" Sylvia asked.

"Same as always kind."

"Oh!" Larry laughed. His chuckle was contagious. Even Mimi smiled and lifted her soft shoulders, shrugging. They were almost at the front door when Feng turned and said to the servant, "The war is over!"

"I thank you very much," the boy said aloud and closed the door behind them with a sigh of deep relief.

"Not at all," Larry answered, in a tone to deprecate his own nonsense. "Now please to pass the peace."

"What a ridiculous evening!" Feng exclaimed, as they walked back toward the gatehouse.

"What a place to pass out in!" Larry said. Sylvia thought of the huge house—the living room had been like a museum of Chinese art, barely softened by the gigantic leather couch and armchairs, impersonal furniture that might have been suitable in an exclusive men's club. Mrs. Bruno, apparently, had not been allowed to express herself at all. The front lobby had smelled pleasantly but puritanically and severely of tobacco, lemon oil polish and floor wax. Somewhere in the house—perhaps in one of the guest bedrooms (which must have been like a hotel with excellent towel service)—Robert was sleeping off a drunk. Perhaps he was sleeping it off downstairs in the den, relegated to the lower floor for bringing disgrace to his father's well-ordered life.

"I hope Bobby's all right."

"Of course he is," Feng said reassuringly. "He might have chosen to pass out in his own place, but I guess he wasn't thinking of our convenience at the time."

"Bobby is a transcendentalist," Larry said. "Here's to him," and tipped an imaginary hat.

"What do you mean?" Mimi asked, protectively, not certain that the description was complimentary.

"Lushes have an urge toward transcendence. They desire a release from self-hood. Lo and behold, you drink and you are freed from your inhibitions, your self-consciousness. Drinking is both a religious experience and a sedation. It's an aspirin that carries you one step closer to the godhead."

"And now," Feng put in, "shall we do something practical, like looking for a couple of pedicabs? I don't think we should make the girls walk back to the Jastrows'." They were standing on the corner of Paul Henry and Doumer. It was so dark Sylvia could barely make out forms across the narrow street.

"Bobby is not a lush," Mimi said, taking Feng's hand.

"No, of course not."

"I didn't mean anything bad," Larry protested. "If I could afford Scotch, I'd be a mystic, too."

"Just be a realist and keep your eyes peeled for transportation," said Feng.

They found a pedicab turning the corner and another came presently. "Prosper Paris Lu," Feng said and bargained adroitly with the men. Sylvia and Larry took the second and followed the dark form of the pedicab in which Mimi and Feng sat. Mimi shouted back, "You remember what tonight is all about, don't you?"

"The war is over!" Larry and Sylvia shouted in unison.

"Yankee Doodle went to town," Mimi ordered.

They cleared their throats and began to sing, "Yankee Doodle went to town, riding on a pony. He stuck a feather in his cap and called it macaroni." Even Feng joined in, the pullers grunting with their efforts and dismay. One just didn't make a racket like this after curfew. It was bad enough, Sylvia realized, being out in the streets, without singing American songs. The Chinese pullers must have remembered what American tourists had taught street urchins to sing, as they begged for alms, "No mama, no papa, no whisky soda." They knew it meant something irrepressibly witty in English.

Avenue Joffre seemed to be seething, not that there was much traffic about, but Sylvia thought she saw clusters of people at a broad intersection. Of course—the White Russians would have got the news first, from listening to the Russian newscaster on the Soviet Station.

"My country 'tis of thee," Larry shouted.

"My country, 'tis of thee, sweet land of liberty!" they sang; Feng was not fighting for accurate identities tonight. But as soon as they left Avenue Joffre, the possibility of the war ending seemed a hallucination. Nothing was changed. To remind herself it was true, Sylvia repeated what Feng had told her—that the Allies were demanding Japan's unconditional surrender. Larry defied any listening Japanese ears and sang "The Star-Spangled Banner," Sylvia trying to keep her hand over his mouth. But he only bit it and kept on singing.

They were on Rue Prosper Paris again, going abreast in a straight line toward the Jastrows. Suddenly their pedicabs jolted them as they were stopped abruptly. They leaned forward and peered into the horizontal bayonets of six Japanese sentries.

"Get out," one of them ordered in Japanese.

Sylvia saw Feng step out of his pedicab and help Mimi onto the road. She and Larry followed. The four of them stood, not daring to move. She could not see, but felt surrounded by many more soldiers, stomping in their heavy boots. The pedicab drivers had disappeared, and they seemed to be standing in almost utter darkness. Feng had moved back and put the girls between Larry and himself.

"Certificates," they heard, and a hand came through the dark to take their identity papers, which were not returned.

114

"Move," they were ordered, but none of them understood Japanese, so they were pushed ahead into the darkness like a pit and almost walked into the tailboard of the truck before they saw it. Feng climbed on first and then Larry. They dragged Sylvia and then Mimi up awkwardly. There were about twenty others standing near the head of the truck—mostly foreigners, Sylvia thought, mostly White Russians caught celebrating the setting of the Rising Sun. There was a conspicuous absence of any Chinese. The Chinese never rejoiced at anything prematurely. It came as a surprise to see another fifty people packed into a second truck which stood alongside.

"Don't separate, whatever happens," Feng said.

"Sure," Larry answered briefly, as if he were saving his voice.

A *keisatsu* swung himself up and peered into their faces, dragging a rifle in one hand. He sorted the people, and with some regulation in mind, barked at a few of the foreigners to stand facing the sides of the truck, while the others were to balance themselves somehow in the center. Unnecessarily, for they were docile, he prodded them with his rifle.

Sylvia turned her face away as he approached them again. She felt she could not hide the hatred she felt. The *keisatsu* turned her face back with one hand and kneed her between her legs in one quick movement. She gasped and instinctively hurled herself against Feng. The soldier pulled her toward him roughly and laughed.

"*Yamu!*" Feng said abruptly and loudly, taking her arm and bracing himself against the side of the truck.

"*Yamu, yamu!*" the *keisatsu* laughed, still dragging his rifle. Feng had used the infinitive "to stop," and the Japanese sneered.

"Yours?" he asked Feng, looking her up and down, and reaching out to touch her breasts.

Feng stepped forward and blocked his way. "Mine," he answered, "my *ane*." My elder sister, he had said, not being able to think of any other Japanese word at the moment.

"Your *obasan*," the soldier answered and spat on Feng's foot. "Your grandmother," and swung agilely off the truck.

The truck started up, shaking them.

"What are they going to do?" Mimi asked.

"Don't know," Larry answered. "Don't know." Mimi moved near him, but he seemed preoccupied with his own thoughts.

Sylvia's knees had buckled under her twice. She put one hand on the side of the truck and held Feng around his waist with the other. His face had set into a look of impatience; she was afraid to tell him how badly frightened she was.

"What are they going to do to us?" Mimi repeated, almost in a moan. No one answered her.

"Stand up," Feng ordered Sylvia.

"I can't," she protested. The truck was rumbling around corners, making wide arcs, for the streets were absolutely deserted now. They were followed by the other truck.

"Yes, you can," he said, and pushed her away.

"My knees." She tightened her hold on him, wanting to feel him solidly there, but he made her let him go. Stubbornly, she grasped the side with both hands and felt some strength come back into her legs. He made her so angry, she felt less afraid.

"Stand on your own two feet," he whispered stridently.

"What did you think I was doing!"

"Hanging onto me."

"I wouldn't go near you under any other circumstances," she retorted bitterly, still shaken.

He actually smiled and turned to face the way she was, putting his hand on the side of the truck, so that his arm surrounded her.

"I know where they're taking us," he whispered.

"You needn't tell me." But she was grateful he stood so close.

The truck swerved by Sylvia's home, where Helen and Liyi and Yennai were fast asleep. The irony of it held her attention for a moment; then she remembered, with comfort, that Paul and Peiyuan were safe at the Jastrows'. At least she hadn't endangered them in this forbidden excursion. Inexorably, the

116

trucks headed for Avenue Petain, for the American School. Outside of Bridge House, this was the most notorious of the Japanese gendarmeries. The trucks backed into the entrance of the Community Church grounds and then rumbled into the school campus. Sylvia clutched Feng's hand and he squeezed hers reassuringly.

The prisoners in the first truck were being discharged one by one. None of them said a word; even the Japanese guards went about their duties silently. Sylvia heard only the sound of boots scraping on the brick walks, and smelled the scent of fear that came from the prisoners, a combination of hatred and humiliation and uncertainty.

Their own truck was being unloaded now. The four of them stood close together, and a murmur of irritation came from the guards below when Mimi hesitated to jump. When she did, she stumbled and hung back, waiting for the others. Feng may have been afraid, but his face was set and he seemed entirely self-possessed. As they were herded into the brightly lit building, which formerly had been the social hall of the campus, he whispered to Mimi, "It'll turn out all right," but she seemed on the verge of tears. "It'll turn out all right," he repeated to Sylvia. "After all, they are the defeated ones."

They stood in the blinding light of the main room. A large cement trough had been built in the center for watering horses; it now lay stagnant, breeding countless singing mosquitoes. They could not see into the other rooms, but it was apparent that the Japanese Gestapo had thoroughly changed the character of the building. Sylvia, remembering how it had looked only three or four years before, felt that they stood in the midst of a nightmare that had solidified into reality.

It was one-thirty by the school clock when the *kempetai* came down the stairs. The officer walked with his legs apart and peered into everyone's face as though he were nearsighted. Every third one he questioned in English, "Tonight, what were you doing on the street?" It was obvious the Japanese had been listening to their own newscasts. An adjutant laughed sheepishly, adjusting his thick glasses, and handed him the identity cards. The officer clearly did not know what to do with the seventy prisoners, but he decided to put on a perfunctory show.

"Kalganov," he called, and a drab-looking Russian in his early thirties advanced toward him. "Tonight, what were you doing on the street?"

"Visiting my sick mother," the Russian answered in Russian. The officer, not understanding, waved him aside. "Stand there," he ordered, pointing to a corner of the large hall.

"Borovsky," "Pavlovitch," "Alexeieff." He read through the names, including a couple of Danish ones, and they all muttered their excuses for having been out after curfew. One by one the foreigners joined Kalganov in the corner.

"Huang," the officer suddenly called in Chinese, "Feng." Feng walked up and said briefly, "I was enjoying the air."

"You are Chinese!" the Japanese asked wonderingly, glancing back at Feng's photograph on the certificate. "Over there," and he pointed to the corner opposite the Russians. Feng stood alone, self-consciously defiant, and turned to look back at Larry and the girls.

"Don't move and don't lean against the wall," a sergeant ordered him.

Sylvia's heart began to beat faster.

"Lambert," he called out. "Missie Mimisan," he giggled, and everyone suddenly understood why the officer stood with his legs apart. He was more than a bit drunk.

Mimi walked forward tentatively.

"You are English?" he barked. "Yes or no?"

"Yes—no, I'm Australian."

"Why not in internment camp?" he asked, sucking in his breath.

"I—my aunt, she happens to be Chinese. She is my guardian."

"Ah-so. You are foreigner, but too young. You are Chinese, however not exactly so."

"But my father was Australian," she said firmly.

118

He waved her to the corner where the foreigners stood. "The Chinese look like white devils tonight," he said to everyone at large, but only his simpering adjutant tittered.

"Casement." Larry walked forward quickly.

"I was out looking for a friend," he explained almost eagerly. "A Swiss friend."

"Ah-so! Irish is neutral. Swiss is neutral. You have best excuse of all!" The officer bowed ironically, presenting Larry's card. In a lightning-quick gesture, Larry put out his hand to take it. Sylvia was astonished at his audacity, and then she understood. His certificate was more important to Larry than theirs—she included Mimi and Feng—were to them. The card seemed a symbol of all his avenues of escape. It was a visa that would help him through the transition into peace.

"So," the Japanese said, pulling his arm back, "you insult me!" and tore the card in four parts, tossing it into the trough. Larry blanched visibly. "Over there!" He moved and stood alone in a third corner.

"Chen." Sylvia moved toward him, staring him down with a neutral look in her eye. If anyone tried to touch her again, she'd fight back, and she was afraid of what might happen then.

"Another Chinese, but not exactly so!" he said to his adjutant. "Look at her. She stares like a European woman. Tonight, Miss Chen, what were you doing?"

"Riding in a pedicab with a friend."

"With enemy national?"

"No," she said, thinking quickly, "with my Chinese friend," pointing in Feng Huang's direction, though actually he had ridden with Mimi.

"That is correct," the Japanese mused. "The Chinese are not enemy nationals. The Chinese are friends."

"No one was celebrating," the adjutant put in.

"Not one person celebrating," the officer continued. "Ah-so, everybody is sorry for Japan. Chinese, especially. Everybody is riding in pedicab weeping for Japanese like myself. Go," he said to Sylvia, "go to the other white Chinese."

Sylvia hesitated, not certain what he had meant. The other white Chinese. But her heart leaped inordinately with something close to joy.

"Over there," he said, pointing to Feng. She walked to him slowly, relief flooding her. Suddenly she knew that the Japanese were not going to hurt any of them tonight. The officer returned the cards to the adjutant, who climbed the stairs and then was out of sight.

"You will stay here and obey my men," the officer said. "You will stand and not move. If you move, there will be punishment. You will stand until I change my orders." He stalked out of the door, letting in a breath of fresh air.

Everything about the evening was two-dimensional, a caricature. From where Sylvia and Feng stood they could see the clock moving infinitely slowly. It was five past two, then two-thirty, three-fifteen, three thirty-five. Sylvia's feet ached in her high heels. They were hot and swollen. She could see Mimi among the foreigners, twisting her legs. Larry was all alone, like a slightly tainted hero. He had outlasted his most courageous act; he had survived the war. He seemed without a name, forlorn, lost, and yet, he was unapproachable because he did not want to forget his private glory.

They heard a great clatter and raucous voices coming from beyond the swinging doors. The two guards relaxed and went past them to peer out.

"Edge up to me," Feng said in a whisper.

Sylvia moved back slowly, inch by inch. Her feet were thick feverish stumps.

"Closer."

She didn't realize that he was about a yard behind her. She had felt protected, as though he had stood beside her.

"Now lean a little to your right."

She did as he said and found she was leaning against him a little, just enough to make standing less strenuous. The guards returned, grinning. The door was flung open and the officer who had examined the prisoners came in with two of his confreres. Arm-in-arm, they staggered, holding saki bottles in their hands.

"Ah-so!" they said, staring at the crowd in disbelief. Their eyes bulged red, and they sat on the edge of the trough and began to drink systematically. The guards still stood with bayonets drawn, but no longer pretended to be severe. They chatted with each other in Japanese, sucking in their breaths. At four-thirty a couple of officers clattered down the stairs and joined the others in aimless conversation. They all smiled the same smile—of embarrassment and self-hatred. One of the Japanese opened his fly, walked halfway up the stairs and urinated from the landing. The drunken *kempetai* suddenly seemed to come to life and, reeling, tried to climb the stairs to reprimand him. The foreigners moved back against their wall and Mimi seemed to have found a part of it to lean against. Larry watched with an almost incongruous detachment. But the officer only staggered down the stairs and put out his arms for the trough. He leaned against it and retched, vomiting over and over again. Then he lay down and went to sleep, covered with his own filth. His two confreres hung over the trough in sympathy and finally collapsed on the floor beside him. The officer who had urinated on the stairs minced around the hall, waving a large banner like a scarf dancer. He swung his hips and staggered delicately as a woman. He imitated the gestures of a geisha girl or a Chinese female entertainer. It was a performance of utter self-denigration. The Japanese defeat was explicit in his identifying himself with a woman, a woman who surrendered her personal dignity to the pleasures of men. He danced a gavotte of Japanese psychology, and it was as painful to Sylvia as if he had been nude.

"I go home," he said, smiling now and then the tortured smile of a clown. "I go home," he sang over and over again.

Sylvia tried not to look or listen, but she could not avoid breathing in the sour stench of vomit. The clock moved to four forty-five, five, five-thirty. At six, as she felt she might faint, a bugle was blown.

A new commanding officer walked in, blinking in the strong light. He ordered the officers carried out and looked around him with distaste. He was jittery and pale, as though he, too, had not slept.

"All of you," he ordered, "begin walking." One of the guards led the way. They walked, light-headed, through the chilly dawn, past the pergola, the track, the dormitories, the classrooms and the baseball diamond. At the gate, a young soldier handed them their certificates, all except Larry's. The officer stood unsmiling, waiting for them to disperse. He was still in charge, he was still the conqueror; he did not move.

They were on Avenue Petain and did not know what to do. Slowly, some of the White Russians began to leave the group and head toward Avenue Joffre.

"My feet!" Sylvia said. They had swollen so much the flesh bulged over the front of her shoes which cut into them. Mimi looked ruefully at her own. Fortunately, she had worn flats, but her legs moved stiffly.

"We'll take you home," Feng said to Mimi, while he bent down and pulled off Sylvia's shoes. "You can walk barefoot. It'll cool them."

"Then I'll go back to the Jastrows'," Larry said, "and see how they're getting on."

"You can't go home like this at this hour," Feng said to Sylvia. "You better come back to my place."

She nodded and said to Larry, "Tell Paul I'm all right. He can tell my parents I'm staying at—well, tell him I'm at Mimi's place. I'll phone home later, when the sun is up."

"The sun is down," Larry commented, "good and down." But he said it unhappily and over his face passed a look of negation and fatigue. Sylvia thought it was as though he realized his own rootlessness for the first time.

He turned to go, and Feng said, "Don't worry about that certificate. You won't need it where you're going," but Larry didn't seem to be listening. He turned and left.

"Where is he planning to go?" Mimi asked.

"He's already gone," Feng answered. "He's already halfway to America."

"I feel sick," Mimi said. "Take me home quick."

They put her between them and half supported her home.

"Don't go throwing up like those Japs," Feng said. "It isn't done in polite society. Anyhow, it has something to do with their fish diet."

"That's a new theory, I gather," Sylvia said, her mind surprisingly clear. His talking about the Japs in this manner took away so much of the night's ugliness.

"There's too much iodine in fish," he said, as though that explained it all.

"And iodine and alcohol don't mix?"

"They don't."

"I think I was really disappointed," Sylvia found herself saying. In some undefined way, she would have liked to have been purged, she thought, purged of her own stagnation of the last few years—purged by excitement, if not by violence. "In a way, I was hoping for some real action."

"But this is just the beginning," Feng answered, for he thought she was referring only to the end of the occupation.

"I'm going to sleep until tomorrow," Mimi said, "a whole day and night," and kissed them both sleepily. "Good morning to you."

The male cook had let Mimi in the gate. Sylvia felt his eyes linger on herself and Feng. Her shoes were in his hands.

"This is my home," Feng announced, after he had closed the door carefully on the brown and muted lobby with the heavily carpeted stairs leading into a part of the house Sylvia imagined to be dark, musty and inhabited by faceless relatives. But she knew Feng lived alone except for his mother. He hesitated now, looking at her, and quickly moving around from turning on a lamp in his living room, bent to kiss her on the forehead. But he missed and planted his lips awkwardly on her eyes. The lamp was upset as they seemed to leap apart, but he caught it in time with his knee. They were both elated and tense from lack of sleep. Sylvia started laughing hilariously and couldn't stop. She sat on the arm of the couch and laughed until her eyes streamed tears.

"I'm s-sorry," she apologized, as he pretended not to have been affected. "I don't know what's the matter with me," and she continued laughing, submitting to the convulsions that wracked her like an agony around the ribs. She reminded herself of Mimi, somehow. Feng had gone into the next room and, beyond that, she could hear water being run. He came back with a fresh towel in his hand, which he thrust at her as though it burned him. "I'm running a bath for you," he said. "It'll help those feet."

She hesitated now, feeling strangely moved. Was it his concern or his clumsiness which so affected her?

"Go on!" he ordered, and pulled her up roughly, giving her an unnecessarily brisk shove in the direction of the bedroom, while she seemed to tread six inches above the floor. His bedroom was bathed in a clear white light from two simple lamps. It was as white and uncluttered as a cabin on a ship; the one chair and bookcases and desk had been planned to lend an air of quiet efficiency and yet a kind of linear energy. Her senses were sharp and completely naked. Light, shadow and forms stood out in a severe, underlined third dimension. She felt sure she had been there before—in this place and at this time. The particularity of the event was as minute and precise as her scrutiny. It was as though, without her knowing, her imagination had inhabited Feng's home before.

Feng seemed to be following her. She turned before she closed the bathroom door.

"There's a—a dressing gown on the hook, if you want to use it." He looked pained—that was the only word she could find to describe it—pained with his own gaucherie.

"Thank you," she said solemnly and saw how relieved he was that she did not seem self-conscious—how really relieved, as she slowly shut the door. She had laughed at his clumsiness, for

124

she was half hysterical this morning, but she had not smiled at his inarticulateness. How could she? Suddenly, with her heightened senses, she understood everything about him—his inability to make small talk, his need to carry on humorless arguments.

"Feel better?" he asked, when she finally came out in his dressing gown. She had rolled up the sleeves and tied the belt tightly around her waist, tucking in some of its length.

"Much better, but my feet are still hot as blazes."

He had been sitting on the edge of the bed, as if waiting for her abstractedly. The lamps were no longer necessary. A dim light came in the one window, partially muted by the white curtains. It was seven o'clock on the morning of a gray day.

"The war is over," she said, depressed suddenly after so much buoyancy. She slumped into the one large armchair and put her legs over the side. "And I feel awful."

"You're more than a strange girl," he said, staring at her, his eyes closing in a long, timeless blink. "You—"

"The war is over," she said, her depression somehow exciting her. "You know what that means, don't you? It means 'there' and 'where,' 'shall' and 'new,' 'yes' and 'to' are all possibilities again; all the possibilities are there for everyone's picking. Oh, how simply terrifying," she wailed and covered her face. "All the companionship of the war is over, the safety of the occupation gone!" She had never thought of it this way before. "I wish I were dead," she said. The sharp focus of the room hurt her beyond expression. The objects, the beauty of their separateness, the things populating life seemed to injure her, seemed to threaten her personally. "Death is so logical, so neat, so perfect. It's the final effect of every cause—you know that, don't you? It's the way to survive life!"

"You have a talent for dying," he said drily, "and so do I." He pointed upstairs. "My mother is a true genuis at it. She collects things; she doesn't live life. I've got a lot to unlearn."

"Feng," she said quickly, trembling with tension, "you are so much nicer than you ever let people know. Why, why?"

He looked away almost shyly and got off the bed. "Look,

125

you and I better get some sleep, uh? Don't you think we better get some sleep?" he repeated matter-of-factly.

He looked down at her upturned face; her eyes suddenly filled with tears and her mouth moved involuntarily, but she stared back at him unblinkingly.

"Don't you think we ought to get some sleep?"

She turned her face away and the tears flowed down her cheeks. Puzzled, he stood above her.

"Why did you?" she asked.

"Why did I what?"

"Why did you say 'we'?"

"Well, I think we ought to get some—"

"No one has ever said 'we' to me before. I never thought there would be a 'we' in the world for me, that I might be half of one 'we'."

He sat down in the armchair, facing her, thinking. Words came slowly to him.

"And I always thought you were so self-possessed. You've made me furious because you seemed so self-possessed."

She shook her head.

"I loved you for being scared on the truck."

"You had a funny way of showing it," she said ruefully.

"I couldn't have you collapse first thing."

"We two white Chinese."

They smiled into each other's faces, touching foreheads. He held her two feet, blowing on them to cool them. Bending over, he kissed her legs and knees and thighs. The dressing gown fell apart and they both seemed to gasp.

"I love you," Feng said, gripping her by her shoulders and kissing her fully on her mouth. "I didn't mean to, but oh, God, I love you." He shook her in what seemed a moment of blindness and fierce integrity. He stood up and carried her to the bed and laid her down gently on the white sheets. Then he lay down beside her and buried his head between her breasts.

Her breath caught; she felt herself go wild. It was like running downhill pell-mell; it would be such incredible delight to

126

let go—he could rescue her from her own ambivalence. He leaned his weight on her lips; their teeth grated against each other's.

Brutally, she wrenched herself away, afraid. They looked at each other like enemies. She couldn't be sure of anything, not even of herself. She knew suddenly that she had always been haunted by doubt of her own existence. She felt a fraud, an illusion, where *she* should have been. And if she wasn't there, how could he make love to her?

But another fear, a new one, made her heart race suddenly. Supposing she was wrong? Supposing she looked in the mirror and discovered her own face there? She was also afraid to be real—it would demand too much new courage of her.

Raising herself on an elbow, she looked directly into his eyes. "I can't, I can't!" Her own disappointment with herself was oppressive. "Do you understand?"

Feng stared at her with skepticism, wondering.

"I don't know why," she added, because she could not explain it to herself yet. "I can't."

He breathed slowly as though to stay his anger, and then kissed her again, carefully; he seemed almost untroubled. Starting to ask her something, he hesitated, and changed his mind. She was grateful he did not question her. Instead he turned and switched on the radio by the bed. Holding hands, they waited for the news. It was the morning of August fifth in Shanghai and also across the waters in Hiroshima. In America, where Larry was going, it was a day later.

"It's eight o'clock," Sylvia heard herself saying. She felt her fatigue suddenly. Feng seemed still awake as she fell into a bright and airy sleep.

CHAPTER ELEVEN

Mimi Lambert thought she had herself well in hand, which was good, since she felt as if she could do *anything*. She seemed to fizz, like an uncorked bottle of sparkling wine. She felt grateful for the small weights of reality that kept her from "taking off." She tried to imagine a depression, "an unhappiness," for there seemed something perilous, outrageous in so much sheer delight in existence. But she could not feel unhappy; she could not even recapture ordinary tranquillity—the kind she had enjoyed for almost all of her nineteen years, the kind that made her rebel occasionally just for the sake of scandalizing people out of their placidity or to make a small holiday out of a customary twenty-four hours.

"I cut off the *amah's* hair in her sleep one night," she boasted to Robert. "I cut off her braids and put them in her hand. She woke up the next morning and screamed around the house like a crazy Chinese Ophelia. She staggered around quite theatrically—all Chinese servants are theatrical, you know—and swore vengeance. I surprised her by readily admitting that I had done it. I was seven. Her new haircut was rather becoming to her."

"I was out dancing once," she had also told Robert, "when my panties fell to the ballroom floor." She had thrown back her head and laughed delightedly as she retold the story for the hundredth time. "You know the kind of ladies' panties with a dainty pearl button on the side—no elastic to suffocate one. My panties fell to the nicely waxed floor of the Paramount Ball-room. I stepped out of them—had to, you know—hung them from the crook of my elbow, like a lace-edged handkerchief, and we danced on. The young man I was with—oh, that was two years ago, when I was young—blamed the accident on the tango we were doing."

"I wanted to be an orphan so badly. The year before Mother and Dad were killed, I used to go out of my way to try to get lost. Railway stations, market places, sightseeing trips helped a little, but not enough. I wanted to be a beautiful orphan, a mysterious orphan, for no one would be able to guess my nationality. They'd think I was a lost princess, and the orphanage would be my castle, and they'd serve me oatmeal on a golden platter. But Mother and Dad never did lose me, and finally when I lost them, it was different. Yes, it was," she had said, with insistence, as though Robert had doubted her word. "You know," she added seriously, "and this is a big cliché, but we live only once." And she had thrown up her arms and embraced herself fiercely. "We live only once," seemed a passionate avowal of creation itself.

And all Robert had done as he listened to her prate about herself was to stare at her as at a rare phenomenon, stare at her with wonder, not quite believing she was true. She didn't know exactly what he was thinking, but—unlike normally intelligent people—he didn't think she was "silly." It seemed to take imagination and special intelligence to encompass true naïveté, and she thought of herself as naïve. He had once said something morbid about his feeling "unreal." His comment had gone something like this: "You seem real, legitimate, certified, branded with a hallmark. I'm a window standing in the middle of a ruin." She had not "pooh-poohed" his unpredictable sententiousness, for his self-deprecation always held a compliment for herself. "You're so vivid," he had also told her, "and I always feel that somewhere else I truly exist, and am only poorly represented by a proxy here."

His father, she knew—for he had told her—was responsible for a great deal of his unhappiness with himself. Robert was thirty-four, and already felt like a worn sock, he said, entirely stretched out of his original intentions. He wore a flat, severely plain watch, the ultimate in chaste, expensive understatement, neutral in platinum. "It's like having my father's hand on my wrist," he had told her, "guiding me even as I shave." His day was determined by the "time" his father's business enterprise disseminated throughout the Far East. Colonials and natives alike flexed their elbows, pulled up their sleeves and stared at his father's Swiss watches. They ticked so quietly, only a sundial could be muter, but they were quite relentless in marking the wasting of Robert's days and nights.

They were in a garden. One would think that the war had never taken place. The gramophone blared. While Mimi waited for Robert to bring her a drink from the punch bowl, she moved into the shadow of the house and sat on a ledge under lilac bushes no longer in bloom. To the right was the small pond, in which the fish lived their egocentric lives, sealed within a watery world, deaf—she thought—as well as silent, coming up to the surface only to bite the air. Two pet monkeys chattered in the tree above her head, now and then squatting on a branch to concentrate on scratching themselves. Their lipless mouths were like tobacco pouches; their bottoms looked scorched. She felt sardonic, considering them: you could not be certain whether they imitated men examining their own armpits, or men were closer to animal than one wanted to admit. Cicadas orchestrated in the west, making a furnace of summer sound.

Mimi felt self-contained, yet light-headed. She felt almost as though Robert, looking handsome in a tuxedo, was held to her by a thread, that he was a kite. All she had to do was tug at the thread gently, tug-tug at his heart, held to her by the silver spider's thread of their secret, and Robert would feel it across the garden and come toward her. She would bring him in lovingly, winding the thread on the spool of her third finger. The third finger of her left hand, the finger of betrothal.

In the garden, guests coughed, made declarative sentences, addressed less to the person at whom they were ostensibly directed than at the real entity of the evening: the party. The party had a life of its own; it was made up, true enough, of the separate selves of the guests, but it dominated with its own being. But she felt so strong, so full of power, that she wanted to outrage that being. A party was more than the sum of the people invited to it. It was more than the talents of the host, more than the festive decorations hung from the arbor, more than the fountain of glass, silver and favors heaped on the large banquet table. A party was all of these, Mimi thought absent-mindedly, not exerting herself, but breathing it in through her pores. A party was a kind of play in which everyone had a role. Everyone was required to deliver a finished performance without rehearsal, simply on improvisation.

Mimi's heart lurched now as she saw Robert turn, his two hands held out before him like a blind man. But in his hands he held full glasses. She felt suddenly that she knew infinitely more than he, that she held his fate in her hands.

"They're talking about draining the sewage system," he said, handing her the pink punch drink, while he held his whisky and water high and looked through it to the fat lantern beyond them. "To keep the city from flooding again."

"What a thing to talk about!" She did not know any of Buenos Aires Wong's friends. A group of them stood around the table, the ladies billowing like curtains in a breeze or standing stalk-slim, their heads turned up femininely, speaking to the men about the sewers.

Mimi sipped slowly, enjoying the sensation that every moment was lasting an hour. Of late, every day had seemed so long, endless, spacious as a huge glass house. There was no sense of pressure or crowdedness. She found herself so relaxed that she could contemplate starting a new activity at ten of two, knowing that she had an appointment at two sharp. And she was always able to complete the activity in those ten minutes. "You have all the time there is," her father had said to her a long time ago, and for the first time she understood the expression.

"I've been feeling recently almost as if I've slowed myself down, and am watching myself unreel. The motion is so slow I can see where I was ten minutes ago, and the next hour will never come, so I don't need to hurry."

She could tell Robert appreciated that. He drank to it, unstrapped the watch around his wrist, and moved his arm back as though to pitch it into the bushes. Instead, he dropped the watch into his jacket pocket.

Mimi laughed and watched some of the guests begin to dance. Buenos Aires Wong, their host who had been born in Argentina where his father had been a Chinese ambassador, was changing records on the gramophone. He swung into a rhumba and demonstrated that the Chinese took to syncopation as easily as any twentieth-century Westerner. He was dancing with *Yiao ching*, the schizophrenic Miss Chu, who sidled in high wedge shoes. She jigged unhappily, a small brocade purse swinging from a chain on her arm, her white fox stole sliding off a scrawny shoulder. In the dim midnight light, her bleached hair looked like a blond fur cap with an extra length in the back.

"Let's dance," Mimi said. They moved toward the patio, and said "hello" to a couple they had been introduced to earlier. Robert knew some of Buenos Aires' friends, but this was the first time Mimi had ever attended one of his functions. Their host affected riding clothes, even at this time of the evening, and his sisters were in modified "foreign" dance frocks. One of them wore a full pink net skirt with a tight bodice that had a high Chinese collar ("low necks make us look Japanese, somehow"); the other one wore a smart black harlequin skirt and a steep bib of jewelry.

"You're my consort," Mimi thought, pressing against Robert. Her body seemed to reign over her mind these days; she felt all thoughtless sensation, crowned with immediacy and womanliness. After her daily bath, she dusted herself all over with talcum. Her breasts were tense and sensitive. Robert moved against her as they danced and she wanted to respond with a cry. Yet, over all her desire, a mist moved, softening the

132

edges of it, making her feel blurred yet alive, removed yet vulnerable.

"Shall we?" Buenos Aires asked, as he tapped Robert on the shoulder, suggesting that they change partners for the next record. Robert smiled meaningfully at Mimi and turned to take *Yiao ching* for a turn around the patio.

Later, Mimi returned, jogged by Buenos Aires' brisk movements, and Robert took her hand to lead her away. "You're disturbed," he said, frowning, but she was not deeply distressed, just pleasantly irritated, gracefully provoked.

"You certainly seemed to like her," Mimi said. "Would you care to dance with her again?" She threw back her head and surveyed him, secure in her hold over him.

He laughed. "We had a fascinating conversation about the dead animal around her neck."

"Admit it, admit it," she pursued. "You didn't miss me a bit!" As they walked toward the house, Mimi realized that she wanted a small quarrel to bring them closer together. The garden was too abstract; the garden was Robert, and *she* wanted to dominate. She quickened her steps, and they entered the deep lobby of Buenos Aires' house. Passing through the formal, dark living room, they found a small study lit with one lamp. She sat on a window seat and drew him toward it.

"You haven't told me how I look," she complained. "You don't see me any more!"

He said nothing, looking at her and then past her through the window to the small swirl of color that the guests made outside. To her, they were simply a disembodied, swarming wreath hung in the night.

"You don't even listen to me any more. Be nice, Bobby." To answer her he sat down, crushing part of her dress. The gramophone was repeating, over and over, "the conga, and the lessons are free; the conga, and the lessons are free"; finally someone released it from its tantrum. The house was so quiet that they could hear voices clearer here than outside.

Mimi whispered, "I've changed, Bobby, see," and took his hand, placing it under her heart, where her breast was heavy.

He spoke at last. "You'll never change," he said, kissing her hand.

"I've changed already," she whispered, and slid his hand down to her stomach. He moved his hand back to her breast and kissed its softness through her dress.

"Darling," he said. "I can't keep telling you how much I love you. Not every hour on the hour, anyway. Can't you tell I do? Who could help loving you?" he asked, holding her face in his hands and examining it like an artist, turning her chin this way and that. He put his hands on her breasts again, and kissed her neck, where the pulse jumped like a bird's heart.

"Let's get married," Mimi said. "I want to be your wife. Let's get married and really, really live together."

He seemed to breathe faster, then inhale deeply; Mimi waited for an answer. Instead, he took her hand and rubbed it over his face.

"I don't go proposing to everyone," she said, in mock self-pity, "and I'll have an answer."

"Yes," he said. "Yes, of course."

"Yes?" she asked. "Yes, we will, we will get married?"

"Must we talk about it now? Let's talk about it some other time." He suddenly seemed garrulous. "We'll talk when we are really alone. I promise. Let's join the rest of the party now," and he stood up to lead her outdoors.

"No, Robert. We're going to talk about it now."

"Now, at a party? Now, at twenty minutes after midnight?" he joked, looking at the clock over the mantelpiece. She had to lean forward to peer at it—she was a little near-sighted, not enough to require glasses, just enough to give her eyes what Aunt Juliet called "a soft, disturbing look."

"It's twenty-three minutes after midnight," she corrected him, and all of a sudden she lost the sense of unhurried time she had enjoyed for two weeks. All of a sudden, it seemed there was no time left.

"We've put it off long enough," she said unreasonably. "Too damn long." Actually, they had never really brought up the subject of marriage. If she had been compulsive about anything, it was in an effort to measure the intensity of his love for her. And that was only because he could be so elusive. "I'm not going to put it off another minute!" She had got hold of one small aspect of the truth—that time was passing—and she would explore that truth.

"I have reason to say so," she said. "After all, I'm a woman and I know better about some things. We've simply got to get married and soon!" She was still whispering, yet her voice was cutting and shrill.

"I don't understand why," he said, seeming frightened, "we have to discuss this right now. Why now, of all times? Let's go out and join the others."

"No," she pouted. "No. I—I don't think it's good for me to dance." She grabbed his hand. "Robert," she exclaimed, "I'm going to have a baby!"

He stood perfectly still, his eyes bright with a splintered light. Something crossed his face—not a shadow, but a stain; his face looked soiled as though with long sleeplessness and anxiety.

"A baby? Our baby? Oh, my poor child!" he exclaimed and seemed to remember everything.

"I've been to the doctor. It's been confirmed," she said happily. "Feel," she said, taking his hand again and putting it where he could feel the softness of her flesh just beneath her waist. "It's just begun to grow. And I won't look pregnant for months yet."

"Then it's not too late," he said, relieved. "You're just a child yourself, Mimi. You're too young to have a baby—even ours."

"We'll get married, and have babies and love each other forever. Oh, my darling, darling husband."

He closed his eyes, and she thought his lids had covered

135

them to indulge in a coma of love. She stood up to reach for his face.

"That's one possibility," he said. "You've just recounted one possibility, but—"

"But we love each other," she protested.

"Why don't we just go on the way we have been? Marriage sometimes ends a relationship, instead of cementing it. Why don't we just stay in love?"

She laughed, looking into his face. She loved his seriousness, his groping ways, his gloom, the way he explained things to her. But it was up to her to be practical and adult.

"But the baby? Babies like to grow up in a home. Oh, Bobby!"

"You don't have to have the baby, you know. Something can be done about that, you know. It happens all the time. If we do something about it right away, it may not even be so terrible."

The full impact of his words did not reach her, only the expression of self-preservation which now discolored his face. Suddenly she forgot about the child, and thought of herself.

"Do you love me or not?" She stepped away from him and repeated, "But do you love me or not?"

"Of course I love you," he said between his teeth, as though vindictively. "That's not the point."

"That's the whole point, the only point!" She moved away deliberately.

"Mimi, I love you. I love you more than anyone I've ever loved."

"We'll get married then," she said. They were passing through the empty living room. "Nothing is going to stop me from having our baby. Nothing!"

He seized her arm from behind. She could feel her own face light up.

"I do love you! I do love you!" he breathed into her neck.

"Oh, my darling!"

They hung back in the shadows, clinging to each other.

136

"Believe me, believe me!" he demanded. She could feel nothing beyond his body pressed against hers. There was suddenly something wonderfully truculent in the stance of his shoulders—what she felt was a new assertiveness.

"Oh, I can't stand it!" she whispered, pulling away, while he tried to keep her against him.

They still had the whole night before them in his house. She laughed, and called over her shoulder, "Catch me, if you can!" and ran into the garden. She'd outrage them all and that entity, the party. She wanted to shout, "I'm going to have his baby!" But she only looked back once more at Robert—who would come seeking her later—and ran past the dancing couples (Buenos Aires Wong tried to hide his astonishment with an unwinking superciliousness) until she reached the pond. She knew what it reminded her of—that wading pool in the old Peking house. She pulled up her skirt, kicked off her slippers, and startling the fish, began to splash around.

CHAPTER TWELVE

Helen, Helen, Helen, Sylvia kept thinking. Helen Ames, her mother. Helen Ames Chen, her mother who had married her father. Until this very moment Sylvia had not known she was more than a little obsessed with her—because Helen subtly planted herself between everything Sylvia was now and what she wanted for herself. Helen was an only child, disturbed by the intrusion of her own two children in her own home. Both Paul and Sylvia apologized for the space they took up, had learned to neutralize themselves when the occasion demanded invisibility. They had brought themselves up, explaining themselves at every stage to their youthful mother, explaining her to herself. Justification had become second nature, a reflex.

Helen's recent elation had been contagious. The peace rumor, which five days later had become a fact, had seemed to make her ten years younger overnight. She talked constantly of the States, her face melting into uncontrollable smiles, like a young girl thinking of her lover. She was inspired and loosened the tight ring of her habits. For three days she did not empty ash trays and smooth invisible scuffs on the living-room rug, following in the wake of the children. She did not make them feel that the value of the furniture—which she considered her possessions rather than the family's—was being depreciated each time they sat in a chair or ran their fingers over the piano keyboard. Their nerve-ends began to seem less raw. She did not look challenged when Sylvia announced she was going out. Sylvia did not feel she had to defend a simple wish, "But I want to," and launch into a paragraph of explanation. "Don't be impudent!" had been Helen's favorite retort—her eyes glassy and bulbous suddenly—when the children were young. They had felt their very existence was an impudence. Sleep was a beautiful negation Sylvia indulged in every night. She was safe and nullified as long as she slept.

Sylvia felt that her own breathing was different, less constricted. She realized she had been girded for crises that might never occur again.

But then she heard coming from the hallway, "Secrets again, boys?" Her mother's clear high voice carrying through the apartment. Her mother's voice had a bell-like quality, it rose and stayed near the ceiling. Sylvia could sometimes hear it days after a remark had been made. Sometimes she heard her mother calling her, only to find she was not even at home.

"Honestly, Mother!" Sylvia could hear Paul answering her, but the exchange still had the quality of something remembered or imagined.

"I know what you boys talk about. Speaking Chinese doesn't fool me in the least. I'd think you'd have more sense than to stir yourselves up."

"She has no delicacy; she also allows one no face," Sylvia remembered Peiyuan having said two days ago, muttering it through his large teeth.

"I'm sure I don't know what you think we're talking about," Paul answered, and added "Mother" reluctantly, as if to soften his retort. He was being very careful.

"You know perfectly well what I mean, so don't lie in my face. Why do you keep the door closed all the time, if you aren't talking about what I know you're talking about?" Then the door slammed sharply, and the voices disappeared, seemed to have been swallowed up.

Sylvia stood up in her room. Her hands suddenly began to shake a little, her palms, which had been dry, were moist. But all she was aware of thinking was: this is not something left over in my consciousness, they *are* talking now. All her mother's past rages seemed called into existence again. Each new incident only reminded Sylvia how tenuous her own hold on herself was, how easily she could be shattered. She couldn't make out any of Helen's words, but the air hung agape, the way the air-raid sirens left it after they declared their violence.

Time seemed speeded up. The door was flung open again. "Your stupid nephew!" Helen screamed, going into the living room to attack Liyi. It all sounded terrifyingly familiar. "Oh, I tell you I can't stand it! I can't stand it another second! He's got to go! He's got to go this very instant!"

Sylvia forced herself to breathe slowly. She looked at herself in the bureau mirror. Her eyes were dark—as though the cornea had disappeared—with a bleak hatred.

"And look here, understand this once and for all, I'm not going to have any more queer Chinese staying in this house! Sleeping with their big teeth showing! They revolt me!

"Chinese relatives making a good thing out of my generosity. What is this—a free Y.M.C.A.? Oh, no, he can't get a job, he can't do this, he can't do that, he's too, too precious I suppose to earn a living, but he's not too precious to sleep and eat and talk about sex to our boy. That ugly brat is getting out, getting out, I tell you!"

Sylvia felt her own cowardice. She forced herself to leave the bedroom and refuge. Liyi was blinking in the living room from shock and alarm. The two boys stood paralyzed at the door of their room.

"Oh, you Chinese!" Helen exclaimed, choking on her tantrum, and she pushed Liyi out of her way.

"*I* am Chinese, too!" Sylvia shouted. "I—I—I! Chinese, do you understand!"

"I hate everything you stand for!" Helen screamed, looking at everyone in general. "No one, no one"—and she pointed vengefully at Peiyuan—"no one is going to keep me from going back to the States! No one, no one!" she moaned shrilly.

"You outsider!" Sylvia sobbed drily. "You poor stupid fool!" and savagely struck her own breast twice. Her breath caught

140

as she heard herself. She was her mother's daughter—nothing would change that. She could not think or separate the strands of her own duality.

"I *am* Chinese!" and she was running down the stairs as though she might betray herself. Her chest hurt from her own blows. Her eyes felt inflamed, for no tears would come. Her head ached as though her senses wanted to burst out of the confines of her skull.

It was growing dim outside, the world balanced between the beautiful day and the attentiveness of night. A figment of new moon hung low on the horizon, where the pink-gray rooftops dipped down and let in more sky. The new moon hung in delicate, precarious balance, the sky around it all reverence for its young life—still uncoarsened, still hung on the first intake of breath, still unknowing and so cruel in its own beauty.

Sylvia ran, and though the sidewalks were level, her legs stiffened and slipped, as if she ran downhill and uphill, unevenly, stumbling against air. She did not know how long she had been running. The streets were corridors that might allow her to run out of conflict; the corridors would lead her out of herself, out of the red glare that filled her head and her eyes, and there was no way out of the corridors, except to run farther into them.

She ran for Avenue Petain and, when it opened before her, wondered why there had been such an absolute need to reach it. It was a huge hallway, a nightmare place, and the occasional rickshaws and passers-by seemed suspended in dusk, floating down the River Styx, and the sky above was a funereal Milky Way. Now she must run and leave this corridor and enter the next, but her breath came in gasps, and stung her chest, and her running feet dragged in an agonizing, slow motion.

Yet she must keep running; her very life seemed to be at stake. Stumbling, she struggled across the side streets; the breaks in the sidewalk seemed to threaten her errand, but there was no safety in making the other side. The trees bloomed large heads and faces, and each home and garden as she passed it seemed an insurmountable obstacle, a huge unmapped estate lying between her and her goal.

Then she seemed to hear a scream and clapped her hand to her own mouth, thinking she must truly be out of her mind. She recoiled, holding out her hands for support, and ran to the other side of the avenue, and leaned gasping against the fence.

She clung to the fence and listened, hoping she would not hear the scream again from across the street, forgetting that the occupation was over. The Shanghai American School, where she had been under arrest the night of August fourth, had been taken over by the Japanese Gestapo three years before, and between these headquarters and Bridge House on the Bund a steady stream of victims had trickled. The vans did most of their work at night, and at night the campus used to come into hideous life. By day, it slept like a cat with its claws curled in, a light sleep with one eye watching.

Blindly she ran toward and then away from the fence. The low moon, circling her wherever she ran, had tangled with the trees around the squat church behind the enclosure. It was her mother's church, non-denominational, the Reverend Ssu-tu blessing everyone alike with the Christian equation. What had he, the Reverend Ssu-tu, given up for the Holy Trinity—was it Buddhism, Taoism, Confucianism, ancestor worship, or had he never had any of these? Was his Christianity an accident of a fellowship to Cambridge, and did he believe in Jesus truly, wholly, completely? Reverend Ssu-tu, Sylvia cried, and she sounded half demented to herself, save me from my trinity: my father, my mother and myself. Reverend Ssu-tu, save me from my duality: my flesh, which believes in life; my spirit, which belongs nowhere. The screaming which she had imagined had cleared her own throat, and part of her was only a hair's-breadth from praying.

She ran more easily now, the corridor grew smaller. In two languages the cicadas chirped, counterpointing the arrogant West, with its sterile sidewalks, and the Chinese houses which

hung back among their trees. Two Chinese houses, blind to the
street and extending back into courtyards, pressed upon her
path. Strange habitations, eccentricities, in this quarter of the
French Concession. Was this where some Kuomintang official's
wife lived, under house arrest? Was this where the Japanese
used to house their spies, preparing them for a Chinese disguise? The houses were not sinister, but mild, leaning down to
the earth they sat upon, understanding the limitations of their
defiance of gravity. Chinese houses ran along the earth like
vines, branching east and branching west, courtyards extending
beyond courtyards. They did not stand brave and white, conspicuous and self-reliant, like American houses, looking at one
forthrightly out of frame windows. A Chinese house grew inward, but included the outside—the air, trees, rocks and rain—
in its very entrails; it lent itself to the landscape, trying not to
draw attention by its difference. It humanized the earth around
it, and the earth gave it its clay and its tiles.

Peiyuan, Sylvia thought. Exhausted, she was walking now.
Out of such a house Peiyuan had come to Shanghai, a Chinese
house, not scrupulously clean, but its untidiness was organic to
life: it fertilized his family's conversation, their thoughts, their
careless, impersonal regard for each other. So lax the Chinese
were—his mother and his relatives, who were also her relatives,
Sylvia reminded herself—they accomplished nothing, their
nerves were never in a white gnarl. They were landowners, and
had had large holdings in the past; they were landowners, who
sat in leisure amid melon-seed shells, playing mah-jong, and
clucking their tongues, now over the servants, then over the
twentieth century. Sylvia could hear their voices in the steady
hum of the evening. For these relatives, to die was incipient in
having been born, to have been born was not to be questioned.
With all the years in between one fulfilled the function of a
link between the last generation and the next, with time out for
simple duties and simpler pleasures.

"Poor Peiyuan," Sylvia cried, and then changed her mind.
One must always be accurate, discipline oneself to apprehend-

ing the truth, and nothing but the very truth. Anything else compromised one in cheap emotions. She was not sorry for Peiyuan, not for the boy Helen called Albert, who had no father, but had a way of existence, even in the schizophrenic East of the twentieth century. Not poor Peiyuan, but enviable Peiyuan; not poor Peiyuan, rejected so forcibly by his American aunt, but fortunate Albert, not to be claimed by something he was not, not to be involved from his very conception and to his very marrow.

Poor Paul, Sylvia thought, and that was more accurate. My brother, she thought, seeing him as he had been at six, angelic and so beautiful (part porcelain and part flame) he had been painful to look at. At their best, half-breeds who had Chinese blood in them had fine features, thin skins and eyes that caught the light in a blaze. So much tragedy seemed to lie beneath Paul's physical perfection, his puzzling Chinese-Western looks, which seemed like an optical illusion. Now, at fifteen, he was awkward, shy, bereft of some of his purity, and given to biting his nails and gnawing at his lips, his eyes gazing absent-mindedly into nothing. What part of his change was adolescence, what part his growing awareness of his own conflict, what part was Paul himself, perhaps? People were so complex, she despaired of ever knowing anything about them. The more she knew, the less she could act upon the knowledge; the more she considered them, the more there was to take into account.

Still tired from having run, she moved very slowly, wondering. How did people who acted, act? How did they take the initial step? Did they close off a part of themselves, close the drawer on the confusion inside, and present an entity, an acquired one perhaps, but an entity and a position from which to act? And she thought of Feng, of his directness and his blindness, of his energy and his brutality—yes, she could see brutality lurking under his warmth—and she gasped with the realization. Her breath caught and she started running again, crossing the street and seeming to head for a house she knew so well.

A Chinese family she and her parents knew lived in the house.

A pure-blooded Chinese family, the head of which had been her father's schoolmate at Tsinghua University. They were the kind of Chinese she hated—the *nouveaux-riches,* ostentatious, without conscience. Chefoo Liu (they called him Chefoo because he had made his money on Chefoo raw silks) passed off his concubine (since concubinage had been outlawed) as a cousin twice removed, while professing to be liberal and enlightened as he listened to American jazz in his concealed opium den.

But why was it, and what did it mean for oneself, that these people, and there were lots of them, caught in the vacuum between generations in China, robbed of all values, could yet rob you of what you were? What they owned could be added up on the abacus; they had a nest to which they added possession upon possession, concubine upon wife, child upon child. They looked at Sylvia from all their hideous exuberance and made her feel like nothing. And her running by the long wall that protected their grounds—hadn't she run from them in many other ways? But weren't they right? She was blown by the winds of every emotion, while they could not be blasted from their safety. She felt she could not justify her life by any of their terms. They had no sense of reality; if they had, they would find themselves ridiculous. Yet their feet were planted firmly in life. She had a sense of reality, but it made her recoil, as she had recoiled from the screams of the campus. They had possessions, and they brought forth warm, living children, and what they did not know only helped them enjoy what they had.

It was too much; she could be anything, experiment with any possibility. Living between two worlds had made her sensitive to the nuances, the innuendoes of everything between those two, all the variations. From a single clue, from a shard, she could fill out the whole pattern. Her mother hated the Lius, as she did, but for different reasons. Helen suspected that their vulgarity perhaps had something to do with their being Chinese, since she did not know the *nouveaux-riches* anywhere else. The Lius liked Helen Chen, but simply because she was foreign, exotic. As for her—she appreciated their spotless Westinghouse kitchen, which some found pretentious, and she was not too staid to dance to the second son's drumming.

And Peiyuan—was Sylvia not partly committed to Peiyuan; he was an untainted Chinese, more foreign, but dearer to her, than the Chinese of Shanghai. He was old and new, and touched off a rhythm in her blood taught her by her father. It was taught her by Yennai, the *amah*, so wise and so gentle, so uninquisitive, and so ignorant that she did not know a door was made from the wood of a tree. Sylvia was each of them, so right for themselves and so wrong for one another. But she was also none of them, for they all seemed partly criminal. But where was the crime, and had there been one, except in her own heart? She was so many different people, and she could no longer maintain the balance among them all. They would have to become one soon, they would have to begin to act as one soon, and it was almost as though she was murdering parts of all the different people she was, all the parts she did not want to retain.

But she was running again, her legs carrying her past the houses. She was running like the criminal. She had denied herself not thrice, but a thousand times since she had been born. She had denied her parents and questioned her own blood. But tonight she had not questioned once where she was going, running until her legs did not seem to belong to her. She turned the corner onto a back street and discovered that she had run all the way to Feng Huang's front door.

In a flash she saw, but the flash seemed to take hours to detonate inside her mind. Her eyes were filled with spirals of light, from having run too long and too hard, but her breathing was strangely controlled, as though the flight had purged her of a stumbling pulse.

What am I doing here? she would have asked herself in another age, long past, as Feng was asking her now without speaking. He had hastily put on his shirt, and any embarrassment he felt had changed to surprise, naked amused surprise.

"Feng!" she said, as he closed the door and she moved back and leaned against it.

He approached her and she stretched out her hand to take his.

"Help me!" she cried. "Can't you help me?" But he didn't move. "Why can't you help me?" she cried angrily.

He pulled her toward him, looking down at her possessively.

"Kiss me!" she ordered.

He pulled her abruptly against his hard body. Predatory and fierce, he kissed her, holding her arms pinned to her sides. She felt blinded, sucked away into a simple universe. His hands dug into her arms, made her a victim at her own crucifixion. She wanted him to expiate her violence with his primitiveness. He pulled her away from the door, embraced her and drew her, as though she were unwilling, into the bedroom.

Love seemed an amulet against living; she clung to him as though he would save her from drowning. But she wanted to die, to die under the calvary of his body, to pass away, out of herself. Undressing her, his hands touched her with an agonizing tenderness; she clutched the torment to her, and cried out, her own moan sounding strange to her.

"Feng, Feng, Feng!"

She felt dependent and a great rush of glory in her dependency. Her body was bright where he caressed her. She had to close her eyes against the glare. Her heart seemed to fill her whole chest and even pound in her head. All her emotion sang in her breasts. She felt invalided upon him. She wanted to be invalided upon him, now and forever.

"I love you."

"We," he answered, "we do."

He hid all existence from her, except the one they now shared. He moved and encompassed her, and the sweet, specific joy and torment swept her out into a vast, shining Pacific. They floated near the rims of a young world. They came back from far away, and afterward lay with their arms around each other and smoked a cigarette and watched the street lamp make a world of dark and light squares outside.

She felt she was one at last, she was herself—Sylvia—having traveled all the paths to a single here and now. She gazed in wonder at Feng's face, his singleness, his pure and masculine identity. He seemed entirely true and real, endowed with grace. He had given her back to herself but she wanted him to lead her life for her.

"Why do I suddenly want to live through him alone?" she thought achingly; she wanted to transfer all her past longings and hurts to him. It was wrong and false and dangerous, but it was an irresistible urge.

She whispered only, "I feel so alive, new-born."

"Then, happy birthday, Sylvia," Feng replied.

CHAPTER THIRTEEN

"Guess what?" Peiyuan cried.

He could feel his eyes blinking as though he were bewildered. "I—I," and he broke into a helpless grin. "I'm staying! I'm staying! Oh, not here—not with you. But Uncle Liyi is giving me a job at the plant. I'm going to stay in Shanghai. I'm going to get a room downtown near work. I'm staying. And what's more—I'll be earning a living."

He rolled up his sleeves in a typically Chinese gesture and blew on his fists. He started to shadow-box with Paul, executing slow elastic movements like a sleepwalker doing calisthenics. Then he leaned against the bureau to regard his future.

"Suddenly I've got myself a job. A job! Do you understand?" He laughed. "I'll be a wage-earner! I'll be running those presses single-handed in a year! I'll show old man Bruno what we Chens are made of! I'll work day and night."

"Don't work too hard," Paul warned, "or you'll put Dad out of a job. Though, of course, I've really no serious objections to your supporting us."

"Wait till Feng hears of this," Sylvia said unexpectedly.

"Ironic, isn't it?" Peiyuan began while the three cousins looked at each other, and he wondered whether he should go on. He was too happy to introduce a sour note; he didn't need to, either, he thought. Both Sylvia and Paul had looked away quickly, when he said, "Ironic, isn't it?" for giving him the job had been Helen's idea all along. She hated him, but in the end *her* plan for him was the one Uncle Liyi had had to resort to—just because she had rejected him. She had wanted him to get a job immediately, but Uncle Liyi had not wanted to be guilty of favoritism and make a place for him at the printing plant. He had decided not to help him—in this way—for the sake of a principle. But when Helen had literally turned him out of her house, Uncle Liyi had sacrificed that principle for him. It made Peiyuan ache; it made him feel older; it was almost too much of a burden for a sixteen-year-old heart. He knew his uncle loved him, and he loved him in return for the compromise he had just made. It also made him suffer with him, for all things in this life were imperfect, involving passion, pain and half-losses.

He felt a wildness in him which he could not express. He flung up his arms and squealed; flung them up again and hugged himself. Not only his own happiness, but everything else, too, seemed unbearable. For peace had really come, and Shanghai had begun to thaw from the numbness of the occupation.

"Where have you been?" Paul would ask him as he came in late for supper or disappeared in the evening and did not return until midnight.

"Walking," he'd answer, saying it as though it were a secret he could at last confess. "I bet I walked twenty miles." He had forsaken the bicycle that Paul and he shared: "I can't stand that old piece of plumbing any longer." During the war, bicycles had been made from old lead pipes and discarded bits of metal; they were hardly precision instruments, and moved only with the application of hardy calf muscles. He would have pulled the bicycle apart physically had an ingrained sense of thrift not inhibited him.

"I walked all the way to the Bund and sat looking at the river. Then I walked practically all the way to Chapei, and back again." He did not tell Paul that he wanted to hug the buildings to him, embrace the people he passed, spread himself over the whole city, like a rug, so that he could touch on life everywhere. He couldn't understand what was happening inside him, but he felt himself the center of an ever-widening circle. He felt capable of doing something insane; he felt his body might grow an extra limb. Life and energy seethed in him as in a tropical swamp. Supposing, he thought, supposing he woke up one day with a third eyebrow growing in the middle of his forehead? Supposing he shot up a foot overnight? It frightened him, and he was shy of everyone, for the unpredictability of his growth and passions seemed to leave him open to committing any sort of possible disgrace.

Before Uncle Liyi had decided to make a place for him at the plant, he had confessed to Paul, "I think I'll join the navy." But the next week he confided that he wanted to be a construction engineer, giving as a reason, "I want to work with my hands, get them in dirt and mortar," and even as he said it he knew it sounded heretical. A generation ago no Chinese aspired to work with his hands. Another time he threw himself into a spasm of radio transmitting, sitting hunched over Paul's equipment, purchased many years before, and feeling that his forefinger was on the pulse of absolutes, such as time and space. Between these bouts, he hiked all over Shanghai alone, blind and driven, as though he were out to accomplish murder.

"Escape, escape," had rung through his brain, but he sat rooted in the family. He went out on the terrace roof and swung from the overhead railings. Chinning himself, he felt like a giant thrusting himself into greater being. When he hung by his knees and looked into the sky, he felt that he plunged into the universe. Dilated with consciousness, he swung down onto the cement of the terrace and returned to the apartment to sit sullenly through a meal. He was all nerves, and Uncle Liyi and Helen seemed like incredibly dense entities that nothing could reach. They seemed resolved, impossible creatures that should have been buried long ago.

Though he stalked through the streets blindly, his senses guttering like a fire in a high wind, he came back able to tell them simple facts. In one district, he watched the Japanese move their belongings onto the sidewalk, and pack them into cars, rickshaws and carts. In another, he saw pale prisoners being released from years in jail. He read the stories refugees wrote in chalk on sidewalks, the elaborate literary accounts of their decline in fortune. These stories the effete beggars had in the past written for alms. Now they wrote them to tell how the Japanese brought about their downfall, and pedestrians stepped into the gutters to avoid smudging the essays. The houses of well-known collaborationists were plastered with obscenities. Men in Japanese or Nanking puppet uniforms moved furtively, going through the last gestures of their missions.

"The city is terrific," he said, "but it's going to take more than peace—more than the lack of war, that is—to return it to normal. It's—it's"—and searched for the right adjective— "it's seething," he ended anticlimactically. He didn't know exactly how to describe it. "It's dangerous, sort of," and he did not know whether it was threatened or threatening.

He felt he should tell Uncle Liyi about it. But he hardly knew what he had to tell. As he thought about it, he knew he wanted to promise himself to justify his uncle's love for him. And as something in him welled up, something he could not describe—it was such a complex of emotions—he suddenly wanted to reassure Liyi, tell him with the sureness of youth that life could be really very good and simple. Adults—and the thought struck him with great surprise—were actually so much more needful than the young.

CHAPTER FOURTEEN

It started raining slowly, a cool drop falling on Sylvia's forehead like a greeting out of the half-clear sky. She looked up quickly and saw that the clouds were moving in from the river. In half an hour it would really start pouring.

The odor of dust that always preceded the real downpour had begun to rise around her. She hurried across the street and presented herself before Mimi's gate. "Well, I'm here!" she wanted to announce. "Here I am!" But instead, she rang the bell and was let in by the cook. Behind her, he was saying, "*Hsiao-chieh* is not in." Sylvia walked quickly out of earshot and was already in the entrance hall.

The house was silent, waiting. Sylvia had walked around the living room once before remembering why she had come. Finding the door ajar, she ran into Mimi's bedroom, but she was not in. Aunt Juliet seemed nowhere around either.

Again in the living room, Sylvia encountered the *amah*. "They're out," she stated flatly, as a dismissal. There was no mistaking her tone, but Sylvia only widened her eyes and, without thinking, left the house. Now the drops were coming down more frequently. They were forming a large wet pattern, each dot two feet from the other.

"Well!" she said to herself, but she was not reacting specifically to her disappointment at not finding Mimi in, or to the *amah's* strange unfriendliness, or to the fact that she was going to get thoroughly wet. "Well!" and it did not occur to her that she could have questioned the servant. Why hadn't Mimi phoned her recently—not even returning her calls? And why had she herself taken the trouble of going over, if she did not pursue her purpose? Couldn't she have waited for them? Even if she had thrown herself on Mimi's bed for a nap, the servants would not have questioned her behavior.

She looked up into the gray sky and smiled. She realized with delight that her life was divided into simplicities. An utterly banal one occurred to her now: she was always either indoors or out-of-doors. Yes, of course! Indoors generally meant either in her own home or someone else's. Out-of-doors was a cultivated quarter, which held few surprises after these years of living in such limiting circumstances. It was either day or night, dry or wet, hot or cold. Everything was very simple and very rich—for within these bold opposing states there was all the room in the world for a million shadings, variations, tones and values. It was so *interesting* to be alive!

She laughed. She was mad, yet never so sane. Her heart suddenly missed a beat, as she jumped back onto the sidewalk. She had been about to cross the street without looking. Almost losing his balance, a bicycle rider cursed her and then rode on. She watched his narrow back move away. She suddenly felt she had a painter's vision. The man's cramped stance, his thin black Chinese trousers flapping around his ankles, his human irritability still ringing in her ears—it seemed a moment that wanted to say something to her, a moment she could argue with. Everything that came within her purview, everything was unique, irreplaceable, its meaning dancing before one's senses like pointillist brush strokes. She thought how all her life she had been afraid to look. She had done things out of a routine of habits, a structure of symbols. Today (and she added, "from now on") she saw things as a visitor might, alive to history and the specific present, a visitor who saw things in their actuality, not colored by the impositions of his own myths.

She felt different. She felt quiet, grave, happy. All day long

154

her body had been singing, for, yesterday, she had been with Feng again. . . .

The air was lighter now, fresher. Steadily filling in the patches on the ground, the rain fell with an even tempo. Frogs behind the hedges began to gargle their throats; sparrows fluttered heavily close to the ground. Sylvia's dress, damp and cool, stuck to her. She walked slowly, feeling refreshed, as after a swim.

They had lain together most of yesterday afternoon, until she had got to know the angle, feel and weight of every part of his body and, through him, of her own. They had had the intimacy of talk, and the intimacy of silence. They had had everything. She now understood the healing power of luxury. She felt she could never again be lonely, greedy, fragmented, at odds with herself. Now she understood temptation and fulfilment, good and evil, men and women. Her own decidedly too-hasty arrogance pleased her. She felt wreathed in love and her own secret life.

The rain was coming down thickly as she reached her own gate, as if shielding the apartment from the world. As she went up the stairs and into the living room, she left the sound of its falling behind her. It was like walking into a deep part of the forest where the storm could not reach you. Dripping wet, she stood at the entrance and looked into Feng's face. He had turned around from the window; Peiyuan and he had been visiting.

"Look at you!" Peiyuan exclaimed.

She and Feng laughed. She said, "I didn't know you were coming over!"

"Neither did I . . . until I just happened to," he answered.

There was nothing more to say, but she still stood unmoving. Then, "I guess I better change," and she went into her bedroom. In her shoes, her feet made a sucking sound every time she took a step. She undressed slowly and wished she had a towel from the bathroom to dry her arms and legs. But she was already naked, and used a handkerchief instead. Peiyuan was outside the door, exclaiming. "We've discussed everything!"

She heard Feng approaching. "He means he let me talk! And I did! I guess you know how much I like hearing myself."

She snorted a little with pleasure. They couldn't hear her behind the door, but they did not require an answer. She could tell they were back in the living room. Feng and Peiyuan had had a visit, since everyone else was out. She wondered how long he had been here, waiting for her. She was glad she had not stayed away at Mimi's.

Sylvia put on a fresh dress and backless slippers. Her hair was combed out straight, lank as after a shampoo. Through the windows a muted light came, and the sound of the rain. In Paul's room, Feng was leaning over Peiyuan's atlas, while the boy tried to tell him about his father's experiences in the interior. Everything was perfect and poised. Feng interrupted him, his exuberance dominating the room.

"They're off on politics!" Sylvia thought. Her contentment would last forever. She stood in the doorway watching them. She looked forward to being alone tonight. To sleep and maybe to wake up briefly. To wake up inside the weather and think of Feng.

CHAPTER FIFTEEN

Liyi felt an unfamiliar irritability, and assumed an extra affabi-
lity to hide it. He felt tired and beset, as with gnats, and
couldn't understand it in himself.

"Yes, of course, we'll do that," he'd say, hardly hearing
Helen's suggestion.

"Just as soon as we can," he'd promise Paul, or "of course,
of course—now that we'll be able to move about," or "we're
all due for a rest and a change, certainly," when the last thing
he wanted was a change. He wanted to scream a little, to let
go, but "it isn't in me," he'd argue with himself, feeling naked
in his inadequacy. "Can't even raise my voice, let alone scream.
Can't even get angry, really," he thought, tasting the full horror
of this revelation.

"Sweetheart, look out the window!" Helen shouted, and her
voice carried only elation and delight.

Why am I so afraid to let go, Liyi asked himself. Am I afraid
of something ugly in myself, some violence that has never been
ventilated. His deepest feelings had never been allowed to air
themselves like night clothes, clothes that are freshened merely
by a shake in the sunlight of morning. If he ever let go, he
might never be able to put himself together again—the explosion of pent-up, unresolved feelings might destroy him utterly.
He shuddered at the thought, at the untidiness, at the sheer
ugliness.

There was no beauty in bare truth. There was no beauty,
in the Chinese sense, in Helen's expression of joy and eagerness:

"Look out the living-room window, love!" she had exclaimed again. There was exuberance, extroversion, but no beauty.

A Chinese painting or poem was beautiful, for it skimmed only the vapor of the unconscious; it did not express the rock-bottom unconscious as those modern Western paintings attempted to do. A single blade of grass suspended in space—that blade in that space transcended the disorder of life. It expressed the essence of the painter's aspirations for a better order, an essence skimmed off in one deft stroke of a brush, skimmed off and recorded on a scroll. And Chinese poems said nothing really, came to grips with very little. They were merely suggestions demarking the location of an emotion. Yes, that's what they were, he thought happily, but the gnats of his irritation returned immediately. He felt alone, somewhat depressed. My children, my children wouldn't understand any of this. My wife—she unquestionably wouldn't understand. Perhaps Peiyuan would. Suddenly he realized he was closer to his brother's son than to anyone else he loved.

But Peiyuan exhausted him, his hopefulness enervated him. "Leave me alone," Liyi wanted to say, "go away, go away," but he could not. Peiyuan, after all, was his favorite nephew, and he saw himself in him. He reminded Liyi how far he had come.

"I want you to keep out of politics, now," he admonished the boy. "There'll be time enough for that." When Liyi had been sixteen—in 1912—he had hardly known what "politics" were. A revolution had just taken place, an empire had been overthrown, a republic declared, but in his innocence he had not understood that by merely being Chinese and alive he was engaged in politics.

He had laughed delightedly and self-consciously when he had had his queue cut off, his generation thus thumbing its nose at the Manchu Dynasty.

"I suppose you'll be wearing buttons next," his mother had said ruefully in Sunkiang. "Buttons" signified everything modern: the trousers, jackets and vests, the foreign suits that

158

modern Chinese leading modern lives were wearing in modern cities.

"I suppose so!" he had replied, expressing only one-hundredth of his glee. The queue had been a symbol of slavery under the Manchus, and revolutionaries had cut theirs off in the last few years, but Liyi had not had his shorn until his parents had been convinced that it was no longer subversive to do so.

And now Peiyuan was telling him about a strike that might take place at the printing plant, not *telling* him, but warning him. "It stands to reason they'll be breaking out all over."

Liyi felt only a wave of nostalgia for his father's days. It had been possible to be a scholar, a member of the gentry, and know nothing of politics, to avoid the subject as soiling, degrading. "Do you know anything about labor unions?" his daughter had once asked him and, involuntarily, he had replied, "No, I'm above those things," and moved his arm in an ancient gesture. It seemed he had wanted to fling back a nonexistent silk sleeve. But his shirt cuff had merely rested stiffly on his wrist.

"Liyi, you simply must look out the window. Oh-h-h," and in their bedroom, Helen yielded to silent rapture.

He stood up reluctantly. He realized fully now how tired he was. Yes, perhaps he needed a rest. The ending of the war, the releasing of tension, the drabness and scarcity of the last eight years had taken their toll. He could barely make himself face the beginning of a new era.

He leaned against the long window sill in the living room. Why couldn't Helen leave him in peace? Nothing fazed her. She now seemed twenty years younger than he. It was a discovery that almost made him cry out in anguish.

A large bloated shadow swept across the sunlight that flooded him and the sill. He pushed back the thin curtains and leaned out, straining his head upward.

"A zeppelin!" Helen exclaimed from the other room. "An American zeppelin!"

"No, it can't be," he protested. "Zeppelin" was a word that denoted the First World War to him. He peered up.

"That's a parachute," he pronounced, disappointed. He had wanted to be transported back a generation. He passionately wanted to be surrounded by the familiar. And the familiar always went back to one's first twenty years.

"Look at the others! There's a whole swarm of them coming down in the west," Helen said and the catch in her voice was unmistakable. Parades, "welcome home" signs, men in the well-pressed uniforms of their countries, all these made her weep. Now she wiped away a tear because American parachutes were dropping K-rations on the internment camps, dropping them to Allied citizens who would not be released until V-J Day was actually announced.

Liyi had always been filled with a shy hopefulness for everything new and modern. His generation had been almost glad (or perhaps they had not let themselves consider the ultimate consequences) that their children grew up writing with fountain pens rather than brushes, knew English better than their own Chinese, explained all the latest techniques, inventions, medicines in American terms. "But, Father, there's no word for it in Chinese. Chinese is too unscientific!" Their girls were bold, stood with arms akimbo, like men. They spoke rapidly and to the point and treated everyone like a sibling.

The bloated shadows kept swarming by. The balloons of brilliant nylon were still high, but their downward drift would land them within the compounds of camps in Lunghwa, Chapei and other outlying districts. An American plane, like a jagged splinter from a huge mirror, swooped down low, buzzing the French Concession. "I can't go along with any more changes!" Liyi wanted to weep. "I am tired, tired, tired."

Peiyuan's fresh, untired voice cut across his mind, "No, but it stands to reason they will. Li Li-san did his work in 1927, but Liu Shao-chi picked up where he left off."

"What are you talking about?" Liyi had asked, secretly

admiring his own testiness. Of course he remembered, but he was burdened by his memories.

He's only a child, he thought. Why listen to Peiyuan? The sun made the window sill glow, the thin gold curtains (just recently reinstated to celebrate the end of the brownout) flared in the breeze. The room trembled with light. The balloons outside drifted down steadily, boastfully, on invisible guide lines of gravity.

How beautiful and how ridiculous! Liyi thought. How sentimental and how embarrassing! These balloons, these gifts, these rewards to "those who have suffered." He found an aspect of everything too abashing. It made him want to hide in a closet, to save himself from regarding a world that did not realize its own dubious taste.

His mind flew back to two unconnected incidents. At the University of Missouri he had sat transfixed on the bleachers watching a cheer leader almost dislocate himself as he led the cheers and the applause. Liyi had been driven then with the belief that everything which was extroverted and American was better than what was Chinese. But he had not looked at the cheer leader; he had looked into him. He had envied him his uninhibited entity, and died with shame for him at his ludicrous performance. He had sat transfixed on the neutral November day more than a quarter of a century ago, trying to understand that shouting, self-comforting young man's sense of mission, yet trying to hide behind himself as he stared.

Then he remembered the five weeks he had spent in prison in Manchuria in the early thirties, arrested by the Japanese in a case of mistaken identity. He had spent thirty-five days deep in the bottom of a well—so it had seemed—sharing a *kang* with forty other prisoners, occupying only the narrow space he required to lie down in. After getting over his initial fear, he had had time to think, to realize how close to feeling a derelict he was.

The family, waiting for him in Peiping, might have been a dream: Helen drying her hair among the oleanders, his young children seemingly strangers against a background with which only he and Yennai, the *amah*, really blended. He could hardly bear to pronounce the word "Eurasian"; it was as though his seed had produced mavericks, a mutation. He slurred over the thought quickly, thinking he had gone up to Peiping first as an adolescent on a freight train; years later, he had returned with a family. But the first trip had seemed much more vivid: he had gone up to Peiping as a candidate for the highest in a series of classical examinations. Other young competitors (all of them had distinguished themselves in the *hsien* and provincial examinations) were picked up from different parts of China. If they passed the finals, they would receive scholarships to Tsinghua, an American-sponsored university. From there, they might even take a ship and go to the United States of America.

He remembered looking out of the freight train at China's landscape. "You're putting your foot on the big wheel," his father had said in Sunkiang, knowing his eldest son would make it all the way to "Beautiful Country," to *Mei Kuo*, as America is called. He had taken it for granted that Liyi would return from abroad to hold a high government post; he had never understood his son's lack of interest in the traditional civil service. He had never understood "professional" life. And his lack of understanding was understandable—China (so ancient, so long settled by human inhabitants) was a frontier country for pioneers in journalism, architecture, advertising, industry.

Liyi had put his head out of the freight car door to buy some steaming refreshments, and he had gasped. Northern Chinese had white eyebrows! Then he laughed, abashed again at his own naïveté. It rarely snowed in Sunkiang, and when it did, the flakes disappeared in wetness the moment they reached the earth. Suddenly he realized his smallness, his innocence—he who was the eldest son of the most well-established family in all of Sunkiang.

In a sense everything he had learned was brushed aside in the ferment of those years. His tutor had taught him and his brothers and cousins to memorize the old literary texts. They committed every character to memory, and after a few years of chanting page after page, his tutor began to explain their meaning. Sometimes the meaning of an abstruse paragraph leaped whole into his consciousness, a passage which had meant nothing until the students had been given a clue. But a literary "renaissance" was taking place in the universities, a revolution of another sort. The dead hand of the scholar was being repudiated, the modern spoken language was advocated over the classical literary language for all forms of art and communication. The roots of the language were struck a blow—systems were being evolved to make the learning of Chinese itself easier, in order to combat illiteracy.

There were other evolutions and renaissances: Confucius was being supplanted by Christ and John Dewey; free love was taking the place of family-arranged marriages; emulation of the West was replacing ancestor worship; birth control, Imagism, proletarian literature, co-education, divorce, the doing away with the subtleties of a double standard of morality for men and women—Liyi was in the midst of all these changes. Being among them, he was not fully aware of the cultures he was straddling, of the props that were being pulled from under him.

He smiled now in the sunlight. K-rations were floating down from a pragmatic sky, generous gifts from America. So much of his thinking and his world was a gift from America. He remembered, too, learning how to eat with a fork and a knife a month before he left Peiping for the University of Missouri. The American professors had arranged to serve one course in each of their homes. The Chinese students, warned that they must speak English only, had soup ("we drink it silently in America") at the residence of Dr. McGuire, the main course in the home of Dr. and Mrs. Daniels, salad at Mr. Whitehead's, and dessert and coffee at the Dean's place.

The best most of them could say for American cooking was that it was "interesting"; Liyi remembered thinking it was "basic"—he could imagine getting hairy and robust on it. Chinese food left one somewhat delicate, one's skin translucent.

"I've come a long way from my alarm over those white eyebrows," he thought, but the core of him was still open to wonder. He left the window sill and sat passive in his favorite armchair.

Why listen to Peiyuan indeed; why let the boy's words set up these fears in him? He was Bruno's manager; he was on the side of management; he would not have to engage in the rough-and-tumble of any strike that might come up. So he comforted himself uneasily, and it did not occur to him that he wanted to withdraw from life, to get into the bed of his childhood and pull the covers tightly over his head.

"They're not afraid," Helen would say, pointing at some of his schoolmates, "why must you be!" and he had felt her admiration for them. She would have liked to have been over-powered by some of those men, put in her place, dominated and reprimanded. Instead, she had married Liyi, whom she over-powered and empowered. The others were aggressive, dynamic Chinese, moguls and would-be tycoons in industry, mining, advertising, real estate and publishing. They had returned from studying abroad, and had been inoculated with Western drive and pragmatism, vaccinated against their Chinese *laissez-faire*. They were men of accomplishment and fourflushers, exuberant and ruthless. One of them wanted to be both an empire-builder and a Casanova. Helen had been impressed because he had copies of *Esquire* magazine in his bachelor apartment. Such was the extent of his worldliness. His wife and children wore diamonds to breakfast, but lived in another city, out of his way. Like J. P. Morgan, these men, Liyi's classmates, were known by their initials, D. K., M. Y., K. L., T. F. They took the raw material of their own lives and the lives about them, and were able to fashion it to their own ends: factories, mining camps, billboards, city developments, news agencies and journals.

"Helen," Liyi called softly. He wanted to evoke a simple world: a world in which men and women were plain, labeled categories, and a father-emperor ruled with benevolent tyranny. A world in which a cow moved in the fields, and one drank tea to the sunset, one stirred the sky in a bowl and swallowed all of nature. I in nature, and nature in me. All the rest was a hideous delusion. Only the child in one was real. He looked up and felt small; the furniture of this Shanghai apartment, the home of his adulthood, dwarfed him.

"Yes, dear," Helen said, coming into the living room, her face lovely and passionless, as after an uplifting emotion. He knew she felt hymnal; the gates of tension were swinging loosely on their hinges. She had been uplifted, and drifted with the nylon parachutes. "I just saw a jeep swinging down," she exclaimed, "the first one to enter Shanghai!"

"A jeep?" he asked, his accent particularly Chinese with the new word. "What is a jeep?" A small seed of enmity germinated in him.

"There was an item in the paper about it. There'll be more coming in from Chungking. But they expected the first one today. Oh, Liyi, let's go back to the States! Let's go just as soon as we can."

His eyes closed in the sunlight. He felt like a tourist who had seen too many different sights; his senses had absorbed to their full capacity. He could look no more.

"Are you getting old or something?" she asked, laughing. "Dozing in the sun like someone senile!" This time courage did not blow in the gap her breach of delicacy made.

This time he merely said, "Leave me, leave me alone, please. Why can't you leave me alone?"

"What's wrong?" she retorted. "I can't understand you these days," and walked out of the room.

He kept his eyes closed. Under his lids large circles of red opened out in ever-enlarging circumferences. He clenched the sides of the chair tightly, feeling that at any moment centrifugal action might rob him of everything he had accrued for himself over the last forty-nine years. Parts of himself seemed to peel off and fly away into a void. He wanted to speak, to cry, to scream. But the house was bathed in warmth and total indifference. He held onto the chair desperately and saw himself very small, being helped into bed, a Chinese bed, by his mother in Sunkiang. His own family suddenly seemed hideously alien, nightmarishly foreign. I must go back, he thought, I must go back. Everything else seemed artificial, corrupt; everything else seemed contrived to remove him farther and farther from himself.

CHAPTER SIXTEEN

No one can do this to me! No one can do this to me! Mimi had cried. She felt she was sinking into illness. Some tyranny had kept her from crossing the street and touching his car. She had felt that just to see him walk out the gate and bend down, fitting his body into the front seat, would be enough. Come out; oh, come out, come out! Oh, come out now, come out, Robert, while I'm here to see you. Come walk into the street, just once into the street, before my feet take me away. Just to see him would be enough. It would help her come together again, keep the suppurating wound, which was her chest, from draining away her strength.

"I love you, I love you, I love you," she had said over and over again on the phone, blaming herself for his negation. She had thought that her loving him would help him, would bequeath him the ability to give the way she had always wanted him to. To give wholly, not self-consciously (the ego applauding its own performance), but singly and simply. Not to "have" love, but to "be" love. To be the very act of loving: selfless, abandoned, never absent, always growing.

In the last four days (it was almost two weeks since the party at Buenos Aires Wong's), he had refused to come to the phone. And somehow in the dusk of her agony, she had had the strength not to force her way into his house. The sun and the trees had made a dappled light, spotting the street with a circular, floating pattern. Across the street had been Robert's car, parked close to the sidewalk, slanting a little into the gutter on one side. And behind that was his gate, brick columns blending into the walls on either side. Mimi had walked by slowly: "For it is hot," she told herself. Everyone walked slowly in the heat—it was only common sense. And why shouldn't she walk on this particular street if she wanted to. Her own belligerence had been a relief, steadying her. She looked across the street—just a matter of a few feet, but it was a few feet nothing could make her cross. She had felt she would not be seen, if she remained on this side. In three days she had "accidentally" found herself strolling on Rue Delastre eight times.

She had hardly been able to breathe. She had envied everyone who was not in love, who was not in sickness but in health. She envied the beggar, whose dark form scurried across the sidewalk like a crab, deformed, but not ill. If only she had been able to allow herself to touch Robert's car, her life might have swung back into focus. She would not have asked for anything more until today, when Robert arrived to "talk things over" with Aunt Juliet. But that final brake of pride had held her back: she had sensed that if she lifted even that, there would be no return to safety.

She now sat in the living room, having made herself migrate to another area of her consciousness—a part that might better survive what was ahead of them. She felt stripped, made naked, on display.

She sat in a chair, watching Aunt Juliet extend her hand, exclaiming, "Ah, I didn't hear you come in!" as Robert hesitated at the entrance to the living room. Mimi looked up, but his eyes did not meet hers, and she found herself gazing at his mouth.

"How could you, Robert," she wanted to say. "How could you!" How could he deny her like this. "How *can* you, Robert?" she also wanted to ask—how can he still look the same. His flesh was an extension of hers—she wanted to put out her hand to touch him—as she had wanted to touch his car the last few days, to touch him and put her in contact with herself again.

She had been right to stay at home, though "I don't want you in the house," Aunt Juliet had said earlier that day. "You will please absent yourself. It'll do more harm than good having you around. My dear niece, be *gentille,* and spend the afternoon with Sylvia or someone. My dear child, do listen to common sense and spend the afternoon amusing yourself elsewhere.

"You do trust me, Mimi? You must trust me. I will do everything in my power, I promise you. I am your *yi-ma,* after all. Your one and only." But Mimi had stayed stubbornly, determined, prepared for the final mortification. Only that could convey her necessity.

Her *yi-ma* had scolded her sporadically for days now: it was as though they were separated by glass. Mimi knew she was on the inside, deep in the aquarium, locked. *Yi-ma* lived in thinner air, but *Yi-ma* did help her. She had definite margins to her emotions, straight lines which she never overstepped; and her precise admonitions were like invisible surveyor marks keeping Mimi out of quagmires.

"My dear, it's all a matter of patterns, patterns by which we live. You—you are so middle-class—so charmingly conventional, but conventional. So modest (except in the name of love), so sentimental. You are pure Lambert," and Mimi heard Aunt Juliet suppressing a sigh for her sake. "We Hongs . . ." But for her sake again, Aunt Juliet had desisted from making what would be a comparison favorable to her Chinese aspect.

"You lack clarity, a liberated clarity. It comes of drinking milk." And *Yi-ma* shivered with repulsion. No proper Chinese could stand milk or cheese. But Mimi thought—and she had discovered that she loathed her aunt—Juliet Hong was hardly "proper Chinese." She was full of clarity, mirth and improprieties. And because Aunt Juliet so enjoyed her own fall from grace, Mimi knew she must even be past decadence.

"Only puritans experience tragedy," Aunt Juliet let drop another time. "They can't accept their own weakness, their own humanness. They are always overcome by fatal accidents," and Aunt Juliet had stolen a surreptitious glance at Mimi's stomach. Mimi's fist had clenched, and she had had to use all her strength to keep from doubling up. "I can't, I can't, I can't . . ." she had muttered within herself, but what it was she "couldn't" she did not know. She felt debilitated, disordered, and could hardly finish a thought or sentence.

Now Aunt Juliet was looking at Robert just as she looked at everyone—appraisingly, mercilessly, her matter-of-factness a kind of sadism. Mimi could almost hear her comment later, "Yes, he was meticulously dressed, his tie correct, his attitude one of understated concern. His handshake? Well—too warm for the occasion." Mimi knew that Aunt Juliet had only extended her hand, and let him do what he would with it. *Yi-ma* would not return the pressure. She had a talent for demanding that others go more than halfway. She played on their sense of inadequacy.

Aunt Juliet chattered on. "Shall we have tea, in the Chinese manner?" and shook the cloisonné bell on the coffee table. "Our secondary characteristics are still native. Our primary ones? Who knows?" She leaned back against the cushions of the couch, while Robert sat in a straight tapestried chair.

"You are most punctual," and she glanced at the clock. "I suppose that is Swiss; certainly it is not Chinese or French. About other peoples I can't say," and began to pour the tea that the *amah* had brought in. She leaned forward, uncrossing her legs. Mimi watched her unblinkingly, feeling herself grow ugly with fascination. It was as though she could cause *Yi-ma's* extinction just by staring at her with a pure purple hatred. She felt herself sick, hideous, malevolent. She looked at Robert, who avoided her eyes, but all her passion was directed against *Yi-ma*; she wanted to be cruel, despicable. To destroy.

"Mr. Bruno," Aunt Juliet was now saying, "you know why I asked you to come. It wasn't to speak of the weather, or how to celebrate V-J Day, or to discuss the five-tone musical scale. It was—" She laughed lightly (incredible! Mimi thought) and

170

continued, "To get to the matter at hand, what are your intentions toward my niece?"

Robert glanced up, bided his time, looked at Mimi as though to encompass her forever, and then said, "I cannot marry her." He looked at her again and said, "I cannot."

Mimi had never seen him so at one with himself, so ingenuous, so peaceful, so courageous.

"I don't understand," Aunt Juliet exclaimed, amused. "You cannot, or you will not."

"I cannot."

"If you cannot marry her, if it is an impossibility, why did you, why did you make her—make her *enceinte*?" Again Aunt Juliet laughed delicately. "What is she to do, have the child, unmarried?"

"Oh, no!" He almost leaped out of his chair, shaking his head in an agony. "No, no! She must not have the child! That's what I've told her over and over again!"

He seemed to remember that Mimi was there. "You mustn't! You're mad to think of having it! I can arrange—you know—the very best of care . . ." His voice sounded shrill and tedious to her, for she had heard everything he had to say two weeks ago; she had heard his voice splinter into a kind of hysteria, desperate because she would not listen to reason.

"She wants to have the child to prove how much she loves you. She wants your child." *Yi-ma* turned her head away to smile a little. Mimi thought that the Chinese could always smile at another's agony, could always deride what was not sensible.

"I don't know what else there is that I can say!" Robert cried. "Do you see what I mean!" He extended a hand to Aunt Juliet.

"You cannot marry her, but you love her. She loves you, so she insists on having the child. Everything would be fine if only we could solve one of two points. The first—if only you *could* marry her, everything would be all right. Second—if only she could be persuaded not to have the baby." Aunt Juliet sighed. It was a relief from her loquaciousness.

"Supposing," she continued, "supposing she did not have the child. What—"

"Why, we could go on forever!" he exclaimed, begging Mimi with his eyes. "You know we could!"

"But you must answer one question," Aunt Juliet put in. "You cannot marry her, but it's not because of someone else. Then, why? There is no insanity in the Bruno family, is there?" and she tinkled over her own joke.

"There is someone else," he said flatly and circumspectly. "There always has been."

Mimi felt herself harden; the mask of her own evil intent— she wished her Aunt Juliet would shrivel before her eyes— filled the room. She felt that she herself was growing into a nightmare, that her bulk of ugliness was reaching dangerous proportions.

Aunt Juliet controlled a snicker, and stared at Robert archly, sizing him up in the light of this additional information.

"There *is* someone else. Ah, perhaps this will effect a 'cure,' " and she made a slight motion with her head, indicating Mimi. It was as though, Mimi thought, she were in collusion with Robert against her own niece.

"No, no!" Robert said in alarm, turning to Mimi. "No, no! It's my father. It's my father. He has—he has other plans for me. You see," and his sigh seemed to come from all of his thirty-four years, "my father has always been 'the other person' in the picture." He looked down at his foot again, shaking it. "You see," he added lamely, as if despairing of conveying what only he knew, "you just don't know what he's like. He isn't like anybody else."

Aunt Juliet stood up; her disdain was implacable. Mimi feared it like a physical blow. She began to pace up and down before them, letting them see the profile of her figure, as she turned left, then right. Her contempt for him included Mimi, her niece who loved this—this— Nothing but disdain, Mimi thought, could make some Chinese passionate.

"Love!" Aunt Juliet began. "So much nonsense goes under

the name of *amour*. It's nothing except a mutual hypnotism, a temporary illness or delusion. Most people in love make the loved one the victim of their own dissatisfaction with themselves. That is called love!" She seemed rhapsodic, inspired, turning and twisting her figure before them.

"Most people in love are just grinding their own axes, trying to rid themselves of themselves, to acquire a new self. That's why I think the whole business is uncivilized. Don't you agree with me, Mr. Bruno?" But she did not need encouragement. "It all comes down to the interplay between *yin* and *yang*. You know what I am referring to, don't you?"

Of course he knows! Mimi wanted to shout with malignancy. He knows more Chinese philosophy than you or I or three other people put together. *Yang* and *Yin* represented the opposite forces in nature: male, female; day, night; light, dark; love, hate; self, selflessness.

"Mimi needs you because she has no father, and you are father, lover and husband to her; you need her because you have the kind of father you have, but you cannot help her make the family she wants because you already belong to a too-strong family. She made you feel safe, originally, but in the end she exposes you to your own greatest—greatest weakness."

Mimi gripped her knees; so much loathing would surely destroy her. She began to be afraid of her own power to abominate. It seemed to have begun to sweep her past the shallows of safety.

"You found a girl, and loved her for her freshness, but you have brought out the tenacious woman in her, and will leave her not quite a girl any more. She is bourgeois, quite narrow. You, on the other hand, are free from prejudice, yet . . ." and she hesitated.

Aunt Juliet looked straight at each of them. Mimi could see she would not withhold what was coming. *Yi-ma* was like a child, finding it impossible to keep her own cleverness a secret any longer.

173

"And yet you cannot marry her because—because your father will not," and she spaced out the words slowly and raised her voice, "your father will not countenance your marrying a Eurasian!"

Robert stood up, his neck taut, his eyes wincing. Mimi screamed once. She put out her hand accusingly. She put it out as though it were a sword on fire.

"Can you deny it!" Aunt Juliet challenged. "Nothing will change the fact of her Eurasianness!"

"You!" Mimi screamed, staring at them both, but she was pointing at *Yi-ma*. "You—ou!"

Blind, enraged, poisoned by her own self, she moved. She felt herself staggering, as though her shoes adhered to the floor. Awkward, she hated her own clumsiness now, now! when she wanted to excel, to glory, to outlive their smallness. She lunged toward Aunt Juliet—she wanted to hit her, strike her down. Startled, she found she had thrown herself at Robert. She clawed at his clothes. Vindictive—she clawed at him, clung to him as though a shred of his clothing were her ultimate desire.

"I won't let you go!" she cried. "I won't let you go!"

She had seen lichen cling to a rock. Their small caps of suction were tenacious beyond belief. She began to laugh. She hung on him, wrapping her arms about his neck, locking her hands behind. Laughing uncontrollably, she threw all her weight on him, and screamed and struggled. Behind her Aunt Juliet was tugging and saying more. But her voice was no longer mincing. From deep inside her, Mimi felt something warm as joy begin to sear her. She was glad, glad, glad. She exulted that she had defaced their day! She shook with an agony of love and hate. Robert's face suddenly began to deteriorate into horror. She was choked by all she wanted to inflict on him; she felt that she had begun to slip into space and danger. Her last scream sounded smothered to her as she fell into blackness.

174

CHAPTER SEVENTEEN

They began the evening with Feng asking Sylvia some questions.

"Do you love me or not?" secretly amusing her with his greed. She merely kissed him on his neck.

"Then why don't you say so, girl?"

"I've other things on my mind."

He sat on a low stool, and stared at her, piqued and attentive.

"What do you plan to do, now that the war is over?"

"I really don't know," Sylvia answered, surprise in her voice. "When there was no possibility of doing anything, I seemed to know perfectly what I wanted to do. But now I guess I just don't know."

"Would you like to include me in your life?"

She looked up, perplexed.

"Marry me," Feng said. "How about it?" brusquely.

"Marry you?" she said weakly. "Marry you?" and threw her arms around him so she would not have to give an answer yet.

"My wife! I'd take care of you. We understand each other. We're the same, don't you see!"

To embrace him, she knelt beside the stool, and now he held her face in his hands, a demanding vise.

"Don't talk," she said. "Just let's be."

"I be; you be; he, she, it be," he conjugated playfully. "Present, future and imperative." Then he shifted gears and she missed him, lost him between his moods.

"Why didn't you tell me Peiyuan was working at the plant? He's been there almost three weeks, and I didn't know till he told me the other day!"

"Tell you?" she asked, totally surprised. "Why it never occurred to me you'd be interested."

"I don't know what does occur to you."

"You don't!" she wanted to retort, hating the familiar feeling of deficiency which he could inflict on her. Involuntarily, she wanted to apologize, except there was nothing to seek pardon for. Involuntarily, she felt in the wrong and hurt, too. She therefore thought of toughness and imperviousness as an ideal, something she could never reach. But she could keep trying. Then Feng changed again.

"You will marry me, now, won't you?"

"And if I don't?"

"There'll be a sit-down strike right here in this house. I won't let you go home. It's really very simple."

She examined her prison. It was Feng's two rooms, white and efficient, and at night it glowed with a clear light, like pale tea. It was no longer his, but theirs; the bed seemed a vast place. She felt nothing could rob her of the actuality of these days here. The future was no longer an anxiety, the present no longer something that passed through one like air, nor the past a dream.

"Really," Feng said again, "you might have mentioned Peiyuan's working at Bruno's plant," and Sylvia unaccountably laughed. She was amused by nothing more than the fact that Feng was Feng, and he was mysteriously preoccupied with the subject of her cousin.

He kept on talking, seeming displeased with himself. But she was too happy still really to notice. Shall I tell him, she thought, how the boy got the job? It seemed years since the day she had run to Feng's house, years since she had returned home that other night to find her mother asking, truly concerned, "And where did you go so abruptly?" Her father's face had drained her, leaving her empty.

176

"You'll be happy to know," Liyi had pronounced, "that it's all been settled for the best. Peiyuan is leaving us—he'll see the wisdom of it in due time. He is a reasonable young man, like all us Chens." Her father's defense was so deep that he had actually relaxed a little while speaking, his own rationalization comforting him so.

"I'm certain this idea of his—this childish idea of coming to Shanghai—did not meet with his mother's approval. As eldest son, he certainly should remain close to home, the ancestral home, and look after things from there." Sylvia had not interrupted him to point out that as eldest son, Liyi had not remained close to home. He had cleaved unto his foreign wife. Not only her father, but so many Chinese had this double focus, and your argument could get lost between the changing of their lenses.

But Feng was saying now, addressing, she felt, an invisible crowd, "Speaking of sit-down strikes, we can expect a rash of them soon in craft shops and industrial plants. The workers are going to demand their rights, too long ignored. Chinese workers have to start taking their place among other workers in a modern industrial world."

Again unaccountably, she kissed him, for he was so solemn. "Do you think I'm crazy?" she asked, smiling into his face.

"Workers here have got to create a new tradition, new formulas," he pursued.

She forced her face into seriousness. "Isn't it true, though, that some workers refuse to break with the past?"

"Whatever gave you that idea?"

"I've been hearing things," she said, waving her hand.

"I don't know where you got that idea," Feng said, sitting up suddenly and transferring himself to a chair. He sat astride it and leaned forward against its back.

Since he was so tenacious, she would satisfy him. She told him plainly that her father thought there would be trouble soon at the plant, for he felt that Bruno Senior would not be able to meet the demands—traditional ones—that the workers would try to exact.

"You know a little, but not enough," Feng declared. "It's too bad." He stood up and stared out the window, turning his back on her.

"Do you love me?" she asked for the first time. But he did not hear.

"Peiyuan has taught me a great deal," she submitted in an effort to please him.

"Peiyuan, speaking of Peiyuan," but the name seemed only to distress him. He stopped speaking to turn and stare at her, as if appraising her before he spoke again. She returned his gaze, hoping she would pass his test, be admitted into his confidence. What he had to confide, if anything, she knew nothing of.

Her father, the other night, had returned *her* gaze—she had had him under her scrutiny. She had said to him, "Actually, I'm not thinking so much of Peiyuan as I am of Paul. I really think you should" and she repeated it bravely, while her father listened with a kind of filialness, "I really think you should ask Peiyuan to stay for Paul's sake. Paul needs a Chinese cousin to remind him he is half Chinese. And maybe I do, too."

Liyi's face had moved into an expression of delicate alarm, for, after all, there was Helen to consider and himself, who needed Helen so much, and there was no pursuing a middle ground with her.

"Dad," she had said later, "Dad, Peiyuan is your brother's son." Liyi had turned away, as close to rudeness as he had ever come. But she had won: he found a solution for the boy. For his nephew he made a small compromise. He had given him the job, so that Peiyuan could stay on in Shanghai. He had found him a room downtown. Helen had been satisfied, too.

"Well," Sylvia said to Feng, "to get back to my cousin who seems to be a great deal on both our minds," and Feng's eyes seemed to dilate, "he told me about Chinese workers who are already asserting themselves in your modern industrial world.

In Free China there are hundreds, if not thousands, of industrial cooperatives. The Nationalists have been quite successful there."

"Peiyuan ought to know better—and you too. Those industrial co-ops were organized by Rewi Alley, a New Zealander who should keep his hands out of China."

"What does it matter who helps the Chinese set up these things?"

"It matters a lot," Feng said. "Everyone wants us to make ourselves over in their image."

It was quite true, Sylvia thought, and she thought especially of American missionaries, missionaries who thought themselves so rich in God, and looked so poverty-stricken in their senses. Their blood seemed an essence distilled from musty prayer books and the wax used on pews. Their kind of chapped cheerfulness was impersonal, all intimacy censured out. They were the inheritors of the kingdom of God, yet their legacy on earth seemed an atmosphere of scarcity. But they had also brought modern medical practice and modern educational methods to China. There was no denying that.

"Well," she said, putting her hand through an imaginary cowlick, a habit she had picked up from Peiyuan, "these co-ops are self-managing workshops and small factories. They are a truly democratic organization, organized by the workers themselves. My father told me."

"Your father?"

"No, Peiyuan's. I was quoting him. My uncle Litan, who died in Chungking."

"He's impossibly naïve."

"Technology, not politics, is what will help here most."

"Technology, democracy, peace, you love general terms, clichés, platitudes, meaningless abstractions. You sound as if you are selling a dish of Western tea. Well, if you are, let's get down to brass tacks, to uncomfortable things like imperialism and white chauvinism. What about them?"

His face, against his will, was contorted, but Sylvia was too afraid of alienating him further to realize that Feng was not aware how much rage showed in his eyes.

"I think we Orientals are schizophrenic," she supplied meekly.

"Whatever that means! Isn't it just typical of you to hide behind a psychological phrase."

She found herself shaking a little. How she wished she could argue swiftly and easily, objectively, as if someone else, someone sure and pat, were speaking through her.

"Maybe the ascendancy of the West is over—at least, the abuses of that ascendancy. Maybe, Feng."

"We'll see that it's over!"

"But while we hate their material and technological arrogance, we want their material and technological benefits, don't we? I'm only trying to be fair," she protested, knowing it only stranded her from the comfort of a point of view. "And—and as for human rights, well, we Chinese have taken life pretty cheaply through the centuries, haven't we? Oh, not that we want to continue to do so. I don't mean that. Please let me talk. I only mean that right has not always been on the side of the East. What about the horrors of the caste system in India, what about the arrogance and chauvinism of the 'chosen' people of our Middle Kingdom, what about the imperialism of the Japanese? And what about the past history of Chinese and Indian colonization? I mean you have to think of these things, too, Feng."

"I believe you'd excuse your own murderer. That's the surest way to become a victim."

"Oh, please, Feng, what is it you'd have me think? I don't quite understand."

"Just don't settle for what other people think we are. Do you know what Chinese communism is?"

"The Communist party, the Kunchantang?"

"Chinese communism," he seemed to hiss. "The Chinese Communists are Chinese first, remember that. First they are

180

Chinese, then they are Communists. You can't underestimate their real, authentic nationalism."

"That's not what I've heard," she said.

"You've got to be re-educated. And I'm going to do it."

"Feng darling," she said, "you might ask me if I want to be—to be re-educated first." She laughed. "The right to revolution is part of the Chinese tradition, too. When the emperor ceased to rule by precepts of virtue, the people could revolt. This is one difference between the Chinese and the Japanese. I do know something, darling."

"Don't you darling me!" Something in him seemed to be unleashed. "You women with your darlings and dears, your soft cajoling voices and words. I won't have it, you hear!" he shouted, quite beside himself. "I know what I'm saying and doing! I know I'm right. What makes you think you know anything about it? Why, you aren't even interested. You— you presume to tell me what Peiyuan's opinions are. Why, you might just as well be lying. How do you know what he thinks? He told *me* what he thinks! You don't even have a frame of reference. And stop looking so benign!"

"I'm not benign!" But with a woman's instinct for living a lifetime in the plunge of a single emotion, she felt alone again under a large sky.

"You mumble stuff about revolutions, but you don't feel them here—here!" and he pointed fiercely at his diaphragm. "What do you know about China and her stifling traditions? What do you know about any of this? I ask you, Sylvia!"

"Very little," she admitted. What did she know about China —and she was Chinese. "You're right," she said, glad he had pronounced her name.

"You think so?" In the sudden pause, he put out his hand, but she did not take it.

"Come here."

She did not move. Uneasily, she pushed back the thought: why did she love Feng?

He sat down on the couch and pulled her toward him.

"Come here and stop being bitchy."

Why did she love him? For she sometimes allowed herself to realize she could not justify her love even to herself. But even the violation of her feelings seemed like a blessing. Some people, after all, could not even be healthily infuriated—their emotions were never purged, but swarmed in them like a pestilence.

Then she thought she knew why—partly. "You're right, you're right, you're right," she wanted to repeat in her mind like an incantation. "Feng, Feng, Feng." She wanted him to be "right," and to inflict upon her his aggressiveness. She knew why. For she felt her father's gentleness was his deepest armor; it had kept her and Paul from the simplest truths. He made the truth seem brutal. His sensitivity and inclination to withdraw had constrained them. As a result, she thought of herself as overprotected, a hot-house plant, a daughter of safety and know-nothingism. Feng's very unmannerliness seemed only courageous and disinterested. He could plunge her into the market place of life. He seemed pure and strong and completely free from ambivalence. She was a little afraid of where their relationship might lead her, and thought her fears were cowardice, her own desire to withdraw. She wanted adventures into experience, into more consciousness. Through Feng she would not accrue comfort but knowledge.

"Come over here!" he commanded.

"I don't want to," she answered slowly, and tried to maintain the dignity of her original position. She moved away, sitting bolt upright.

"Who asked you what you wanted?" he asked. She struggled with him until angry tears came. But she could hardly breathe and quickly, roughly, he was beginning to undress her.

She pushed his face away and began to ask why, why it had to be this way—always "force," always "force" in his world.

"I love you, you fool," he said, and embraced her so decisively she could do nothing but go along with him.

"Marry me, you pretty fool," he demanded later. "You. You."

She buried her face in the pillow, then raised her head to look at him, and found herself sighing.

182

He ran his hand lightly over the length of her arm, over the soft and angular curve of her waist and hip as she lay on her side.

"You are beautiful!" he exclaimed. Suddenly he was tender, pensive, articulate. "Your body is so delicate and tensile, sensual and informed. You are entirely beautiful."

Sylvia forgot her doubts; she felt only like a photographic plate which was less than nothing unless exposed to light. And Feng's love was her illumination.

CHAPTER EIGHTEEN

"This son of mine is amazing!" Peiyuan imagined his late father saying of him. "He knows so much about everything."

He couldn't visualize the circumstances in which his father might have pronounced the judgment on him. But his voice came from a corner of the room, as from a hidden loudspeaker. His father had been rather elegant, unlike himself who took after his plain mother, and even unlike Uncle Liyi. His father had been both more conventional and more selfish.

He's gone, he thought: died in Chungking, in one of the bombing raids. He had not seen him in more than six years—Peiyuan had been under ten when his father left for the interior, never to return. He had left the family, cloaking his selfishness in heroism, in an act of patriotism. Peiyuan knew how his mother had tried to persuade him to return—always in the name of the children—and how his father had always answered the same way. "I have a job of work to do here. When I can, I shall send for you." But he had never kept his promise. His mother must have thought even his dying had been egocentric.

It was as though a record were playing in his head, something he could not turn off. Peiyuan had never felt surer of himself. He was certain he had reached a plateau of self-confidence, based on a fusion of knowledge and action. One can live on so many levels at once, he thought. Take today, for instance. He had never felt more alive. Nor more empty. He had also never felt more self-congratulatory. His arguments with himself were reaching a crescendo of self-exhortation, yet, he had also felt dangerous with doubt. He missed his father, whom he had barely known. He found himself admiring him for breaking away from the family and participating in the struggle in Chungking. He found more to love in his father's cruelty than in Uncle Liyi's kindness. And thinking that, he knew that he must find perfection in himself. He could find it nowhere else, in no one else. One was, after all, entirely alone.

He leaned out of his narrow window into the heat that pressed thickly about the semi-tenement of his home—a furnished room just a block and a half from the Bund. Uncle Liyi had found him this neat but tiny room. He had been almost as excited about it as Peiyuan was—it had been part of his own dance of justification. After all he had said against nepotism, petty or otherwise, Uncle Liyi had truly made a compromise by giving him the job at the plant. Even if a principle were not involved, Uncle Liyi had given him the right job for a poor reason. He had placated his wife and helped his nephew in one stroke, but . . . and Peiyuan made himself stop considering it. He was exultant about working. Wasn't that enough? Peiyuan was grateful; he knew that he was truly fortunate.

He felt that he had reached adulthood like a shore. There was no more growing to be done, no more to be "gone through." All improvising was over. From here on in, the game of life would be played with the utterly singular, but easily mastered, rules of grown-upness. "There's nothing to it!" he wanted to sing out like a refrain. He knew it all; what there was left to acquire was merely virtuosity.

All day long he had milled about the streets. Shanghai had exploded with bursts of sound. It was September second, V-J Day. The tugboats on the Whangpoo let out piercing calls, too raucous to be even faintly mournful. Bands had passed through the streets and parades appeared like mirages only to melt again into the crowds. Flags decorated every building and the front balconies of homes. I am nothing: just a listening ear! He had been proudly self-abnegating in order to get the feel of the victory. He had also participated lustily, screaming at the top of his lungs at the officials, soldiers and others who paraded at times militantly, but mostly haphazardly and always jubilantly. Now it was all over. He was trying to catch a breath of fresh air. And he felt dejected.

It did not occur to him that he was despondent because he was lonely. He sought his window not only because it might afford him a breeze, but also because the flickering of the neon sign was company of sorts. It blinked on and off, and the arm of the sign that extended under his sill let out little sizzling sounds that were almost like speech. He was tempted to look down at the brilliant, delicately spitting tube and make faces at it. He tried once, and losing self-consciousness, carried on a terse conversation, spraying the tube with saliva. He didn't laugh. He felt he was discovering the ultimate in resourceful, adult behavior. Felicity, he thought. All of life was felicity. His despondency evaporated as the record in his head began to play again.

"Now, you see," he said, and he could not be certain whether he addressed Uncle Liyi, Paul—his alter ego—or his late father, "the war certainly set things back. Yet, even under the puppet regime, certain advances were made. That is not to say . . . well, as a matter of fact—" and his face assumed a clownish blandness, as attractive clichés distracted him from his didacticism and stopped him altogether.

"Look here," he went on, as though he were being challenged, "the labor movement has always been linked to political motives. Unfortunate but true! If the Nanking puppet government strengthened it, it was only to help incite anti-foreign feeling. We know this, but it is salubrious to review even the immediate past. And, if I may impress you with facts, we know that the All-China Labor Federation, established in 1927, was an affiliate of the Red Trade Union Federation.

"In all fairness, it must be stated that the Kuomintang's unions, if the truth must be known, are not much more than a kind of *yamen*, a government department—you might say—
186

which doesn't really look after the interests of the rank and file workers.

"But—" For he suddenly remembered his enthusiastic endorsement of the industrial co-ops, information that had impressed Sylvia. There were "buts" to every issue in China. That was the price one paid for being liberal. His father had been aware of the dilemmas the country faced. He had said, "Let's be fair, but not lax; and let us not confuse broad-mindedness with an overflexible conscience."

Peiyuan sighed, thinking of going to bed. He would have to work tomorrow. He leaned out of the window for a last look at Shanghai at the end of V-J Day; he leaned out far to look at the word in the sign he had been arguing with. Upside down, the word was just an entrail of illumination. He leaned and peered. It said simply, "Kuan," the last word in a restaurant's name. Across the street a figure moved; it seemed part of the landscape of something he had recently read. But the man had a distinctive air, neither Chinese nor totally foreign, though he walked with an assertive stride. Then he knew who it was. He did not have to see his face. It was Feng Huang, turning the corner of Avenue Edward the Seventh.

He knew immediately Feng was going toward the printing plant. The bend led to the deserted street of warehouses, it led nowhere else, and for a moment he did not think it strange that Feng Huang should be down in this part of town. But it was midnight, and Peiyuan fell back into his room and almost squealed with joy—the joy of awakened curiosity. That was interesting! This was peculiar in the nth degree! This had to be looked into! All his earlier fatigue left him—it had never been. He seized his shirt, putting it on in the hallway, and skidded down the narrow stairs. All at once, Feng seemed the image of perfection that he sought in himself.

The street was dark. He leaped across it, turning the corner, mimicking Feng's stride. He ran swiftly, hugging the walls. He could see Feng entering the side door; a small crack of light appeared in the alleyway and then quickly disappeared. Peiyuan clucked his tongue in irritation. The door would be closed on him. He had wanted to reach Feng before he entered the building. He felt along the dark wall and found the door. That moment he heard the click of the light being snapped off inside. His curiosity stiffened. It dawned on him that there were others inside, for Feng had entered a lighted corridor.

He hesitated, thinking. The darkness thickened about him like fur. He moved, keeping one arm extended before him, and rounded the building. The sky dipped low here, where one of the improvised shelters that surrounded the building of the plant had lost its roofing. Getting a foothold on a window, he easily pulled himself up onto the straw matting that kept the rain from penetrating. With a light thud he jumped into the inner court and pushed his way through an unused iron folding gate.

How strange things were at night! He passed through the stock rooms, the accounting department, and it was as though the place had slept for years. Yet, just a few hours ago and in a few more, the mere presence of people would put the deserted rooms into focus, would make an unearthly stage set turn again into a scene of life. The boards creaked under him as he bumped into counters and swivel chairs. Insensitive to everything except the sounds his own feet were making, he pushed open the swinging door that led into the long, low press room. He ducked as he passed through the door, for the shifting spot from a flashlight almost caught him. Trembling with surprise and anticipation, he crouched behind a heap of unused machinery and listened.

"I could swear I heard something," a voice whispered.

"The place creaks at night. And there are rats besides."

The voice of authority continued in tones that were conciliatory and adamant at the same time, "Then, are we all prepared? So now it's just a matter of waiting."

No one answered, for the question had been slipped in like a hackneyed order.

"Are we still listening for rats, or shall we go on? I think we should review our actions for each other and then disband for the night."

It was an unctuous, almost tender voice, used deliberately and through the teeth. Peiyuan strained to place it. The men were sitting absolutely still in a small circle of light, gathered about the main linotyping machine. There was the smell of fresh ink and damp paper.

"As soon as Lao Yuan has handed the petition to Bruno, we stand ready for our orders. I as *kung t'ou*—" so it was Tang, the foreman, speaking, Peiyuan thought—"will order a cessation of work. There will be a complete strike throughout the shop, led by you people. Anyone who resists will be dealt with, but there is no fear of that. Bruno will see we mean business; but more important, the workers will realize our strength, and whether or not we get all their demands, they will be persuaded to join the union."

"Within the next week, then?"

"Probably."

"But Chen Liyi . . ." and Peiyuan raised his head slowly. It was Feng speaking. "Chen Liyi is away. He won't be back for ten days."

"Why do you suppose we chose this time, this particular time. Not, of course, that he could hinder us." The conciliatory voice had turned impatient. "And you," he said, "your job is to keep alert to any moves you may hear about that Bruno plans to make. Don't let anything slip by again. This is just the beginning," he added scornfully. "The workers haven't been activated in more than fifteen years. It's time we got started again."

Peiyuan's mouth hung open, as his heart beat faster. It hung open as though to catch the drift of the conversation, which seemed to escape him. If Tang was something of a union leader, why was the air of conspiracy necessary? And what did Feng, Sylvia's friend, have to do with it all? He didn't work in the plant. Wasn't he a lawyer, with an office somewhere near by?

Outside, a child wailed, and the intonations of a Sikh policeman could be heard. It was so quiet that the sounds had traveled the length of almost two blocks. The men moved around, putting things away, and because they might be passing his way, Peiyuan decided to step toward the wall. He tripped over some rope, drew in his breath and fell back trembling.

"Who's there!" It was Tang's voice, the one he used during working hours, sharp, fretful, verging on disdain.

The man with the flashlight played it over the room. Peiyuan could see it making triangular patterns against the ceiling, the corners, the windows. *If they find me, what'll I do, what'll I say?* He was not panicky, but wanted to prepare himself. Footsteps approached him, joined by others. Suddenly the light was full on his face, blinding him. He smiled, feeling fatuous.

He was pulled out by an unfamiliar hand.

"It's me," he said, unnecessarily, and smiled again.

Tang swung around quickly, facing Feng Huang.

"What do you know about this? It's that Chen kid."

The men, and he recognized them all, stood around, nonplused. But he thought they were almost glad to see him; he provided them with some amusement.

"Why should I know?" Feng answered defensively.

"I was walking by," Peiyuan explained—he did not want to say he had followed Feng in, "and thought I heard voices. I climbed in."

"Sent by your uncle, no doubt," Tang said. Again he turned to Feng. "It was your business to know these things. How many transgressions are we to forgive you! They—the Chens—were your own assignment, your own idea."

"I know nothing about this. Ask him, if you don't believe me."

"Do you take me for a fool?" Tang asked softly, incredulously.

"He's overheard everything. He knows everything," someone supplied. It came from behind Peiyuan and he could not tell whether it was the machinist who had a small goiter on his neck or Lao Yuan: everyone spoke so softly.

Peiyuan said, "But I'm for the labor movement. I don't understand . . ."

Tang cuffed him swiftly across his face, and Peiyuan could have cried with shame.

"It's not for you to understand or not. You're a child, an apprentice, a hanger-on. You'll be sorry if you tell your uncle anything about this. Do you hear?"

Peiyuan muttered through his teeth, boastfully, "My uncle knows about the strike. He expects one."

"Is that why he went to Sunkiang for a holiday?" Tang laughed, but his eyes darted about tensely, as he seemed to wonder what they should do with him. "I'm afraid I shall have to report this to *him*," he said, looking at Feng and smiling intently.

"Before you do that," Feng retaliated evenly, "I suggest that we place the kid under arrest."

Peiyuan looked up, not knowing which he felt more: the quick anger that flooded him, a resentment of Feng, or a feeling of having been wounded, disillusioned. But a veil of general surprise stood between him and the happenings.

"Arrest him—to keep him quiet, or to hide your guilt?" Tang closed his eyes briefly, his jawbone working like a vise. "Put him away, yes."

The men hesitated, apparently thinking he was merely talking to himself. Then he repeated, "Put him away quickly, and we'll decide what to do with him tomorrow."

The three men seized him, while Feng and Tang stood back and watched. Peiyuan struggled, screamed, and one of them muffled his mouth the palm of his large hand. They half carried him through the dark corridors. He lost track of where they were going; he was dizzy from struggling and having his nose blocked by their hands. He must hang onto one thread. Why the conspiracy? He was all for democratic institutions, and labor unions were going to be an important part in the reconstruction of China.

They flung him into a dark pit. There was no window, just

the broken slats of a skylight. It was a room he had never seen in the plant, and he guessed that it must be a kind of storeroom no longer used. As they slammed the door and padlocked it from outside, he remembered that they did not look brutal or angry. They looked amused, and he hated them for it. They would not have looked amused if he were an adult. They would have taken him seriously then. He suddenly thought of Paul, whom he hardly realized he pitied (yet Paul seemed too engaged in a hopeless family situation for anything but pity). And now, unexpectedly, he was even sorrier for his cousin, who by his very state would never find himself in a situation such as this. Peiyuan took this adventure as a strange reward— an unsought-for experience that did him honor.

He did not sit on the floor right away—there were no chairs —but paced up and down and was not at all depressed by the strange night he would have to pass. Feng Huang had him all wrong. And the thought made him feel a little smaller. It was Feng's idea, having him thrown in here. But he knew something about Feng Huang no one else did, not even Sylvia, and the secret made him feel as exhilarated as a child let out of school.

CHAPTER NINETEEN

In the midst of a busy day, Feng became nostalgic for himself. He suffered from a sense of regret, of things left unsaid, as at the departure of a dear one. Of an extra dimension to the air, the way one felt when a train pulled out from a station. A little extra awareness adding a feeling of dissatisfaction to the heart. He found himself unexpectedly remembering the Feng who had been in love, but had been too young to have anyone to love. The thin air had returned his desire as an agony of longing. He had been in his teens—and there had been days when he had given his soul to a passing smile, a pair of female legs, a blur of femininity inhabiting a dress.

He had been reminded of the young Feng by what had happened last night. Had Feng sat down and examined himself, he would have realized that the question and the attendant anxiety were really academic. But he thought, saluting himself with Sylvia's words or her near-words, "You make everything so simple," and he had done just that.

He had seen two clients during the day: one on a matter of divorce—the wife regretting the "mutual consent" advertisement she had published in the paper; the other on a suit against the city by an American who had fallen into one of the many manholes no longer protected by a cover. He had dictated letters to the secretary whom he and his senior partner shared, and had even called Sylvia about seeing her tonight. And now that he was old enough to love specifically, he was both happier and more cynical. He had also coolly confirmed over the phone the fact that Liyi would not be back for another eight or nine days.

He congratulated himself on his control, as he had often done, when his mother shook his emotions or his values. "You are my son: be good to me," she had only to glance at him in order to convey. "Feng, darling," and he could never be certain whether he raised his hand to stroke her or to hit her.

"Are you listening to me, dear?" and he wished to be deaf, dead, beyond any linkage with the human kind. I am *not* hateful, I do *not* hate, he would repeat to himself. But he wanted to say to his mother, to whisper into her ear when she slept, for the unconscious, they said, was most receptive then: *I hate you, I hate you, wrapping yourself around me like fern. I hate you*—and he was as committed as he would have been if he had loved her. *I hate you*, but it was only because he must love, he must love and give himself to *one* reason to live. Except for that faint taste of regret, he had been able to close off love, hate, doubt, anxiety. He had always been able to compartmentalize himself. All day he had gone about his work without any leakages in his valve-tight system.

His self-congratulation was there in direct proportion to the intensity of the anxiety which he thought he was shutting off. Last night he had done a dreadful thing, and even in the soundproof rooms of his mind, he could contemplate—though not feel—that dread. He had said, "Arrest him," and Tang had acted upon it. He had slipped, he knew, into an arrangement with fate. It had been as easy as sliding downhill on snow. He did not believe in "fate." He believed vaguely in "free will"; he believed he could choose his own necessity. He *knew* what he was doing, yet fatefulness leaked in like light under a door.

Oh, Mother, he thought involuntarily, but did not hear himself. He hurried home, walking. He tucked his chin in sharply (he would never have admitted to self-consciousness), as though aware some glory was about to be bestowed on him, aware that he must shrug it off for the sake of not antagonizing the public. He walked with a spring, almost leaping the gutters, seeing

194

everything before him in the quivering quality of five o'clock light.

As he approached the house, his pace slowed. Soon he would have to sit in his room and open the valve on last night. And in direct proportion to his dread of that "facing up to the facts" was a knowledge that in so facing it he was being moral—in fact, righteous. He was being good. The word did not embarrass him. He knew he was right, because when he thought honestly, he seemed to feel the spade of his intellect scraping rock. He would think about Peiyuan and extricate the boy from Tang and the others.

He would not procrastinate. He entered his apartment quickly, taking off his jacket and tie and tossing them on the couch. He went to the refrigerator and poured himself some grape juice left there by the cook upon his mother's instructions. I am all she has in the world, and sentimentality made him relax his neck. He accepted the sentiment, and flung himself onto a chair, only then completely realizing that he had not been dreading this interview with himself at all.

His spirits suddenly soared. He was thinking of Tang, not of Peiyuan, and he wrinkled his brows, as though in wonder. He hadn't realized until just now how bracing the whole incident had been. All his poor efforts at self-justification were now unnecessary because of that one suggestion he had made: "Arrest him." Tang, in doing what he had suggested, seemed to be under obligation to him now. He began to feel that he was no longer afraid of him.

He felt so good now that he no longer was interested in being good. He went to the bathroom to toss some water on his face. He rubbed it briskly, and brushed back his hair. Still holding the grape juice, he went into the lobby and called, "Mother," and when she did not answer, called again.

Audrey had been sleeping, and came to the head of the stairs with her fists in her eyes, as though she would rub them out for being drowsy when her son wanted her awake.

"What time is it? I must have dropped off for a few minutes."

"Almost time for dinner. Let's have it together."

"Why, yes!" she said, almost alarmed. "Why, yes! How very nice," and began to get flustered.

"Get dressed and come down, then. We'll eat in my apartment. I'll tell the boy." He felt peremptory, precise, and almost rubbed his hands together. After dinner his mother would go back to her rooms, and then Sylvia would come. At midnight, after taking her home, he would drop in on Tang and see what he could do there.

"What are we celebrating?" his mother asked a half-hour later, as she entered his living room like a guest. "Today's not a special day I've forgotten about, is it?"

"No, no," he said, thinking of the evening he had met his mother coming into the house from their little hedged-in garden.

That evening she had peered at him suspiciously. "Going out at this hour, dear?"

He had nodded.

"It's so breathless in my room," she'd said. "Funny how this tiny plot takes over all the feeling of the countryside at night. Oh, only at night. It's the night that takes over, I suppose. The night takes over and the dark is almost animal. Yes, the dark does peculiar things." She had shivered and seemed to want to communicate, to express what their garden meant to her after the sun left it desolate of light, but populated with a ferment of motes.

"I've been out here too long," she'd said, teetering on the two low steps that led to the entrance. "The night doesn't—doesn't occupy the same space. It's a district set apart, a county." She laughed. "Audrey Huang in Night County, Shanghai, China. I wonder, don't you, what the post office would think of that?"

She had called to him just as he was stepping out of the opening in the hedge. "I'll have a hot thermosful of tea left in your room, Farthington," and the scent of roses followed him. He might have been turning a corner in a small English town,

196

sunk in dampness and carefully tended nature. That night he saw his mother as his father must have originally: when she stood with the light behind her, her hair was an auburn flame. She had the beauty, fire and spirituality of an overexposed photograph.

"No, no," he said now two weeks later. "Just an idea of mine. We don't dine together very often, and I just felt like it today."

She went up to him and kissed him lightly on the cheek, as though to wish him a happy anniversary.

"There are days when I just feel like it, too," she said, without any rancor, "but we don't." Then she jumped to a conclusion and became vaguely imperious. "We shall do this once a week. It'll be a lovely habit. All of life is made up of habits, you know. Just waking up into a new day every morning is a habit," and it seemed she might turn into a large, middle-aged bird, her head turning this way and that, as her hands began to smooth the tablecloth before her.

His buoyancy had left him. "Serve dinner at once," he said to the servant who hovered at the door.

They ate in silence. Feng still felt vaguely dissatisfied with himself. Tang had asked for him two weeks ago, the evening he had left his mother in the garden. And because Sylvia had not told him about Peiyuan, Tang's tongue (Feng always imagined that the red tip of it was hooked) had flickered in an unpleasant laugh. Abruptly, Feng now made up his mind.

"I forgot an appointment," he said, lying to his mother. "I must go."

"Do you have to?" she asked, resentfully, between two bites of dinner.

"Of course I *have* to," and he looked at his watch. "I wouldn't have suggested eating together in the first place, if I hadn't completely forgotten about this."

"You always have to go, don't you?"

"I won't have time for dessert," he said, getting up to put his wallet and pen into his jacket pocket.

"Couldn't you be ten minutes late? We were celebrating!"

"No, I can't be ten minutes late!" and a wave of irritation almost choked him. "What you need is a boy friend!"

"I hate your girl friend. I've always hated her. All of them!"

He turned back, preoccupied. "Oh, by the way, Mother, do me a favor. Call Sylvia and tell her for me that I can't see her tonight. I almost forgot." Without waiting for an answer he left the house.

"Every other half-hour he starts fighting," Lao Yuan said, sucking at a missing tooth, "yelling and screaming at the top of his lungs, pulling at the door, acting crazy."

"He's a kid," Feng said, and went toward the storeroom where Peiyuan was still imprisoned.

"I've fed him well," Lao Yuan said. "Pretty good food, even if I say so myself. Everything I like to eat. What more does he want?"

"To be let out," Feng answered.

"All day we have to work up front, and back here he can take it easy, and he fights it. Doesn't make any sense."

Lao Yuan knocked on the door, but Peiyuan did not answer.

"He's sulking. He fights, sulks and eats, and then starts all over again."

Feng had to laugh. "Open the door," he said to Lao Yuan, "and lock us both in. I want to talk to him."

It was dark inside, and it took a few moments after the padlock clicked before Feng saw Peiyuan sitting on the floor in a far corner of the narrow room.

He's been here all alone, Feng thought. In a leap of his imagination, which upset the rhythm of his pulse, he felt the boy's loneliness, his imprisonment.

"You!" Peiyuan exclaimed, standing up quickly, his voice irritatingly happy.

"Look," Feng said matter-of-factly, "I want to talk to you. Do you want to listen?"

"It's on account of you I'm here," Peiyuan answered, half admiringly.

Feng saw two images in Peiyuan—the boy whose singleness he envied, and the sixteen-year-old for whom he had compassion, as he had compassion for himself at that age. The prison Peiyuan was in was nothing compared to the invisible prison every child had to pass through before reaching adulthood. A prison of no bars, but of so much possibility, it defeated you. He thought of adolescence as an endless age of yearning. The world was a paradise beyond one's reach. One was all alone, unrelated, impotent to make meaningful choices.

"I want to talk to you, too," Peiyuan said. "Look, I wasn't born yesterday. I know what this strike is all about."

"Sit down," said Feng, but he felt at a loss for words. That gaucheness he often felt in himself took over, an impasse, a blankness as though a wall suddenly loomed before him. At times like this, he could only be direct—but then he had nothing to lose with Peiyuan; he would not be taking any chances.

"You know how I feel about your cousin. You do know, don't you?"

"Sylvia, you mean?" Peiyuan asked.

"I am very much in love with her. And since I love her, I would do nothing to hurt anyone close to her. And that includes you," he added, on the chance that Peiyuan was wholly literal-minded.

"What's she got to do with this?" Peiyuan was aglow with a canniness that Feng had not thought he possessed.

"Nothing. Nothing direct, that is. And that's part of it. She doesn't know about this—about you. And won't know. You understand? We—you and I—won't tell her, see."

"They don't . . ." the boy's voice wavered on fright. Apparently it had not occurred to him that the Chens did not know where he was, were not at that moment prevailing on the men to release him.

"No, of course not," Feng answered sharply to neutralize

his sympathy. He felt he would do anything for the boy, whose face was so bright it made him feel almost drab by contrast, and not a little envious of him. "Your uncle's away, so how would they know? Only you know, you and I. And that's the way it's got to be."

"But why?" Peiyuan asked with the most compliant blandness.

"Even if your uncle had come to work today, he would not have known. Does he usually come to this part of the building?"

"I'm sick and tired of being here!" Peiyuan shouted. "Tell them to let me out. What kind of justice is this!" He made for the door to shake it again, but Feng grabbed him by his arm and held him firmly.

"Act grown-up. Stop wasting your energy. I'm here to help you."

You are my brother, Feng had wanted to say. If it would take the burden off your shoulders, I would live your life for you. More than ever, he found Peiyuan an extension of himself. Peiyuan was what he wished he was—purely affirmative, unformed enough still to be poised on action, uncommitted to everything except the future.

"If it were not for you and Sylvia, and the fact that I think your heart is on the right side, I wouldn't be doing this. Sticking my neck out," and Feng looked toward the door, as though Tang were listening. "We've got big plans afoot. You can be in on them if you believe, and if you co-operate. If you promise to keep all this a secret, you can have a part in the strike we're going to pull off."

"You can tell me the truth," Peiyuan said, seeming to want to make it easier for Feng. "I know whom you are working for."

Feng looked at him, but neither of them pronounced the word.

"Now, I've got a job ahead of me. I've got to convince them about you."

Peiyuan nodded. "I won't tell anyone. I promise you."

"We're all for the right things—the workers, the peasants, democracy. Reconstruction from the ground up."

"Sure," Peiyuan said. "Don't worry about me. I wasn't born yesterday, you know."

"You'll be out of here in a day or two."

"A day or two!"

"Look, the easy part is over. I always knew what you thought. I've got to convince the others about you. Sort of give them a guarantee."

"I'll just pretend this never happened!"

"You'll be out of here by tomorrow!"

Feng hated to leave. It was like walking away from himself. He wore a face of plain determination and pounded on the door. Lao Yuan came and let him out. Feng felt a tension in the back of his neck, the constriction of a new anxiety. He wanted Tang to understand Peiyuan, too. His approval of the boy seemed as necessary as life itself.

CHAPTER TWENTY

Mimi stood in the rain on the corner of Avenue Joffre and hailed a rickshaw. She still felt a little weak, a little fearful. She knew that if a friend approached, she would cross the street hurriedly, or pretend to be interested in the contents of a shop window. She had been so full of a nameless shame, she felt she had gone through the last couple of weeks without eyes or ears. It was as though by not allowing herself to see or hear, she trusted others not to recognize her existence. But she had been able to notice that Aunt Juliet had been nice and even kind, hovering around maternally, her cruel matter-of-factness softened with sympathy.

Mimi felt unaccompanied, naked on one side, as if for sometime in the past she had been used to a permanent escort. I feel this way, she told herself, only because I've been ill. One felt chilly after leaving the comfort of one's bed, thrown out into the world again, an orphan. Yet she had made herself get out of the house, had given herself a specific errand, an exercise that would put her back into life again.

She stepped into the rickshaw, saying, "Park Hotel," and wishing the ride ahead were twice as long. She wanted the time to gather strength, to arrange in her mind the reasons for making this trip. She crossed her legs, and as the breeze made by the rickshaw's progress disturbed her dress, she diligently adjusted it and fingered the small veil which covered her eyes. She made certain her bracelets were on, her bag and umbrella safely on her wrist. These things would give her support and reality.

Through the rain hood of the rickshaw, she could see the French Concession swim in grayness. The sky was being washed into the gutters, the horizon obliterated in the downpour. She had known, of course, but never really felt the quality of its streets. Avenue Joffre was wide and noisy with the mixed medley of Oriental traffic: streetcars passed in the center, while bicycles, pedicabs and rickshaws presented an endless entanglement of wheels among the more solid shapes of cars. The buildings on either side were not tall, and there were as many signs in English as in Chinese. A small park slipped by her on the left, the blue-domed Russian church hidden in its trees. She saw it all through the softness of the Shanghai light, misted over with a certain amount of humidity, even when the sun shone, and its clarity always somewhat dimmed by the rich presence of so many inhabitants. The stores made sharp contrasts: some were glassy with modernity, inviting one to linger on the sidewalk among reflections of oneself. Others had narrow entrances and dim interiors, suggesting to her less in the way of atmosphere than of poverty, compromise and decay.

Her puller turned left to dive into the turmoil of a side street. Years ago as a child she had had secret rides down real Chinese streets, taken on forbidden excursions by the *amah* of the moment. "If your father asks," the nursemaid would warn, "tell him we spent the afternoon in the compound," referring always to a compound of homes belonging to foreign embassy families, her parents' friends. But, actually, they had ridden down back alleyways into the heart of Peiping (for it was there that the Lamberts had spent the first years of their marriage), passing market places her parents had never seen. She still remembered the huge brown pickle jars through which they had to wind their way and the bloated pigs' bladders hanging just above their heads as they seemed to stream by. They visited the *amah's* relatives, or a labyrinthian bazaar, or a fifth-rate theater for which the *amah* had a sentimental attachment. Mimi always returned to the safety of home with a sense of guilt and of dangers overcome. These afternoons had no relation to the rest of her life. The pullers always seemed to run too recklessly; her *amah* never quite held her tightly enough on her lap; they were pursued by time ("Now you must return from the compound before dark," she had heard her mother instruct the maid). They were bedeviled by their lies, the ones they were perpetrating at the moment and the ones accumulated from the past. But they had never been found out.

She suddenly knew that she preferred Shanghai streets. Purely native streets seemed unsafe. Macadam and asphalt and tar kept the threat of the Orient at bay. The still archaic "cluck-cluck" or song-call of a vendor was enough against the security of foreign buildings—enough to add a little intoxication. She leaned back, and her body began again to find lines of ease and languidness. The rain made her hair springier, alert around her face. She took deep breaths, relaxed by the odors that dampness released. It seemed the first deep breath she had taken in weeks.

She had fainted the day of Robert's visit with Aunt Juliet. In trying to mutilate them with her hatred, she had hurt herself. She thought of it rather ruefully now. The days in bed after the miscarriage had seemed submarine, subterranean. She was still partly convalescent.

Her thoughts during those days—and she would not have been able to name them—enervated her. She slept all morning, waking up only to look at the clock and close her eyes again. The day seemed rude, raucous with light. At noon she got up, but stayed close to her bedroom. She became braver as the afternoon wheeled toward night. But before supper was served, she had to have a nap. Then the short sleep so filled her that she had no appetite for food. After dinner she sat in her room and imagined scenes of love. She did not know she was engaged in fantasy. The background music of her daydreams both fulfilled her and purged her with their demands. She re-enacted moments with Robert, and created from her inverted energy sequences that brought tears and relaxation. Sometimes the object of her affection was an unfamiliar man who had no name, but whose arms kept her warm. He would be waiting for her at imaginary terminals, lobbies, lake sides, bridges. Or he would be Robert dressing her, comforting her; Robert kissing her and denouncing himself as the criminal. The Robert that she knew these days alone in her room was father, uncle, doctor. He was very severe in his judgment of that other Robert, her lover and betrayer.

Though she had not been aware of it, she had watched Aunt Juliet care for her, efficient, self-contained, affectionate. She envied her her neat soul. Aunt Juliet never fell a step behind her image for herself. She had a tidy epigram for every emotion, every situation which came up. She was mature, Mimi thought, sighing. She did not know she also felt a regret for such economy—Aunt Juliet expended so little of herself in misery. She almost denied herself humanness. Mimi was younger, too young to know that youth was a time for despair and torture and the waste of energy. She only thought that nothing lasted forever, neither love nor happiness. Only unhappiness had a quality of permanence. It was as hard to give up as a part of yourself. She then hugged her misery with possessive arms. The pain Robert had given her was like a jewel hung in her heart.

The puller had reached the International Settlement. Again the streets broadened out. As they approached Nanking Road, she could feel the growl of traffic increase. The taller skyline of buildings marched by on her left. On the right was the open oval of the city race course. It afforded a vista and trees that freshened the air. She opened her purse and prepared to pay the puller, who now drew up outside the Park Hotel.

She stepped out onto the sidewalk tentatively, as though into hostile territory. The rain had abated, but she shook herself a little as if to dispose of droplets. The gutters were running with oily brown water, the coolies' bare feet covered over by it up to their ankles. A straw sandal floated by. She looked away, suddenly aware that her heart was pounding fast and she felt faint. Why did I come? she demanded of herself. What made me require this of myself? She almost stepped back into the rickshaw she had just left. But the surprise she would find in the puller's face kept her turned away. All of a sudden she felt herself swept up a few steps into the hotel lobby.

This was what she had come for. The lobby was astir with immediacy. American MP's, exhilarated by their own importance, walked about, entering, leaving and re-entering from their jeeps outside. They disappeared into the elevators, only to reappear. They seemed to be concerned with missions of a holy nature. She would not have wanted to know their secrets, even had they offered to divulge them. The Chinese hotel employees sat at their desks or operated the elevators. They seemed frail, informal, contrasted with the uniformed Americans. Compared with the American boots the soldiers wore, the Chinese shoes seemed as soft and casual as slippers. She stood with her back to the glass front of the hotel and watched, completely absorbed. She was intoxicated with the feeling of power and contemporaneousness the uniformed men exuded. All these years these men had arranged her destiny for her in Chungking, Burma, India. Her own gratitude overwhelmed her. She almost wanted to offer herself in thanksgiving.

She was too absorbed to feel the cue travel through the room. But she turned to stare out of the window as a space was being prepared, a passageway through all the men to one of the elevators. With no ceremony or preliminaries a small guard was formed. A man was surrounded (she craned her neck to see who it was) and was swallowed up behind a door.

"Russell Chow!"

She jumped at the sound of the familiar voice beside her.

"What are you doing here?" she asked involuntarily and peevishly. She had not wanted to share this experience.

It was Larry Casement, who did not bother to answer her question. "Russell Chow," he repeated. "Up for interrogation for collaborating." He shuddered. "That might have been me."

She was still too annoyed to muster any empathy. Why did Larry have to come, too? She did not want to see anyone who would remind her of the last four years. The partial lives they had lived filled her with a sense of disgrace. She was ashamed of his poverty, of his personal but insignificant courage (wasn't he congratulating himself on not having compromised and worked for the Japanese?), of the whole Jastrow group. She wanted to go on to other things.

"I've got an interview," he said, his eyes bright with expectation. "One of the press officers is looking for a reporter."

"I hope you make it," she said mechanically.

"If you wait, we can have a cup of coffee next door."

But she did not hear him. At least, she had to admit to herself, he wants something definite, something specific. A job. He would fit himself in somewhere. Larry Casement would end up working for an American news agency. That was something for a Shanghai boy.

But me? What did she want? She wanted everything and nothing. She wanted to be found. But who or what she wanted to be found by she did not know. She wanted to be recognized and adopted. An enormous wave of anxiety overcame her.

"I'd like to buy you a cup of coffee," he repeated. "Please. I'm going now but I won't be long." He had already left her side. He looked over his shoulder at her, charming her with a look of pleading and teasing. His shoulders were straight and a little tense. She noticed that the bottoms of his trousers were still damp. He walked into one of the elevators.

She had nowhere to go. She seemed to stand on the threshold of surrealist space. She put up her hand to take off the veil. It irritated her. She shook her head, and felt her waves spring back into loose array. Two MP's had been discussing her. She had been aware of it as of a scene in a dream. They were young boys, she thought. Robert had made anyone less than fifteen years older than she seem too young for her. She had forgotten she was nineteen. These soldiers must have been in their twenties.

She couldn't stand there any longer. She knew that. Even pretending to herself that she was waiting for Larry to return would not help. Outside, the pedestrians and the traffic went by soundlessly, like a newsreel with the sound track turned off. She couldn't plunge into that now either.

"I wonder if I can have a cigarette?" she said, walking up to the MP's. She felt her coquetry perform without her.

"Why sure, miss," one of them answered, with simple pleasure in his tone. The other seemed to look at her with a mixture of intensity and cynicism.

"What kind are they?" she asked.

"Luckies. Do you like Luckies?"

"Those can't be Luckies," she said. "I just know they aren't." Through his hands she could see the white and red package.

"Want to bet?" He laughed and opened his hand, and she saw that they were.

"Why, the package is changed!"

"Years ago," he said. "Don't tell me you haven't seen them like this."

"No, I haven't. So what?" she rejoined quarrelsomely. It seemed as though she had been buried alive for years. There was so much to catch up with that she wanted to indulge in a tantrum of desperation.

"Here, take it," he said, offering the pack, as if to make up for having offended her mysteriously.

She laughed briskly, sounding like her Aunt Juliet. "Thank you," she said, "but no, thank you." She looked at his uniform and wished she knew how to recognize his rank. She wanted to stare him down. She ignored his proffered hand, and walked out of the lobby.

What could she do now? She was expected nowhere. Her life was empty except for an infinite longing for things she could not define.

The sky was beginning to clear, the clouds and heaviness retreating in the west like a tide. A few high windows were prematurely lighted against the coming of evening. She felt drained, empty, light-headed, as though she were walking out of her body, her clothes, herself. Men stopped to stare at her admiringly. She walked down five blocks on Nanking Road, gathering their unspoken compliments. She felt nothing but a faint disdain. She felt careless, supercilious. At any moment she could have thrown her life away.

She had involuntarily walked into a large florist shop with which she was familiar. The damp presence of flowers chilled her, but she held onto herself and waited for a salesman to come up to her. The peculiar atmosphere of a flower shop closed in on her like a wet Sunday at a dull resort.

"Can I help you?" the man seemed to ask. He stared at her sideways in penetrating appraisal.

She knew precisely what she wanted.

"A dozen each of the red and white roses, and the carnations, and the gladioli. And fern, lots of it. And let me have four bunches of those," pointing to an assorted array of garden leaves and flowers. On going to each group of flowers, he let his glance linger on her. His eyes seemed watchful, wounded and all-knowing. He is like a detective or a saint, she thought. He wrapped them all in tissue and green paper.

"You'd better help me into a rickshaw," she instructed him. She felt unnerved by him—by her awareness of him. Walking out behind her, his arms full of her purchases, he seemed at once dangerous and protective. Even when she realized why it was so (he had presented the bill silently for her signature), she still could not shake off the eerie feeling he gave her. He was a mute and she felt pursued by his dependency.

All the way home, the flowers surrounded her. She was bolstered by the small pageantry her purchases created. At home, she arranged them in vases all in her own bedroom. The room smelled as cold as nature at night.

She drew herself a hot bath and lay in it a long time. She cleansed her face carefully with Aunt Juliet's cream and powdered herself all over. In Aunt Juliet's room she also found an old red satin embroidered coverlet—a traditional Chinese wedding gift. She spread it on her own bed and lay on it nude. It was silky and soft; she pulled part of it over her. She had no desire to move, no memory. It was as though her mind saw only the bed at that hour, the small spotlight of awareness seeming to close down to the size of a dime. The telephone began to ring. But it had no meaning for her. It rang as in an empty hotel room.

CHAPTER TWENTY-ONE

The city, Sylvia thought, was a beautiful encrustation. She could almost see it as it lay on the plains, an irregular, intricate castle. A castle which had housed them all for so many years. Only cities had a density, a tactile sense of humanity, of each inhabitant's personal history. Only cities whetted your appetites. One walked with one's desire on sidewalks populated with the ghosts of other days and memories. Only cities had true corners and oblique vistas. The sixth-story window created its own scene.

Windows, wall, flowerpots, doorways, the smart movement of shining wheels, angles and vanishing perspectives—she saw them all concretely, as for the first time. She understood why they were there, infinite aspects of a finite world. Her loving Feng made her a respecter of the selfness of others and of things. She was beginning to understand reality, and the holiness of all the five senses could perceive.

Happiness made Sylvia both conservative and mystic. The long day alone with Feng had tired her. Now they rarely saw the rest of the old crowd that used to meet at the Jastrows', and none of the others seemed to want to seek out either of them. All their orbits had changed—only the city still superficially held them together.

Feng and she had had lunch together. After he left his office for the day, they'd met again in the New World Emporium, and wandered through the garish market place of entertainment. They wanted to see things together—it didn't matter what it was. After that, there was an early dinner, and now they did not know what they wanted to do. But small things satisfied her. She wanted only to be with him. With the conservatism of contentment, she wanted to measure out their pleasures. But through her fatigue (two-ness could be a burden for lovers), she sensed his unhappiness. She felt, however, that asking him what the trouble was would be an intrusion. She didn't want words, self-conscious efforts to express the inexpressible. She wanted only the defining of a simple desire. Instead, she found herself initiating conversation behind which he could find some privacy.

"We'll all be gone soon," she said, "and ten years from now think back on it affectionately and a little patronizingly. The Hasan Kemals and the Larry Casements, Bill and Julie, Mimi and Robert Bruno will seem part of a state of mind—something that we created out of what was around during this long war. They'll seem unreal, unless we happen to meet again. We'll feel like those philosophers who think nothing exists unless one's eyes are on it. And if we do meet, we may have changed so much, we won't have anything to say, but just stare at each other. And behind everyone's stare will be the same feeling: I was not there with you—I couldn't have been. See how little we have in common!"

They were walking after the early supper. She felt Feng's bleakness and her own impotence in relation to it. He could die on her every other half-hour when he was unhappy. He just went away, disappeared and took everything with him except his morbidity.

Unexpectedly he said, "Perhaps it won't be that way. Maybe certain friendships last."

She knew he had said it without thought—the very careless-ness of his voice proved how estranged he was from himself this evening. The words were right, but his face was wrong. He looked unhappy, egocentric, petulant and self-pitying. She knew exactly how he looked and wondered why love could not bequeath her more blindness. Her still "seeing" seemed to her to mean that she did not love well enough. She knew only one way for her to make up for her dereliction.

"I want you to do something for me," she said, as they rounded the corner and walked on Avenue Joffre. The streets were again luminous, the shop windows again advertising themselves with lights.

"What?" he asked. "Anything you say, anything at all."

"Oh, it's something very complicated and very strange and very different that I want."

He glanced at her sideways, granting her one of the two expressions she liked most. He seemed most alive when he was righteously indignant, and devastating when his face was like this—docile enough, but really bored over her female wiles. His looking at her this way hurt, but it was part of him and that was enough.

"Do you really want to know?"

"Uh-huh," and this time he looked straight ahead, hiding his impatience over her prolonged coyness.

"I want you to . . ." and now she hesitated in front of a window of ladies' lingerie and costume jewelry. "And you simply must, must, must. You promised."

"Yes."

"You promised, now."

"Buy you something?"

"Oh, no. Something much nicer."

"Come on, out with it."

"I want you to do me the great favor of holding my hand."

She held out her right hand which he took in his left and they continued down the street together. This is all I want, she thought. This is all I'll want forever. Every desire she had ever had, beginning from infancy, seemed fulfilled by his presence. For a few minutes they said nothing in the soft darkness.

"You're worried about something, aren't you?" she asked. "Why don't you tell me?"

He seemed to pull himself up short. "I'm going to," he said decisively.

"What is it, Feng?"

"I'm engaged in some activities. Some activities Peiyuan found out about. He had no business poking his nose in, but you know kids. He's been detained, shall I say. Put away for a couple of days."

She looked up at him, not understanding.

"But it's really nothing to worry about. He'll be let out tomorrow for sure."

"Oh," she said, aware only that her hand was safe in his. "Then it's all right."

"Of course. He'll be fine. He'll probably be having supper in your house tomorrow."

It crossed her mind to ask him what these "activities" were, but she hesitated, afraid she might dispel the look of relief on his face.

"I'm glad I told you," and he no longer looked so isolated.

"I've told you everything," he added, but her instincts told her it was not true. She could not deny them. Her instincts were usually unerringly accurate. But she did not care. Where would you end if you doubted everything? How could love be, if one did not act upon a premise? Feng believed he had told her everything, and she chose to believe in him.

He turned to kiss her gratefully. His face was again breathtakingly pure. It had a childlikeness, a new-born look that was as elusive as a whisper. It almost eluded her now, but her heart felt enlarged by his contentment. He turned to kiss her again and was entirely gentle and attentive.

Through her devotion to him, she might even acquire a self to call her own, she thought. The city surrounded her like beautiful, familiar furniture. The world was her home, because Feng and she loved each other.

CHAPTER TWENTY-TWO

At night the darkness had a way of almost choking him. It was like learning how to swim, to get over that fear of water blocking the nose, that silence in a world of heavy liquid. In the almost total darkness, Peiyuan lost all sense of anchorage. His emotions surged and dashed him against the narrow walls. No one but Lao Yuan had visited him since yesterday. And the old man had not said a word, just pushed the food in front of him and left. Feng had not appeared, had not fulfilled his promise that he would be released today. The Chens did not even know that he was here. Peiyuan laughed the thin cracked laugh of youthful bitterness.

I am a tyro in politics, he thought pompously, but I'm not completely stupid. Yet this action of these Communists—that was what they were—was just too much, though he would have liked to have given them the benefit of the doubt. He tried to remember what he knew about them. They were revolutionaries, reformers. They wanted to wipe out land abuses, change agrarian economy. They also wanted to work militantly in the industrial centers. They were an independent Chinese party, some said. But his own grandfather had said they were strictly guided by the Soviets; he had often been involved in arguments about them—if his grandfather's generation could be thought to have had arguments at all. It seemed only his own generation of students, and those who came a little after Uncle Liyi, were really uninhibited enough, bold enough to engage in politics.

But his grandfather had been jailed once—before Peiyuan was born—and all at once he remembered almost all of it. His grandfather owned farms around Sunkiang, and the peasants came at night to give him his rents, so they would not antagonize the Reds. Then in 1926—or was it 1927—a Red agent demanded that his grandfather subsidize one hundred machine guns for the party in the area. His grandfather had refused and had served over a year in jail. It was all confused, as so much of Chinese politics was confused at the time. How had the party had the authority to punish his grandfather? Who had imprisoned him? Had he been released through the intercession of a high official—the way things were usually done in China—or had the Nationalist government, just established then in Nanking, set him free by decree? Peiyuan wished he had listened to these stories more carefully when he was little.

He also wished he knew what time it was. Was it ten, eleven o'clock or midnight? He went to the door and banged on it, pulling it back and forth by the handle until he was sure it would give way, but it didn't. Certainly they could hear him; it must be that they were deliberately ignoring him. He'd show them they'd have to treat him seriously. He moved back into the room, gritted his teeth and ran headlong into the door, dashing his right shoulder against it. He was furious with frustration and struck the door over and over, making the storeroom shake. Something hard glanced off his head. He ducked and looked up. One of the slats in the skylight had fallen loose.

He threw back his head and stared. There was nothing to scale the wall with, so he put one foot on the knob and another in a broken part of the door jamb. From that height he flung himself off, leaping upward and backward, catching onto one of the slats. For a moment, the slat sagged under his weight, and he thought he would fall. He swung back and forth, judging his distance, noticing that the board moved with him, making a wider and wider aperture in the skylight. Quickly he brought his legs up, almost kicking himself under his chin, and swung them through the laths of the skylight. He righted himself and saw that he was in the equally dark out-of-doors.

He jumped off his seating, the board hurtling down into the storeroom with a crash, and began to run over the uneven roofs of the printing plant itself as well as the shelters that surrounded it. He was looking for the straw matting by which he had entered. From there he could jump onto the street.

He stumbled, making a great clatter even in his sneakers. I won't go home, Peiyuan thought. I'll just keep on running. Exhilarated by the thought, he leaped off, his feet stinging. He almost bellowed with joy as he rounded the corner.

The darkness which had muffled him like a hand across his face seemed now like a ramp by which he was accelerated into freedom. The air, freshened by a breeze from the Whangpoo, blew his three-day captivity from him. He had not lost anything by the confinement; he had gained a new appreciation of life. He knew so much more now. He felt he was beginning anew. He had so much to warn his Uncle Liyi of. There was so much to do. He ran blindly and intuitively toward the Bund, to where the buildings would give way to a clean view of the harbor.

Suddenly he was aware of footsteps behind him, then his name being called. He looked back and saw Tang running pell-mell, almost overtaking him. He panicked, ran across the street and turned back in, away from the Bund.

"Leave me alone!" he shouted, his breath stabbing his panting chest. He sounded immature to himself, defenseless.

Then his knees buckled under him. He was aware of kneeling, of suddenly falling forward. For a long endless second he seemed to be able to see and even to consider a hundred overlapping thoughts.

He was aware of an overwhelming desire to struggle. So much seemed to depend on him, so much that no one but he could accomplish. No one, not his uncle, nor his cousins, only *me*, he thought. "No one but I," Peiyuan wanted to yell out in his sudden fever. Hopefulness pierced him like a nail. Caught between joy and pain, he wanted to scream, to assert his aliveness.

I am alone, he thought joyously. I am young! I am free! But his greatest freedom lay in the fact that he had no more to lose. Slowly, within the blooming of a single, enormous moment, a fourth dimension opened within his aching skull. The blow from behind had killed him almost instantaneously.

CHAPTER TWENTY-THREE

Feng found himself looking at things as though he were memorizing them, trying to retain them for some unpredicted long journey ahead. He did not know that he had awakened that morning with a foretaste of damnation, but he had felt strongly how corruptible everything was. He had little respect for anything; his every relationship produced its own befoulment. He wasn't sure; he wasn't sure of anyone, least of all himself. His lack of respect came from the very core of his being. One corner of his mouth turned up in a partial sneer. Part of him denied everything that lived. It denied even the sprout of pain that reminded himself that he, too, was alive.

Why didn't his own ugliness show? He felt atrophied, wasted, ashamed. But more than that, he was propelled by his own misanthropy. People accepted him for what he appeared to be—a young man with good habits. Those very habits for which he was sometimes grateful—they carried him over his own chaos—now seemed despicable. The fact that people did not see through them only reaped in him more lack of esteem for them.

Every new day, he realized, was an addition to one's history which was rewritten constantly. He looked at everything that morning with the cold eye of cowardice. He remembered that he had done nothing for Peiyuan—the boy was still alone, a prisoner. And careless, Feng did not worry. He shrugged a little in the sunlight, as he shaved. Caught between two dangers, he chose the less extreme. He could not offend Tang. Not even for Peiyuan, his own "brother," could he face up to Tang, who was his disapproving "father." He had tried to make an appointment with Tang two evenings before, after leaving the boy in the locked storeroom. But even filtered through Lao Yuan he had felt the impact of Tang's impatience with him. So he could not be importunate. He would wait a little longer. He could never sufficiently vindicate himself to this cruel master. And Feng had taken on his cruelty to assuage his own need for pain. His love for Peiyuan would have to be sacrificed to it.

Sylvia did not enter his mind at all that morning. Uneasily, he dressed and went downtown by streetcar. They ran more frequently now, and one did not see the scenes that took place during the war: beggars snatching hats as the trams pulled away from their traffic islands. The hat owners would shout and gesticulate futilely in the crowded car. For the conductors would never disrupt their schedules long enough to stop the cars and initiate a pursuit of the thieves. There was less savagery in the crowds now, too. He remembered the times when buses and streetcars, which came only every half-hour even during rush hours, would be boarded through their windows by eager office workers, climbing over the shoulders of anyone standing in front of them. No one cared, neither the ones who were carried away in the bus, nor the ones left behind to wait another half-hour. To preserve one's sanity, one pretended one was not alive. One would save oneself for "after the war."

And now the war had ended, and as he entered his office and heard the telephone ring, he felt he was enacting an old role. He promised himself to handle it all tomorrow. Today was just to be "got through." Today he would rely on a few businesslike habits. Today he would exempt himself from an accounting. It was like sinning, he had thought, and enjoying all its pleasures, with the reservation in mind that at one's deathbed one would be able to wipe clean the slate with absolution. He allowed himself to wonder, however, for a second if the practice of sinning did not perhaps dull the spirit, so that the vision of forgiveness for which one asked on the deathbed would not be so bright as that innocence might have created for itself. It was a Christian thought, a throwback to childhood training, and made him smile. He hated confession and self-abasement.

His secretary picked up the phone and motioned him into the office. He could hear her put down her receiver as he picked up his.

"Yes . . ." he said in a whisper. Not hello, but "yes," as if he had expected the call. It seemed to him almost as though he crouched by the phone on his desk.

It was Sylvia, who had never called him at his office before. He looked out the window, committing the scene to memory. The buildings were a mass of brick dedicated to commerce and mercantilism. Small men appeared in windows and he could look down on the street below and see their antlike servitude. Men had created Shanghai and now more men enslaved themselves to its care.

"The foreman Tang just called me," Sylvia said, but he was listening only to the sound of his own fear. He knew what she was going to tell him next; he seemed to have heard it all before.

"Peiyuan was found dead in the street. A mugging. Hit with a heavy instrument. Did you hear me?" she asked in a moment. "He's dead!"

"Yes . . ." he whispered again. And then, involuntarily, "But why did Tang call *you*?"

"Peiyuan's my cousin!" she shouted. "Why shouldn't he call me—" and broke off, as though she felt his hatred for hysterical women. Then, suddenly, she asked, "But how could he have been out on the streets at midnight if he was 'detained,' as you said? You did say that last night, didn't you?"

"They must have released him," he retaliated quickly. "I'll speak to Tang right away and call you back."

"I'm coming over."

"No, no, not at the office!"

"Then at home."

"But I'm busy, Sylvia. Later on I'll call you."

"No, you meet me at your place right away. I must talk to you."

"But there's nothing to say, Sylvia, beyond the fact of the tragedy."

"There's lots to say!" she shouted. "He's dead," she said hoarsely, "and what are you going to do about it? What are you going to do about it!" she screamed.

To placate her, he said he would meet her at his house in an hour. Then they hung up, and he was appalled that he felt nothing, except that he suddenly found himself wondering what Helen Chen's face looked like when she cried.

He took the streetcar back home. It was apparently an ordinary day, for women were out shopping, people smoked cigarettes, spat on the sidewalks; paid him no attention at all. He was grateful for their blindness, though he liked them no more for it. He had felt suicidal, caught, when he had not been able to reach Tang by phone. He would try again at night, but he realized Tang was not going to speak to him. He tried to be rational. "They will maintain," he said to himself, "that it was a mugging. And why should Tang discuss it with me? They are safest denying to themselves that I know anything. And I am committed to nonexistence in this matter." But the thought of suicide seized him. For ten distorted minutes he felt that the truth derived from one principle: the world murdered its citizens. Not always in the way that Peiyuan was killed, so dramatically that it could be seen. But in the sense that all these people—and the streets produced them like maggots—walked around deadened, blind, deaf. Each one had committed his own murder. Each one was on his way to an appointment with his own death. None of them believed in his own worth; none of them took pride in his own life. And thinking of himself, he asked, "And why should they?"

Sylvia was waiting for him. Once they entered the house, she didn't give him a chance to say a word.

222

"How could I have been so stupid! How could I have been so blind!" Her use of the word "blind" for herself brought him up short. She struck herself sharply on her forehead, as though to let in some light.

"I shouldn't have told you a thing," he found himself saying. "Because I told you—not wanting to keep anything from you —now I'm being accused."

"But what did you tell me? You told me nothing. You held my hand and muttered something about the 'activities' you are engaged in."

"Who asked me to hold your hand!" The infantileness of the retort released him.

"While Peiyuan was being killed, while he was being murdered, you were out holding hands with me. God!" She stared at him glassily.

"Why couldn't he have kept his nose out of it all!"

She whipped herself around and faced him directly. "Why couldn't you have done something about it! You could have if you had wanted to!"

"Tang re—"

"Tang killed him, didn't he? Killed him because he might tell someone about these plans of yours, the activities, as you call them, of this party of yours. Killed him and then pretended it was a mugging."

"No one intended killing him. I know if only he had stayed put, he would have been released—"

"So you admit he was killed in cold blood! You who at first tried to make me believe that he had been let out and was killed accidentally. Now! Now!" and she went up to him and shook him. "Now, tell me the truth! The truth, do you hear me!"

"You don't love me!" he exclaimed, beginning to realize it was true.

"Now you just tell me the truth!" she cried bitterly, and as if in warning.

"You don't love me," he repeated.

"I don't love you!" She stood two feet from him and pounded on his chest with all the strength in her fists.

"You'd have some faith in me, if you did." He seized her by the elbows and held her against him. Her staring at him as though he were a stranger was unbearable. "I love you, I love you. Oh, God, I love you. You are in every pore of me."

She tore her right arm free and hit him across his face, and then ran sobbing to the door. But he followed her and blocked the way. They struggled at the door and he could see that his easy reserve of physical force made her choke with rage. But he couldn't let her go.

"It was a mistake," he said. "But what do you want of me! It was a tragic mistake, but he brought it on himself. And as for you—" He pushed her back, his hands about her like a vise, and put her down in a chair.

"Let go of me!" She dug her teeth into his arm, tearing his shirt.

"I'll let go of you when I want to!"

But he released his hold, his arm recoiling with pain. To arrest her hysteria, he slapped her severely across her cheek.

"I did my best by that kid. I've got into a lot of trouble on account of him."

She struck him again on the chest, and once more fled to the door.

"Murderer!" she screamed. "Murder and horror and hate. You don't know anything else!"

She tore open the door, and before he could seize her again, ran sobbing from the house. His mother was standing in the vestibule with an indefinite smile on her face.

He ran down the garden steps and shouted huskily, "You have no faith in me! You have no love! You don't know the meaning of the word. You have no faith in me!" Then he raced back into the house and slammed the door in his mother's face.

Sylvia was gone, he realized fully. A panic took him; he felt suddenly weakened as from shock. Days seemed to stretch

224

before him like a strange landscape from which the signposts had been removed. He felt that he could speak, but that his throat would produce no sound discernible to the human ear.

Now it was three o'clock in the morning of the next day.

He wrote: *Dear Sylvia, Though I need you,* and it seemed to him he could not capitulate more than to admit need, need on any level. Until he wrote it down, he had not known he felt needful. He thought he had never allowed himself to admit that he was alone. Each time the realization seemed a new one.

Though I need you, I have made the decision to leave Shanghai. All at once tears came, the first in a decade. He clenched his fists in an effort to control himself. No one knows, he thought, what makes us cry. The background music in movies manipulates us; we are obedient to its command. But why tears now when he felt a little ennobled by his decisiveness? *I cannot tell you where I am going or what I shall be doing, but its importance to our future cannot be denied. I leave not on my own account, but with an express purpose.*

He had not been able to see Tang earlier that evening but he had received a letter by messenger. He would leave by train sometime the following day, and pick up instructions outside Nanking. He couldn't tell Sylvia any of this. And he did not have a strong desire to share it. It was as precious as a child's secret life, kept safe from a hostile world. The loss of his secret, the sharing of it even with her, would hurt like mortality. His mind leaped from association to association. When he had been a boy he had dreamed of running away from home as they did in English story books. Boys ran away barefoot and walked into the dawn down damp country roads. But he had always had to visualize himself climbing over a high wall, to drop into the Chinese dust outside. But the walls, he thought now, would be coming down all over China and he would have a part in their destruction. He added to the paragraph: *I am in love with you, despite our misunderstanding,* and wished he could convey in words how much he wanted her.

I must be factual, Sylvia, I had absolutely nothing to do with Peiyuan's death, and I feel deeply about it. Let me add that if one young boy's death were necessary for the new order of things, then honestly I would be the first to mourn but the last to prevent his dying. (I want to be honest, and I tell you this even at the risk of losing you further.)

He could remember clearly each of their times together. Yet so little remained with him of the details—they were swallowed up in the experiencing. She didn't like him to rub her between her shoulder blades. After love, their sleep numbed them like warm snow. She was impossibly lazy in the mornings.

What he felt did not come out in the letter at all, but he accepted this as inevitable. He wrote mechanically: *Don't mock all we have had together by no longer loving me. I ask you this because I am sentimental and because I love you very much.* It was the best that he could do. He signed it, sealed it and addressed the envelope.

This morning he had not thought of her, and now he could summon up no thought of Peiyuan. His lack of feeling alarmed him—it was like a kind of impotence, the facing of the blank wall of self. He thought of blindness again, of how blind the people appeared from his office window, how Sylvia had struck her own forehead. And yet perception was not enough. One needed a code by which to live. Only in blind work and in idealism, he thought, only in the momentum of action could he expend this distaste for himself. At least, he could try. Good things sometimes grew out of strange motives.

He began to pack and prepare himself for the journey. He saw the country bright and hard in the merciless light of the days ahead. He saw himself—as he would be—walking through the aisle up to the front of the lurching train, while China unfolded itself outside the windows. The morning landscape seemed to stream toward the hour of noon.

226

Across the narrow street the tea house glowed like a bonfire. Mimi could smell the vapor that floated off its boiling vats. She had been inside once several months ago. All they served, besides several varieties of tea, was a delicacy stuffed with an assortment of flavors, its juicy contents encased in glutinous rice flour. Its customers were of two kinds, those who dropped in for a quick snack, or the others in the back of the drafty room who made of the tea house their living room, club and rendezvous.

The car protects us, Mimi thought. Here, sunk in the back seat, only diluted odors and diminished sounds could reach her. Hawkers' carts rattled gently over the cobblestones, and soft echoes from strident and incessant Chinese opera found their way from radios to her ears. The low tiled rooftops presented an unstimulating silhouette of almost identical buildings, the night sky bleeding silver around the dark shapes. Some day, she knew, she'd be in another city, and she felt she'd be a totally different person by means of geography. In two years she would come of legal age, and get her inheritance and go away. She somehow visualized herself carrying all her worldly wealth in a brocade satchel and walking from a gray gangplank onto a totally white ship.

The four of them were waiting for Emerson Howell. She took particular pleasure in the fact that the car was marked *Press*. She was in search of labels these days. The two young men in the front seat were crew-cut Americans. The one behind the driver's seat had the quick incisive mind of a lawyer, the other was dough leavened by humor and a comfortable homespun dowdiness. Their uniforms gave them being and entity. She felt unsafe with the soldiers of any other nationality. But these men, though she hardly knew them, seemed like brothers. They were speaking desultorily.

"Town's peaceful tonight."

"Peaceful like a quiet volcano."

"The Jap military are doing a fine job."

"It's too soon to tell—not the Jap part. But the shape of things to come."

The voices of the men in the front seat went by her like certain news items, which she read but could not grasp. She could only understand personal events. She understood that if the Japanese had not remained in charge of local affairs during this transition period, Shanghai would have been a dangerous place to live in. They were going to hand the city back to the Nationalists when things settled down a bit more. But her consideration of it was academic. She knew herself to be one of those girls who cannot comprehend how a committee works or how individual men figure in abstract causes and institutions.

She could trace things only in a straight line. Two nights ago through Larry Casement she had met Emerson Howell. She had seen him twice with Larry, who was acting as his liaison. She trembled with anxiety, an anxiety she could not forego, when she was near him. Howell was a correspondent for a New York paper, and she didn't care or know which paper it was. Foreign correspondents were the knight errants of World War Two; they were the only romantic figures left in an unromantic world. She also knew that he was not interested in her, but the anxiety he touched off in her felt like love.

"What's keeping the character?" the young man seated beside her in the back seat asked. He was Louis Murray, who had adopted her as his own. She pretended to herself not to notice that she did not care for him. He was tense and the palms of his hands sweaty. He and the two others had been flown in from Chungking in B-29's. All Americans—and gradually more and more reached Shanghai—descended like archangels from outer space.

"He's compulsive," Louis Murray said, "ferreting out news eighteen hours a day. Under the guise of conscientiousness, Howell's merely perpetrating an act of hostility on us, forcing us to wait here.

"There's nothing quite so dull as common sense, but it's sometimes a short cut to leisure. Take me, for instance, I know what the pitch is—do the details matter? This place is doomed. The Chinese can't take it over and make anything of it. You'll see what I mean. The war ended not too late, but too soon. Well, no—too late in one sense—Chiang is debilitated. But too soon, too. Corrupt, but liberated, there won't be anything to hold the country together. The war supplied a fiber. Say, where the hell is that character?"

The men up front ignored him, it was their way of showing him the depth of their affection. "That Lou Murray," they said of him, "that pup who is wet behind the ears." She looked at him from the corner of her eye. He had a retroussé nose, too small for his face, soft pale skin and a shock of unkempt hair hanging over his forehead. His foot was always jigging; his nails were bitten down to the flesh. She tried to move away without offending him, but Lou was too quick for her.

"Whoa!" he whispered. "Do I have to start from scratch every time?" He put his arm around her and nuzzled his face into her neck. "Rub my ear," he demanded, and as she obeyed, he murmured, "Oo—oo," and shuddered with pleasure. "Don't stop now. Come be my love," he started lyrically, "and reactivate my manhood." She found him too repugnant for even a smile.

He raised his head to continue his soliloquy, but put his hand on her knee so as not to lose the ground he had just gained. "The Chinese will be looting and pillaging, acting like carpetbaggers, but they won't be vindictive. Venal but forgiving. Mark the words of Louis Cassandra Murray."

She had edged away, but he pulled her back, peered at her with his intelligent, self-pitying eyes. "You must learn to relax. That's the first step in the direction of the Kingdom of Heaven. And how else are you going to learn how to relate to another human being! And relate we must in this year of our Lord—A.D. now stands for atomic death, and H is not for hell but for Hiroshima." His own profundities seemed to have so distracted him that he took his hand off her knee and sat staring morosely out the window. What was the word for him? she wondered. For his combination of callowness and crudity, his false emotionalism and phony bombast? He hung his head down over his outspread knees and put his hand through his hair in a tragic gesture.

The two in front paid no attention. They were all committed to waiting for Emerson Howell, who was down the street interviewing somebody's widow—they seemed to know who the Chinese woman was, but Mimi was not interested. Shanghai was just a stopover on her way toward true living. The less she knew about it the lighter her luggage would be when she left it. Life, she felt, was "out there" somewhere. It resided in an Emerson Howell, who could put her in contact with everything that mattered.

She eased herself down into the seat and shrugged. Just yesterday she had been out on the mud roads to visit the Lunghwa internment camp, and seeing how her friends had spent the last few years had proved to her how right she was. After all was said and done, you had only yourself, an instrument with which to create your own reality. An instrument which, like merchandise, had a price on it. The thought, surprisingly enough, did not leave her frightened. She was prepared to believe at nineteen that most directions in life led to a spiritless cliché.

"You think you're in love with him, don't you?" Louis whispered, putting his face into her hair and sniffing at it like a slightly damp dog. She moved away and presented him with an adamantly indifferent shoulder.

"You want him because he doesn't care one whit. You love him even though he can hurt you. You love him *because* he can hurt you. The story of every magnificent obsession is a large maladjustment. Baby, dear," he said, pulling her toward him, "you can't cope with Emerson Howell. Why try to draw blood from a stone? He isn't interested in girls—exclusively. He's mainly interested in the career of Emerson Howell. Come close and try coping with me."

"Oh, leave me alone!" she declared irritably, and seized her purse as though she were going to strike him with it. Instead, she made for the car door. In a split second she was out, and walking briskly and blindly down the narrow street.

She was delighted with herself, and alternated her pace with spurts of running. The streets were short; she had to keep turning corners that seemed to lead her deeper into the maze. She had no fear, though it was a sordid area, for she felt like a wraith streaming by the Chinese who crowded the sidewalks. She felt she could pass right through them, and she would be as elusive to the grasp as a spirit. The brightly lighted stands of fruit and hot sweetmeats that spilled over into the middle of the alleyways seemed like the décor in a huge ballet. Even when she sensed footsteps behind her, she did not feel afraid, but automatically quickened her own steps. Suddenly the byway widened and she found that she was in the shadow of the blue-domed Russian church.

She ran into its darkness, up a few long steps leading to its porticoes. At the top she was seized from behind.

"What's come over you!"

It was Louis Murray, and her heart lurched in disappointment. She had wanted it to be an unknown, a male who was anonymous.

"What's the matter with you! You flipped or something!"

They stood, panting, as he forced her against the column. His vocabulary was like everything else about him. It made her

231

feel out of things, at the same time that it suggested that he was somehow repugnant.

"Dangerous," he said, pressing against her, "dangerous means unsafe. It is unsafe for the human female to run home unescorted."

Her short jacket had come undone. In the almost total darkness, he fumbled with her blouse, until he found her breasts beneath. He put a hand on each and kneaded them until she moaned, content with his discipline. They were the only life for half a block, the night lapping around them like a broad band of river. Beyond, through the trees, was the other bank, the lighted streets, the people and the noise. She was repelled by him, by his pulling her skirt up to her waist now. But she had nothing to fear any longer. Nothing. She felt cold and public. Deep inside her, she knew she hated the whole act, and because she hated it, she would seek promiscuity as a mortification. She was a willing victim as she leaned against the column, making her body pliant, asking any man to punish her and to find her beautiful.

CHAPTER TWENTY-FIVE

They came out of the Community Church together onto Avenue Petain, a small group, Sylvia thought, just eight in all, besides Reverend Ssu-tu and his athletic-looking wife.

Robert Bruno had attended out of sentiment and perhaps to represent his father. The Jastrows, Hasan and Larry came because of her. Mimi sent a huge wreath of daisies, but stayed away because Robert was going to be there. No one mentioned Feng, as though they knew about his involvement in Peiyuan's death.

The service, arranged by Helen, had been simple and touching. They would have had some sort of Chinese funeral, if any of them had known how to go about one. But a Chinese funeral, Sylvia reminded herself, demanded a family setting and a hierarchy of mourners. The service, among the flowers that Helen had selected, and conducted in English, had represented them, rather than Peiyuan, and that was almost inevitable.

Across the avenue, the school campus stood bathed in the pink five-thirty light. Out of its gates rolled an American jeep. Young American officers greeted each other and walked away as though a late afternoon in Shanghai were an old story to them. Reverend Ssu-tu shook Sylvia's hand with his usual diffident punctiliousness, and his wife clasped it in a warm and bony grip.

Sylvia felt poised between exhaustion and renewal. She had been washed clean, past any more arguments with herself. Now she could again enjoy the disjointed, fragmentary exchanges of life.

"I'll call you later," Julie reminded her. "Bill and I will be talking to you."

"So long," Larry pronounced affectionately, like a brotherly tourist. He rumpled her hair and surveyed her sideways, part of him already turned to go. Every one of his movements these days announced the temporary nature of his stay in Shanghai.

"I want you all to come over on Sunday," Sylvia said, looking at her mother for agreement.

Helen nodded, smiling through her still wet eyes, a brave child. She was innocent beyond all comprehension, Sylvia thought. Primitive and untried, she could hurt and be hurt in ways that Sylvia could no longer be. She felt she understood her mother's strengths and weaknesses for the first time.

"See you," they said in different ways, accepting the invitation. After a funeral everyone made small plans, to prove that nothing had changed. Sylvia could hardly believe that only two days ago she had been in an entirely different state. She had been a different person.

She had come home from Feng's, her mind still screaming. She had wanted to will Peiyuan back into life. She had wanted to beat upon the walls of Feng's deafness. (But he can't hear, she reminded herself. When he so wished, he could turn off his hearing aid, and nothing could reach him.) She had locked the door of the bathroom and vomited into the basin.

Her legs seemed boneless, and when she could vomit no more, she leaned against the wall and made her mind as blank as she could. No one tried to intrude upon her privacy there. The bathroom was always sacrosanct. It commanded more respect than the secret places of the ego.

She felt she had been partially broken at the diaphragm. The top part of her could not seem to straighten up, as she finally had walked into her room and sat upon her bed. Peiyuan was dead. Nothing would bring him back.

But she thought—Feng! Oh, Feng, Feng, Feng—she had

234

buried herself in his name like a pillow. Feng, Feng, Feng, please, please, please! She would plead that he be other than he was, that he be noble and pure and entirely good. But he wasn't. He wasn't these things, and knowing it only seemed to make her want him more. And what did that make her, for having loved him so? What had she done? Her passion seemed to have created what it needed for its own existence. Everything one did—and one had to act—committed one to a circle of questioning. And yet, when all was said of the dilemmas of love ("What happens to the spirit," she asked herself, "when one questions, did he come to me so passionately because of his great love and strength, or was it only great need and weakness?") nothing was resolved. And what of her own motivation? She felt degraded by her own doubts, by her own intelligence, which drove her into paradoxes. When all was said, she came up with only one thing of dignity, one thing in which she could take pride. And that was her desiring. She had wanted him. And their times of being together had been a celebration. She still wanted him. She was glad of it, though it was to be unfulfilled. The longing, too, was something she did not want to kill. It was too easy to be criminal. And as she thought it, she wondered how masochistic she was being, enjoying her own pain. It seemed to her that perhaps people created their own pain because only when in pain were they truly sure that they were alive. "I hurt, therefore I am," and she wondered if people ever became sure of anything.

Whatever the relationship had been for Feng did not truly concern her. "I love you," he had said fiercely many times. "I shall always love you," as though it were a threat. But she had not always believed him. Or perhaps, she should say, she did not always believe in the fleeting world, the always changing present. No one was today what he had been yesterday. Her contemplation of the day and the city left them changed. Even while she contemplated transience she had left part of herself in history. They lived in a moving, floating scene. Feng was human, both weak and strong. Yes, she could reiterate, he had loved her. And no, it was equally true, he had not. He could affirm and deny in the same gesture, he could create and destroy. He was, after all, only a man, alone as she was under the same weather.

She had been blind, and she would be blind again. She could have doubted him from the very beginning. Had she not known even that night at the Jastrows, when he had stalked out in a fury, that his anger was the anger of weak righteousness, not of strength? He would not have become distorted with rage if he were not threatened. But even in ugliness, he had asserted himself, and she had admired that. And his weakness, too—wasn't it only more reason to embrace him, not less? His idealism, she now saw, led him to commit outrages against the human spirit. His social conscience, which had seemed all virtue to her, would violate society. For the wrong reasons, so much good was done—she had learned from her dependency the necessity for being separate. For the right reasons, much wrong evolved—she had acted for herself in this experience with Feng, and between them they had discovered that their relationship, however much they wanted each other, was not enough.

Doubting could lead only to disintegration. She felt a dizziness of the soul when the end of every thought was a question mark. She had thought before, that from the same evidence one could come quite accurately to two different conclusions. For herself, she knew only she must choose to believe. She decided to believe. Her body doubled up in a scissorslike contraction. She felt something snap, leaving a white scar across her consciousness. Like a twig, she had been broken in two, the strong nerve of her attachment and dependency giving way at last.

The egocentricity of me, she had thought, striking her forehead for the second time that other day, and despaired because she was only herself. The pretentiousness of me! In despair all her life without even knowing it. In despair because she was herself. In despair because she did not know what that self was. And as she thought, the next step came easily. Despair

236

was a sin, complete and simple. She knew that it was a sin even as she knew suddenly that she sat in her own body.

Peiyuan was dead. He had died in an accident, so Tang had said, so Feng had tried to make her believe. He had died in an "accident" that involved them all in guilt—Helen, Liyi and herself, not least of all. He was gone; he was no longer a fleshly location. His spirit had left to slip into another image in another plane. For the ones left behind, he was no more.

And quite suddenly, because of his absence, she had realized what life was. Both love and death taught her to revere the body, for the soul lived hand-in-glove with the flesh. Where Peiyuan had been was now only a felt space. The body must be holy! She wanted to cry out her discovery. The body held and contained the aspirations which strained against the necessary limitations of humanness. It provided a home for intangible energies. She had loved both Feng's and Peiyuan's in different ways. She now felt the value of her own for herself. By residing fully and carefully in her own, she would be able to engage her emotions, her mind and her days with pride. Abruptly, she had no longer felt accidental, but responsible. She was Sylvia Chen, and she would speak out for herself—an entity composed of both her parents, but ready to act and not merely react, for one individual—herself. She had seemed to take her first breath of life.

She now looked up into Robert Bruno's face. He seemed to be waiting for her to return to the scene on the sidewalk. He looked at her enviously as though through windowpanes of his own disengagement.

"My father," he said, "would like a talk with you—informal, of course. Do you suppose you could arrange it soon?"

"But Liyi will be back by tomorrow or the next day at the latest," Helen put in. "We wired him. Hadn't he better see your father? I know he will want to."

"He expressly asked for Sylvia," Bruno emphasized. "You know more about this than anyone else. Though, of course, your father will submit the formal report."

Sylvia nodded. She knew very little really, just enough to

put Mr. Bruno Senior on his guard, just enough to embarrass her own father, who would rather not know too much. "I'll tell him everything I know about this murder. I can't do any more or less. . . ." They stood awkwardly, constrained with solemnity. Yes, she repeated to herself, I'll tell Mr. Bruno all I know, for the same kind of thing is beginning to happen everywhere in China.

They had all turned to go. Each one stood out distinct in the floodlight of the sunset. Robert walked away, escorted only by the kind of handsome propriety he had worn during the service. It seemed to her that her brother Paul, made shy by death, was more bereaved than any of them. The others moved away, each thinking his own thoughts. Feng was gone —he had left for the interior without a trace. Only her father, after comforting Peiyuan's mother in Sunkiang, would still have the facts of the death to face.

She thought of Mimi and knew that tomorrow she must see her. Since the day that Sylvia had not found her home, Mimi had scrupulously avoided her, but Aunt Juliet had told her almost everything over the phone. It was as though Mimi had been injured into nonexistence, as though she were acting out her feeling that she had been put aside, disgraced, denied recognition. Carelessly vivid, Mimi had spent herself so generously she seemed to feel faded now, and was dramatizing the feeling of her own invisibility. Sylvia felt she was strong enough to be able to help her "sister" tomorrow.

They were all gone. Sylvia found herself between Helen and Paul as they began to walk home. They knew the side streets of this quarter by memory. The beggars—blind, albino and crippled, who had made it their professional beat—were there in the shadow of the wall that surrounded the small park. Sylvia would have missed them like relatives if one day the three did not appear at sundown. They could not reach into each other's worlds, but they belonged to the same human situation, each isolated beyond recall. Yet as Sylvia passed the

238

three, she knew she inhabited their consciousnesses as much as they did hers.

Her mind strayed back nine years. She remembered moving down from the north when she was eleven. Moving down to Nanking, the new capital on the ancient river. Nanking sprawled in a basin of low land, ridged by the Purple Mountain, where Sun Yat-sen's mausoleum lay in the midst of parkland. The Chens lived in a newly developed area of the city. Around them foundations were being laid for the new foreign-style residences in stucco. Chinese coolies stood in circles holding onto the ropes attached to wooden pounding blocks. They flung the ropes in the air, heavy maypoles, and brought down the blocks, making a thudding sound on the ground. The coolies chanted and sang as they worked. For centuries men had beaten the earth and the earth had borne their planting and their homes. For centuries men had gone back to the earth amid lamentation. The coolie voices were full of anguish and joy; their singing went on from dawn until twilight—ten hours a day of grieving and commemoration.

Sylvia was eleven and pressed her nose to the window, thinking—though she did not know her own thoughts—what chance have I in this old populated land, what chance have I to exist at all? And this feeling of her own worthlessness had revisited her regularly afterward. It seemed she could only beg in this life of other people's riches. When would she feel real, accepted and accepting? When would she feel—as well as know—that her world existed only because she truly existed, that she lived a legitimate life and was her own witness? For each man was his own witness. It was a responsibility and a gift you could not evade. No one else could supply one's own center. Without self, the world would not exist. You supplied your own evidence of it. She had known that as soon as she knew *that* in her heart—and she no longer seemed to want to avoid the knowledge—she would understand life and identity itself.

They turned the corner and she saw their home. The light

239

from the west transfigured the street, the sidewalks seemed to tilt upward into a blinding sky. Though the sea around Shang-hai was not a refreshing one, the ocean seemed to Sylvia to be more immediate than it had ever been before. It felt like an invisible beachhead on a level with her eyes. She was alone but not lonely. She expected a new and sudden vision.

CHAPTER TWENTY-SIX

I suppose I should be glad we took this house, Liyi thought, standing in the warm gloom of the porch. It was the next best thing to going to a resort, which was still out of the question this September. The change in scene and the house itself had given the family a chance to expand, to come alive again. They were only four miles from their own apartment, but in Hungjao one at least had a garden, could hose oneself to the amusement of the servants, and track up the floors just as though a beach were within running distance. Helen had rigged up a rope, in lieu of a net, and she and the children were having a tournament with a rubber ball.

"Oh! I can't any more . . ." Helen's voice in the garden trailed away breathlessly. Through the screening and the bushes, he could see beyond to the open lawn, a small rectangle of yellow light. He caught a glimpse of Helen's red blouse, her back relaxed with exhaustion. She had thrown herself into a cane chair, and now she sank out of sight. Sylvia's and Paul's voices had chorused and screamed, and still lingered like leaves held up by an eddy of air that would neither rise nor fall.

Liyi walked into the living room and stood in the middle of it. It was full of summer furniture, brown rattan pieces, extra chairs stacked in one corner (summer rentals always prepared for the eventuality of large families or many guests), straw matting on the floor, and cobwebs in the corners near the ceiling. He walked through the bedrooms in the back. They were dappled in light like pergolas, those small islands of refuge from sun and rain. A gust of wind blew a window against its frame and seemed to wake up the whole house. In the hallway he could hear the *amah* and the cook in the kitchen, beating eggs with chopsticks. His restlessness could not be assuaged. It seemed to him he had spent hours of the last few days talking to himself. He couldn't stop the voices. They insisted on being heard. He was victimized by the demands of his own soliloquies.

I should not have gone! he cried silently, swinging his clenched fists. I should have stayed! Instead, I turned my back on reality and rocked in the chair of myself. But how was I to know! How was I to think this might have happened! He felt arid and hopeless. His tongue was dry against the roof of his mouth.

His trip to Sunkiang! He shook his head over it. The old scenes had come back effortlessly. This house he was looking at offered a striking contrast. This summer house, though perhaps fifteen years old, was new, unlived-in compared with the old homestead. Its face was unlined, empty of history. In Sunkiang he had remembered and looked for the step-worn slabs, the ghost chairs evoking a kind of intimacy with the dead, the courtyards that led you into the heart of the family. They were all present—it was just that the expression had been changed, as though his memory had suspended an atmosphere over the scene, which he could not find when he was actually there. He had looked at everything as a stranger might, trying to find the meaning that those rambling rooms used to hold. And the people—his in-laws and nephews and nieces—it was as though they were related to another person. They could not be integrated with what he now was. The trip had only made him feel more unreconciled with himself.

He clenched and unclenched his fists. This place suddenly seemed like a cage, a cave in which he could only be sick. Outside, human beings existed, engaged in individual adventures. He felt he must join the world.

He had his hand on the porch door and stopped abruptly. He couldn't face them—Helen whose concern was undiluted

242

and primitive, "You must forget it! Love, you must put Pei-yuan out of your mind this instant!" and the children whose thoughts were too complex for his delving. He decided to go out the back way, through one of the bedrooms.

Without looking at the family, but skirting them through a narrow passage between forsythias, he followed the short path to the road. On one side tall acacias formed a wall of shade above his head. His legs were silhouetted against the dust. He walked briskly, the way he had when he was a young man up north, wearing the jodhpur-type trousers popular then. In Sunkiang a week ago, he had taken a walk, too, through the fields that belonged to the Chen family. But there he had worn a loose Chinese gown, and had felt as though he were at a masquerade.

He had almost asked for death, too, when the news of Peiyuan's dying arrived. He had wanted to cry, "Help me!" but did not know whom to say it to. To God? But he was too self-conscious to pray. "Help me, help me!" sounded too demanding to him. Under that, he heard the humming, "If I could only hurt myself into extinction!"

He thought of the boy, and despised himself. He hated his own failure, his own fecklessness, his own lethargy. His hatred served as a kind of stamina these days. He was like a man who had taken a vow. It stiffened his spine, and made him walk jerkily. His co-ordination was poor, for he hadn't been able to sleep in a week. He felt his sleeplessness could be shared by all the men of his generation. It was as if he were punishing himself for having half closed his eyes before, for not having been strong enough to look the facts in the face, all the changing facts of the world. One must look at things precisely as they are, he thought. Not through the distortions of hope, fear or indifference. It was too late in the century for immaturity.

A car rumbled by, making a loose swerve to avoid him, but kicking up dust that sprayed the road like thick fountains. Liyi choked and blinked his eyes. It was like walking through a mountain fog, an acrid one. Only large shapes were recognizable, bold sterile outlines inhabited by nothing but dust and opaque air. It filled him with a fearful emptiness.

He continued to walk mechanically. His legs moved under him like wound-up parts of a machine. He felt hollow and fascinated by the sheer act of moving into nothingness. He could have walked off a cliff or into a lake, hypnotized by his own fatigue and tension.

It took what seemed a long time for the dust to settle, for small things to appear again. The road grew before him, coarse in the foreground and becoming faint and delicate before it turned five hundred yards away. The trees above reappeared, reborn into the day, getting darker green as the moments passed and the dust withdrew. The long walls of property showed their human flaws—some bore the scars of the early shooting of the Japanese incident. Birds and insects rustled. A chicken ran before him crazily, limping in the uneven ruts, the caricature of a cripple. The dust was gone completely. He felt far-sighted, clear-eyed. With a sharp ache, his despair turned over like a heart lurching at the mention of a long awaited rendezvous.

The miracle was beginning to happen. He was going to feel again. He began to experience that drive toward sublimation, which some call love, others prayer, still others a renewal of striving. There were so many ways of loving, he realized all at once and as if for the first time: large and small. All men's lives were a growing outward of love itself. Specific, precise, it sought the lover and the wife. The thrust of sexual love projected more life into the world, more lives to be loved, one's children to be embraced. The situation of love was their breeding ground, the home their early world. Childhood was both the heart's kernel and the sheath to be discarded upon coming of age. He would soon lose his children—their adulthood would be the thief. He would have to learn to let them go graciously. Only with a yielding toward the inevitable could you rise from the human situation toward peace. Only

244

that way could he grow with his children into their world, a world which was wonderfully corporeal— It could not be avoided. It had to be contended with. Its problems came at one, day by day, budgeted. They provided the necessity by which we grow. Life was not to be resolved, but to be lived— a constant improvisation. He felt he was more prepared to take things as they came—and to act upon them with his senses all awake, responsible.

Another car approached; he turned around to avoid getting the dust full in his face. Without knowing it, he was walking back to the house.

A small leaf, shaped like a woman's eyebrow, hung before him, turning. It landed on his sleeve and he picked it off and held it in his hand. Its edges were turning yellow, all of summer's burning in its chemistry. The vacation house they had rented was almost archaic now that autumn was in the air. In two weeks they would leave Hungjao to return to reality.

Helen and the children were no longer playing on the lawn. They sat under a tree, their backs to him, fanning themselves after the game and drinking iced tea. He looked at them, the bright colors of their play clothes dazzling and fragmented with shadows. That had been the bravest thing he had done— to marry Helen and bring two Eurasians into the world. But that had been done with the courage of innocence. Now the courage of understanding was required.

One war was over, but it was bringing in its wake even more serious issues and, perhaps, another kind of war. Up north, in Manchuria, the Nationalists who had not lost to the Japanese were having a difficult time reaping a victory from their own countrymen, the Communists. To be Chinese was not enough; it did not define one's beliefs any more. The times were demanding new loyalties, more discriminating, more humanitarian. His children, free from any narrow chauvinism, were the new citizens for an expanding century.

He went through the wooden gate into the front yard. The Chens are all together now, he thought, but the future which he felt was upon them might separate them in several ways. But whatever would happen, they were together in this: each would have to explore the humanity in himself.

There was no time for hatred or for any vows except mutuality. He put his hand on the screen door and quietly let himself into the house. They had not watched him leave or return. They did not see the tension fall from him suddenly. He was quite tired. Tired in a different way. He felt that he could sleep at last, and wake up ready for clarity.

ABOUT THE AUTHOR

DIANA CHANG, the daughter of a Chinese father and an Eurasian mother, was born in New York City, but spent some of her childhood in Beijing and Shanghai as well as in the United States. She has taught creative writing at Barnard College, exhibited paintings in solo and group shows, and edited *The American Pen*. She is the author of the novels *A Woman of Thirty*, *A Passion for Life*, *The Only Game in Town*, *Eye to Eye*, and *A Perfect Love*, and the poetry collections *The Horizon Is Definitely Speaking*, *What Matisse Is After*, and *Earth Water Light*. She lives in New York.